# DEADLY LITTLE LESSONS

Also by Laurie Faria Stolarz

*Deadly Little Voices*
*Deadly Little Games*
*Deadly Little Lies*
*Deadly Little Secret*
*Project 17*
*Bleed*
*Blue Is for Nightmares*
*White Is for Magic*
*Silver Is for Secrets*
*Red Is for Remembrance*
*Black Is for Beginnings*

# DEADLY LITTLE LESSONS

A **TOUCH** NOVEL

*Laurie Faria Stolarz*

**HYPERION**

NEW YORK

Copyright © 2012 by Laurie Faria Stolarz

All rights reserved. Published by Hyperion, an imprint of Disney Book Group. No part of this book may be reproduced or transmitted in any form or by any means, electronic or mechanical, including photocopying, recording, or by any information storage and retrieval system, without written permission from the publisher. For information address Hyperion, 125 West End Avenue, New York, New York 10023.

First Hyperion paperback edition, 2013
10 9 8 7 6 5 4 3 2 1
V475-2873-0-13274

Printed in the United States of America
Library of Congress Control Number for Hardcover Edition: 2012013991
ISBN 978-1-4231-3498-5
Visit www.un-requiredreading.com

SUSTAINABLE
FORESTRY
INITIATIVE

Certified Chain of Custody
Promoting Sustainable Forestry
www.sfiprogram.org
SFI-01054
The SFI label applies to the text stock

Sometimes the most important lessons
are the ones that stem from fear.

# I

THERE'S A STABBING SENSATION in my chest. It pushes through my ribs, making it hard to breathe. I've felt this way since last night. Since the phone rang and I decided to answer it.

The caller ID screen flashed: PRIVATE CALLER.

I wish I had let my parents get it. The last thing I needed was another faceless person on the other end of a phone, especially considering everything I'd already been through during the past year.

But instead I picked it up.

"Camelia?" an unfamiliar female voice asked.

My chest tightened instinctively. "Who is this?"

"It's your grandmother."

But it didn't sound anything like my grandmother. This person's voice was less cheerful, more distant.

"Your *mother's* mother," she said, to clarify.

It took my brain a beat to make sense of her words,

after which my whole body tensed.

"I know it's been a little while," she continued, "but I really need to speak to your mother."

I wanted to ask her why—what she could possibly want. My mother hadn't seen or spoken to my grandmother in at least twelve years.

"I heard your mother is staying at your home, is that true?" she asked, when I didn't say anything.

"Staying at my home?" I felt both dazed and confused, like in that Led Zeppelin song from the '60s.

"Your mother," she attempted to explain. "I heard that she's moved in with you. Is she there? Can I speak with her?"

*Moved in with me?* "My mother lives here," I told her. "This *is* her home."

"Well, then, please," she insisted (her voice sounded sharp and irritated now), "can you simply put Alexia on the phone for me? This is rather urgent."

"Alexia?" I said, assuming that she was confused, too. "Aunt Alexia *was* staying here. A few months ago." *But now she's locked up in the mental ward at the local hospital. And the way that you treated her as a child—resenting her for having ever been born—is at least partially to blame for her instability.*

"Do you want to talk to my mother instead?" I asked.

"Your mother." There was a tinge of amusement in her voice. "Don't you know? What have they told you, dear?"

"Excuse me?"

"Alexia *is* your mother, Camelia. Certainly you must know the truth by now. . . ."

*"What?"* I asked, but I'm not even sure the word came out.

"Alexia is your mother," she repeated, louder, more forcefully, as if I hadn't quite heard her the first time.

My heart pounded. An array of colors bled in front of my eyes, and the room began to darken and whirl.

"Camelia?"

The receiver fell from my grip.

I sank to my bed, where I've remained ever since, replaying the phone conversation in my head, dissecting each sentence, word, syllable, and letter, hoping that maybe I misunderstood. But no matter how many times I try to pick her words apart, the meaning is still the same.

There's a knock at my bedroom door. I roll over and bury my head beneath my pillow, hoping that whoever it is will just go away. But a couple of seconds later, the door opens. Footsteps creak across the floorboards.

"Camelia?" Dad asks.

I clutch the ends of the pillow.

"It's almost noon," he says. "I thought we'd go out for brunch. Anywhere you want."

"I'm not hungry."

"Are you not feeling well?" He attempts to pry the pillow from over my head, but he's no match for me.

"Headache," I tell him. The knifelike sensation burrows deeper into my chest. Talking feels both labored and painful.

"Well, can I get you anything? Tea, aspirin, something to eat? I could bring you some toast. . . ."

"Nothing," I say, wondering if he notices that I'm still in my clothes from yesterday; that I never changed for bed; that the phone receiver is still on the floor; or that my pillow is soiled with tears and day-old makeup.

"Okay, well maybe I'll make you something anyway," he says, lingering a moment before he finally leaves.

Alone again, I attempt to let out a breath, but the sharp sensation in my chest keeps it in. I know there are a million things that I should do right now—that I *could* do—to try to ease this ache: talk to him and/or Mom; call Dr. Tylyn; phone Kimmie; or text Adam at work to come and pick me up. But instead I replay the phone conversation just one more time.

# LESSON NUMBER ONE:
## *NEVER GO WITH STRANGERS.*

He slides a tape recorder toward my feet, through the hole in the wall—the wall that separates him from me.

I'm confined underground, in the dark, in a cell made of cinder blocks and steel. The hole—just big enough to fit both of my hands through—is the only visible opening in the cell. There are no doors, no windows.

"Where's the trash?" he barks. His voice makes me shiver all over. He sets his lantern down on the ground; I hear the familiar clunk against the dirt floor. The lantern's beam lights up his feet: work boots, soiled at the toe, laces that have been double-knotted. "I shouldn't have to ask for it every time."

Time. How long *has* it been? Two weeks? Two months? Was I unconscious for more than a day? He took my wristwatch—the purple one with the extra-long strap that wound around my wrist like a bracelet. My father gave it to me for my fifteenth birthday, just before I found out the truth. And now I may never see my father again. The thought of that is too big to hold in; a whimper escapes from my mouth. Tears run down my cheeks. I hate myself for being here. I hate even more the fact that I probably deserve it.

I lean forward, pushing my plastic bowl through the hole, eager to appease him. Hours earlier, he'd filled the bowl with stale crackers and had given me a lukewarm cup of tea. My stomach grumbles for a hot meal, though the thought of eating one makes me sick.

He snatches the bowl and then pushes the tape recorder a little further inside. As he does so, I catch another glimpse of the mark on his hand, on the front of his wrist. I think it might be a tattoo.

"What is this for?" I ask, referring to the tape recorder. Aside from the clothes on my back, my only current possessions are those he's given me: a flashlight, a blanket and pillow, a roll of toilet paper, a basin of water, and a cat litter box. If it weren't for the flashlight, I'd be totally in darkness.

I shine my flashlight over the recorder; it's the old-fashioned kind.

He feeds a microphone through the hole. There's a cord attached to the handle. "Only speak when spoken to," he reminds me. "Now, be a good girl and plug the mic into the recorder," he continues.

With jittery fingers, I do what he says, fumbling as I try to plug the cable into the hole at the side, finally succeeding on the fifth try.

"I want you to record yourself," he says. "Tell me what you love and what you hate. What scares you the most."

"What scares me?" More tears drip down my cheeks. *I'm scared that I'll never get out of here. I'm scared that I'll never get to see my parents again, and that I'll have to pay for what I did.*

I move my flashlight beam up the wall. Unlike the cinder-block back and side walls, the front of the cell has a solid steel frame, consisting of a locked steel door, similar to that of a prison cell (except with no bars to look out).

"As you can imagine, I love a good scare." He laughs.

I huddle into the far corner of the cell and pull the blanket over me, still trying to piece together what happened the night I was taken.

I remember talking to him for at least an hour at the bar and then following him out a side door. We walked toward the back of the building, where his car was supposedly parked. It was dark—a spotlight had busted—and we were passing by some trash cans. I remember trying to keep my balance while standing on a lid. Why was I doing that? And what happened afterward? Did I fall? Did anyone see me? Did I pass out before we drove away?

"Whatever you do, don't waste my time," he snaps. "Don't record how much you hate it here, or how you think I'm a monster. Those opinions are irrelevant to me. Is that understood?"

I nod, even though he can't see me, and dig my fingers into the dirt floor, trying my best to be strong.

"I'll be back in an hour," he says, as if time had any

meaning for me since I don't have a watch.

I nibble on my fingernails, too nervous to care that they're covered in dirt. "Can I have more water first?" I ask, knowing that I'm speaking without permission, but needing to, because my throat feels dry, like sandpaper.

"Not until the tape's done," he snaps again.

I listen as he walks away, the soles of his shoes scuffing against the dirt floor. The door he entered by—the one that leads to a set of stairs (I've seen it through the hole in the wall)—creaks open, then slams shut. Those sounds are followed by more noises: bolts and locks and jingling keys.

I remain huddled up, trying to reassure myself that I'm still alive, and that I'm still wearing the same clothes as the night I was taken, so he probably never touched me in any weird way. Maybe there's hope. Maybe once I'm done with his tape-recording project, he'll finally set me free.

IT'S NOT UNTIL late afternoon that I finally venture out of my room. The light in the hallway stings my eyes. Sun pours in through all of the windows, shocking my senses, because everything inside me feels dark.

In the kitchen, Mom's yoga bag is gone from the hook. She's already left for work. Dad's outside, mowing the lawn. I can see him out the kitchen window, past the growing number of my mother's prescription bottles on the sill. When she first heard about her sister's most recent suicide attempt, nine months ago, there was only one bottle. But now she's up to four medications: one to help her sleep, another to make her wake, one to numb her pain, and another to help deal with the side effects of the pain-numbing pills.

Positioned beside the array of bottles is a supersize jar of almond butter (her edible vice), two sizes up from the one she used to buy.

I head into the living room, feeling my body tremble with each step I take toward the bookcase. You'd think that after everything I've been through this past year—after having been stalked, held captive, and almost killed three times, not to mention having questioned my own sanity—I wouldn't let one measly phone call get my world so off-kilter. I mean, who even knows if what my grandmother said was the truth?

But I fear deep down that it is.

I zero in on the row of photo albums on the top two shelves. Back when life was simpler, before things got too dramatic and complicated for any of us to handle, my parents and I used to go through the albums together, reminiscing about things like my sixth birthday party, the time Mom nursed a baby sparrow back to life after a nearly fatal fall from its nest, and my first lost tooth.

I grab the album that documents my parents' life before I came along, and start flipping through the pages. For all the time I've spent perusing the album, laughing at my dad's dorky bangs and my mom's hippie clothes, never once did I think to question the fact that there aren't any shots of Mom when she was pregnant with me, that there are no photos from a baby shower, nor any ultrasound pictures.

I spend several minutes going through the album yet again, poring over photos of my parents' wedding shower, photos of the big day itself, and then years' worth of pictures dedicated to their exotic vacations in places like Fiji, Costa Rica, and Capri, hoping to find even one baby-bumpified picture that would make everything right. But all I find is my mom's concave stomach in an array of tie-dyed bikinis.

A moment later, my cell phone rings. It's Kimmie.

"Hey." I pick up, relieved that it's her.

"Guess who you're talking to right now," she bursts out.

"Excuse me?" I recheck the phone screen.

"Bonnie Jensen's newest style maven."

"Wait, *what*?"

"Three words for you: New. York. City. This summer. Me: interning for Bonnie *Genius* Jensen. Seriously, can you believe it?"

"No. I mean, yes. I mean, that's great."

"*Great* doesn't even cover it, Camelia. This could be *life*-changing for me."

"Right. I mean, *so* great."

"And so what if I'll be fetching coffee and dusting clothing racks all day . . . as my downer of a dad says. It'll be for Bonnie Freaking J. I mean, I'll wipe her ass if she wants me to, because I'm sure it'll be with designer T-paper, right?" She laughs.

"Exactly," I say, trying my best to sound happy for her. And I *am* happy for her. She deserves every bit of this. But right now, amid family photos that add up to only one possible conclusion, it's all I can do to hold the phone to my ear.

"Is everything okay?" she asks.

Part of me wants to tell her about my grandmother's phone call, but another part doesn't want to ruin her moment or admit what could be true.

I glance up at the plaque on the mantel. It's a framed quote from Don Miguel Ruiz, one of my mother's many earth-crunchy gurus: *Use the power of your word in the direction of truth and love.* Mom made a point of putting the plaque here in the center of the room over the fireplace, to remind us always to be true to our word. But what about hers?

"Camelia?"

"I'm so excited for you," I say.

"What's wrong?" she asks.

"Nothing, I just have to go. My father's signaling for me to help him outside." A big fat lie. "Can I call you back?"

"Wait, have you been crying? Your voice sounds all nasal-like."

"Allergies." More lies. "My dad's mowing the lawn."

"And since when have you been allergic to cut grass?"

"I'll call you later, okay?"

I hang up without waiting for her answer and hurry up to the attic. I start to go through the cedar chest in which Mom stores what she deems to be of sentimental value, still hoping to find that one scrap of evidence that'll prove I'm truly theirs.

I pull out my old tutu, a caterpillar costume, and my first-ever teddy bear. At the bottom of the chest is a scrapbook. In it are photos of my mother and Aunt Alexia when they were young. Even then, my aunt looked out of place—either standing in the background looking down at the floor or half concealed behind someone else.

As I start to put the scrapbook away, I spot another photo at the bottom of the chest. I reach in and pluck it out.

"Camelia?" Dad calls from downstairs, startling me.

I take a step back, bumping into a pile of old shoe boxes. It's a picture of my mother on yet another beach, in yet another tie-dyed bikini, completely bumpless. I turn the photo over, noticing a date printed on the back that falls just three weeks before my birth.

"Are you upstairs?" Dad yells when I don't answer.

I stuff the photo into my pocket and hurry downstairs, feeling my stomach twist. Entering the bathroom, I slam the door behind me and try to catch my breath, but I can't seem to get enough air.

I move to the sink to splash water onto my face. My reflection stares back at me in the mirror, but I no longer even recognize it. My eyes are bloodshot. My skin is flushed. There are red spots all over my neck.

"Camelia?" Dad asks, rapping lightly on the door. He opens it and our eyes lock. He appears as surprised as I am by what he sees.

"Who am I?" I ask him; my voice breaks.

"Camelia . . . ?" He appears thoroughly confused. "What do you mean?"

"I mean, *who am I?*"

"You're not making any sense."

It's like we're speaking two different languages, which makes my heart clench tighter and the air in my lungs feel so much sharper.

"Camelia," he repeats. He sits me down on the corner stool and gets a cold compress for my face. "What is it? Do you still have that headache? Maybe we should call the doctor."

"I don't need a doctor!" I shout.

Dad scoots down in front of me and takes my hands. At first I let him. Because Dad's the one who soothes, who makes everything better, the one person I can always trust.

But then I push him away. Because this time, his touch makes everything colder.

"How could you do this?" I manage to ask. Tears bubble up in my throat, constricting my breath, making me feel like I'm drowning.

"Do what? Camelia, what are you talking about?"

"I mean, *who am I*?" I ask him again. "Who was I before *Camelia*?"

"Okay, now, slow down." His voice goes powdery soft. "Take a deep breath and try to help me understand."

"Why are there no pictures of Mom when she was pregnant?" I blurt out. "And where is my birth certificate?"

Dad's lips part and his expression changes, morphing from concerned to horrified.

And suddenly I don't even need to look at a birth certificate. The look on his face is the only truth I need.

*I* LEAVE THE BATHROOM, pulling the door shut behind me. Dad emerges not two seconds later. But instead of following me, he heads into the kitchen. I hear him from the door of my bedroom, leaving Mom a voice mail begging her to come home early.

Meanwhile, home is exactly where I *don't* want to be.

I phone Adam, even though I know he's at work. I leave him a message, and then stop myself from dialing Kimmie. I know she'd drop everything in a heartbeat for me, but I don't want to ruin her moment, so I call Wes on his cell instead.

"Pizza Rita's," he answers. "Are you interested in hearing about our cheesy bread special?"

His chipper voice almost makes me regret the call. It's not that I don't want him to be upbeat. It's just that I'm on a completely different emotional page right now, and I'm not sure I have the patience to catch him up.

"Camelia?"

I glance over at my desk. The emergency number for Dr. Tylyn is just inside the top drawer.

"Are you there?" he continues.

"Sorry," I say, resisting the urge to slip into old patterns—to keep things a secret instead of asking for a little help. "I'm here."

"And how are you?"

"Honestly," I say, still staring at my desk, "I feel like jumping off a ledge."

"Trust me, it doesn't work." He sighs. "You'll only end up breaking something, which will confine you to bed with your mom's raw-inspired vegan cuisine, and seriously, when you really stop and think about it, does it get any more torturous than her Italian rawsage or her sprouted bean porridge?"

I bite my lip, feeling it quiver, knowing there's no way I'll be able to say the words aloud. To him. To Adam. To Kimmie.

"Tough day?" he asks.

"I think I just need some fresh air. Can I call you later?"

"Will it make you feel any better to know that my day has sucked, too? I feel like I wait around all week for the weekend, but then, once it's here, I'd rather cheese-grate my face than endure another Friday night dinner with the fam. So, what's *your* cheese-grating gripe?"

"Is your father being a bully again?" I ask, much more comfortable focusing on him.

"My father was *born* to bully. He even had that phrase

16

tattooed to his ass. I'm not joking, by the way. Next time you come over, I'm sure he'd be more than tickled to bend over for you."

"Thanks, but I think I'll pass," I say, reminded of Wes's journal. A few months back, he let me read it. It was basically a series of poems that documented his struggles at home, struggles that revolved around his father's disappointment in him.

In a nutshell, Wes's dad has always wanted him to be more masculine, less in touch with his feelings. He threatens Wes by saying he'll enroll him in the Girl Scouts and have his car painted pink. The truth is, as I learned from his poetry, that Wes is gay. Only, aside from me, he hasn't shared the news—*or* his personal poems—with anyone. Nor has he wanted to discuss it.

"Are you *sure?*" Wes asks. "It'd probably make his decade to have a pretty girl take a peek."

"Well, if that's the truth, your dad has serious issues."

"And apparently, so do you, my little ledge-jumper. So, let's hear it: what's your motivation for taking the plunge?"

"Would you believe that I'm just PMS-ing?"

"If *you'd* believe that I'm the sexiest stud in Freetown."

"I'll have to get back to you on that one."

"Don't tease me, Camelia," he growls.

"I'll call you later." I hang up before he can argue and gaze out my bedroom window, thinking about my ex-boyfriend, Ben, of how he used to be able to sense what I was feeling without my ever having to say it. Right now, that would be a blessing.

Like me, Ben has the power of psychometry—the ability to sense the past or future through touch. Ben's power works best when he touches people—when there's skin-to-skin contact. But my power works differently, sort of like what happens when my aunt does her finger painting. When I do my pottery, images come rushing through my mind. I sculpt the images in hopes they'll make sense. And over the past year, since this power emerged, some of the images *have* indeed made sense—at least they have eventually. With Ben's help, I've been able to save a couple of lives, including my own.

But my power doesn't work the same way every time. Sometimes when I'm sculpting, I'll envision something significant. Other times, I won't envision anything at all. And still *other* times, the premonition will be *so* intense that I'll hear actual voices pertaining to whatever it is I'm sculpting.

"Camelia?" Dad calls from the other room.

Instead of answering, I pocket my cell phone, pull on some shoes, and open my window wide. I know that I should probably call Wes back. He probably suspects there's something seriously wrong. But right now, I just need to get away. And so I climb out the window and run as fast as I can.

*4*

*J*TURN ONTO A STREET that leads to Regino's, the restaurant I went to on one of my very first dates with Adam. We sat at a table in the back, and I remember at one point during dinner looking out the window just as a tree branch broke outside, exposing two limbs that stretched out at sharp angles. The image reminded me of Ben—of the scar that runs along his forearm.

I push the door open, surprised to discover that it's no longer an Italian restaurant. A sign above the front counter says, WELCOME TO HALEY'S TV DINER.

I turn back to gaze at the entrance to see if the exterior has changed as well. Maybe I was too distracted to notice it.

"You can take a seat anywhere," a waitress tells me.

"Thanks," I say, looking around. The interior is decorated with posters of new and old TV shows—*I Love Lucy*, *Happy Days*, *Seinfeld*, and *Family Guy*—and there are flat-screen TVs throughout the place, though only one is currently on. It hangs down over the front counter. A group of older people sit huddled below it.

The waitress hands me a menu; it's made up to look like a *TV Guide* with a caricature of Steve Carell on the front. "Is this your first time at TV Diner?"

"Sort of," I say, noticing that the rest of the place is pretty empty, that the old photographs of Florence, Rome, and Milan are gone, along with the red-and-white-checkered tablecloths.

Despite these changes, the table at the back is still there. I head toward it, as if cosmically (and perhaps pathetically) drawn to the infamous tree branch outside the window. But the leaves are at their peak now—lush, vibrant, green—and so I can barely see it.

I wonder where Ben is right now and what he might be doing. After coming to my rescue a few months ago, he decided to go away for a while. He joined a homeschooling group, with the principal's approval, only he hasn't been home in months.

I slide into the booth, suddenly feeling stupid for coming here. Why didn't I go to Adam's office? I open the vinyl menu, thinking back to that first date. After the tree branch broke, I remember how distracted I was, despite how sweet Adam was being. I couldn't seem to stay in the moment, wondering if nature was trying to send me some message.

"What can I get you?" the waitress asks.

I feel a chill, wishing that I had grabbed a sweater on my way out of the house. It may be June, but the air conditioner overhead makes things feel more like late

November. I order some food by pointing to the first things I see on the menu: a raspberry muffin, along with a strawberry milk shake, despite knowing I won't be able to stomach them.

I look up at the front counter. The old people are taking notes as they watch TV, as if keeping score or solving puzzles, and yet it looks to be a news show. A forty-something-year-old woman appears on the screen and starts sobbing into the camera.

"Here we are," the waitress says as she places my order in front of me, along with a couple of containers each of butter and strawberry jam.

"Thank you," I say, noticing a man on the TV screen now. The woman's husband? Her older brother? He's crying as well, which upsets the woman more. She tries to say something, but I'm too far away to hear.

"Hello; *hello*," the waitress says in a singsongy voice.

"What?" I ask. Has she been talking to me?

"You're addicted, too, aren't you?" She laughs.

"Addicted?"

"To *Open Cases*?" Her pixie haircut reminds me of Kimmie's, as does her plum purple eye shadow. "It's one of those unsolved-mystery shows—the kind where they ask the viewers for help. The difference with *this* show is that the stories are all fairly current, which means that the regulars here are totally obsessed with solving the cases before the police do." She gestures to the row of note-takers. "Check them out. They come in here daily to watch the show. You're welcome to join if you like. Just don't be too insightful, or else you're apt to piss Rudy off. He likes to think he's the smartest one of the bunch."

I recognize the girl from news reports: Sasha Beckerman, a fifteen-year-old girl from Peachtree, Rhode Island. She's been missing for six weeks. The photo was taken at the end of Sasha's eighth grade year and shows her with a fishtail braid and full-lipped smile.

I grab my food and head up to the counter, eager for distraction.

"It's the parents' fault," says the guy at the end of the counter to the woman sitting beside him.

The woman pauses in dunking a butter-slathered cracker into her mug of tea. "Don't tell me you think *they're* the ones behind the kidnapping."

"Who says it was a kidnapping?" another guy says, glaring at her over the rims of his bifocals. "I'm telling you: that girl ran away."

"Well, I still think people need to cut the parents some slack," the woman says.

The guy with bifocals shushes her as the host of the show details what the authorities know about the case. Apparently, Sasha told her parents that she was going to a poetry slam with some new friends. But it turned out to be an underground party with no adults present to speak of—except for the one adult she was last seen with: a good-looking guy with a brown leather jacket.

My stomach rumbles; I feel hungry and nauseated at the same time. I take a bite of my muffin, trying to tame the thick lead taste in my mouth. A moment later, my cell phone rings. It's Dad, but I don't want to pick up.

"Your phone's ringing," the guy with the bifocals says, as if I'd suddenly lost my hearing.

I reluctantly click my phone on and mutter, "Hello."

"Your mother just got home from work," Dad says. "Where are you? And since when do you leave the house without checking with me first?"

*Since I just found out that for the past seventeen years, you and Mom have been lying to me,* I want to tell him. *Since I learned that Mom's long-winded lectures about peace, love, and honesty are all just a pile of BS.*

"Look, your mother and I would really like to sit down and talk this out," he continues. "Now, just tell me where you are."

He still isn't denying it. The tightening sensation returns to my chest.

"Camelia?" he asks.

I drop my cell phone. It lands on the floor with a clank. The case breaks. The clip holder goes flying.

"Is she all right?" I hear one of the regulars ask.

I'm breathing hard. The room starts to spin.

"Do you need help?" a female voice asks me.

"Get her a glass of water," someone else says.

Their voices only make me dizzier, so I cover my ears and do my best to remain composed, wishing this were all a dream, that I could wake up and be the girl I thought I was, rather than this person I no longer know. This person who will never be the same.

$\mathcal{I}$ SPEND THE NEXT fifteen minutes in the bathroom, regaining my breath and praying for the spinning to stop. Once I've managed to get a grip, I step out of the handicapped stall and return to the dining area.

To my complete and utter shock, Dad is at the front counter, paying my check.

"How did you know where to find me?" I ask him.

"Don't forget your cell phone," he says, sliding it down the counter toward me.

I glance at the row of regulars, assuming that one of them must've picked my cell up from the floor, answered it, and told my dad where I was. They're all focused on me rather than the television now, as if I were every bit as intriguing as the girl on *Open Cases*.

"Let's go," Dad says.

I follow him out to the car, both surprised and disappointed that Mom isn't in the front seat.

Once inside, Dad locks the doors and turns to me. "We have a lot to talk about," he says.

"Just tell me," I mutter. "I need to know if it's true."

"If what's true?"

I squeeze my eyes shut, resenting him for making me be the first to say the words. Then I open my eyes and gaze out the window, wishing that I could jump out, and that it was a whole lot further down.

"Camelia?"

I look at him again. "Are you and Mom my real parents?" The question comes out in a whimper.

But still he understands. I can tell by the flare of his nostrils and by how firmly he presses his lips together. "We have a lot to talk about," he repeats; these seem to be the only words he can currently say.

Meanwhile, I have no words left.

I get out of the car to give myself a moment. It isn't long before Dad steps out, too. He takes me in his arms, and I reluctantly feel myself melt. Tears run down my cheeks, onto his shoulder, dampening his shirt. I want to be angry at him, but right now I just need for things to be the way they used to.

I'm not sure how long he holds me—if it's for two hours or two minutes—but we eventually get back inside the car and head for home.

Mom is waiting in the living room. She embraces me as well. They both hold on to me as if I were some long-lost treasure that they don't ever want to lose again. But I feel like it's already too late.

Eventually, Mom sits me down on the sofa and gives me some dandelion tea. Her eyes look brighter than normal, as if she might have recently popped a pill.

"Is it true?" I ask, still waiting to hear them say it, part of me hoping that they might somehow even deny it.

"How did you hear about this?" Mom asks, kneeling down in front of me.

I look at her—at her red, corkscrew curls and her angular face—and suddenly feel so stupid. Because what I once thought of as a mother-daughter resemblance—our almond-shaped eyes, our high cheekbones, our pointed chins—I now know is a resemblance between aunt and niece.

"We were going to tell you," she continues, "but our lives have been complicated lately." She starts to prattle on about how fearful she's been for me, because I've been involved with all things lethal (avoiding being murdered, rescuing others, getting saved by Adam and Ben).

"You've reminded me so much of Alexia this past year," Dad says. "I think you've sensed that, too. And I didn't want you to worry."

Worry because Aunt Alexia has a record of attempting suicide.

Worry because she's been labeled by doctors as mentally disturbed and possibly schizophrenic.

Worry because she hears voices, and because now I'm able to hear them, too.

"We were going to tell you when you turned twelve,"

he continues, "but you just seemed so darned young. And so we waited until sixteen came around, but there was such a rough start to the school year, including your aunt's suicide attempt. . . ."

"Your mother told me," I say, focusing on Mom, finally revealing the missing piece. "She called here."

"Did she call just to tell you that?" Dad asks.

"Did she tell you anything else?" Mom jumps in.

I shake my head, feeling the urge to scream, because this isn't about my grandmother. This isn't about what she wanted or what I said in response. "This is about how you lied to me," I tell them. "How I have no idea who I am right now."

"I may not have given birth to you," Mom says, "but you'll always be my daughter."

"*Our* daughter." Dad sits beside me and takes my hand.

"So, is Aunt Alexia really my mother?" I ask, thinking how it was only a few months ago now that Dad looked me in the eye and said that Aunt Alexia and I were kindred spirits.

"She is," he says, squeezing my hand.

I nod, fighting the urge to tear up again and thinking how it all makes sense. My touch powers, for one; both Alexia and I have the ability to sense things through our art. She and I also look a lot alike—blond hair, pale skin, emerald green eyes—even the nurse at the mental facility in Detroit said so. Did the nurse know the truth all along? Did Aunt Alexia tell her? Am I the last person to know?

"*We're* still your parents," Mom reminds me. "We're the ones who've raised you and cared for you and been there for you every day of your life."

And that's when it suddenly dawns on me—as if this could feel any more surreal—not only is my mother not my mother, but Dad isn't my father, either. "Who *is* my father?" I ask him.

Dad takes a deep breath, trying to appear strong, but he looks even more upset than me: his face is blotchy, his eyes are full.

"Why don't we all take a little break?" Mom says, extending her hand to Dad. "We can continue this conversation later."

Without waiting for Dad to respond, I head into my room and close the door, wishing that I could block out my thoughts, that I could restart my yesterday, and that I'd never picked up the phone last night.

# LESSON NUMBER TWO:
## *NEVER LET YOUR GUARD DOWN.*

He says he'll be back in an hour, but how long have I been crying? My cheek is pressed against the dirt floor, and my tears have made a patch of mud; at least it feels that way. I've shut off my flashlight to preserve the battery.

I almost wish he would just kill me. Thoughts and memories are like daggers in my heart. I imagine my mother, worried sick, unable to get out of bed. Then I picture the two of us stringing popcorn on the tree last Christmas. I replay the time this past fall when my father jumped up from the bleachers after I'd scored my fourth goal in soccer. And then the time he brought me a dozen roses on the opening night of *Grease*, when I understudied the role of Sandy Dumbrowski.

I sit up, turn my flashlight back on, and dip my fingers into the dirty basin of water to wipe some mud from my eye. My lips are chapped. I wipe them, too, and my hand comes away with a smear of blood on it; they must be cracked. The corners burn from being stretched . . . from screaming. Two meals ago, I spent a chunk of time yelling, praying that someone would hear me. But no one did, not even the guy who took me.

I'm pretty sure I must've been drugged on the night I was taken. He must've slipped something into my drink when I wasn't looking.

I remember being charmed by him—so much so that I didn't object when he offered to take me someplace quiet. I went willingly, hoping that because he was older he'd actually understand someone like me.

I also remember that Misery had warned me about him—the "creepy-looking" guy seated at the bar. Unfortunately, I hadn't wanted to listen. I'd been so angry that she'd lied to me about the plan for that evening. She'd told me that we were going to a poetry slam, that there was a special boy she'd wanted me to meet—Tommy was his name—but in actuality it was a glow-stick-friendly party at an abandoned sewing factory, devoid of anything even remotely poetic, and no special boy at all. And so I purposely went over to Creepy Guy at the bar, only he wasn't creepy at all. I remember thinking how good-looking he was with his smooth tanned skin and dark hair. I half suspected that *he* might be Tommy after all, that maybe Misery had changed her mind about fixing me up because she suddenly wanted him for herself.

I grab the tape recorder, replaying in my mind what he said he wanted, and curious about why he needs it. Is it so he won't forget anything I tell him? Or because recording my words helps maintain a distance between us, whereas a conversation might make me seem more real, more human? Or—my biggest fear—is it because he collects the recordings of all his victims, to keep them as souvenirs?

# 6

IN MY ROOM, I stare at my reflection in the dresser mirror. I always thought I'd gotten my longish neck from my dad. For years, I'd assumed that the spray of freckles across the bridge of my nose was inherited from him, because he has it, too. I gaze down at my hand, remembering how just months ago, when Aunt Alexia placed her jittery palm against mine, it was a mirror image of my own.

I grab my phone and text Adam to come pick me up as soon as he gets out of work. And then I sit down at my computer, hoping that I might have gotten an e-mail from Ben. We haven't called or texted each other since he left. For now it's only e-mail: a way to keep in touch while still remaining distant.

I check my in-box, but I don't see a new message from him, just the one from last week:

Dear Camelia,

I'm in D.C., just thinking about you. Having a
great time, despite having to keep up with my
homeschool stuff. I went to a bunch of museums
today. There's nothing like getting the education
up close and personal. I'll be heading north next.
I hope things are well with you.

Love,
Ben

I draft an e-mail back, filling him in about everything.
My pulse racing, I move the cursor over the send button,
but then hit the back arrow instead, deleting the entire
message, because sending it would make me vulnerable to
him again, and that's when I get hurt.

Still, I want to write him back. I make several attempts
before giving up and busying myself with the array of news
links on my home page. One of them concerns the missing girl from Rhode Island—the story featured on that
unsolved-mysteries show—as if I needed another reminder
of my panic attack at the diner. But I click on the link
anyway, desperate for a diversion.

A picture of Sasha Beckerman pops up on the screen.
In it, Sasha poses in her soccer uniform, red shorts and a
yellow T-shirt, with a soccer ball under her arm. According to news reports, all signs, including an already packed

bag stashed away in her closet, point to the fact that she ran away. Because Sasha was angry as hell. Because her parents had kept something very significant from her. Oddly enough, it was the very same "something" that my parents had kept from me.

I continue to read about the case, wondering what else Sasha and I have in common—if, at fifteen, a freshman in high school, I could've been so upset by the news about my parents that I'd have behaved like her, that I'd have quit all of my favorite activities, ditched those closest to me, and started hanging out with people much older—people on the verge of being kicked out of school.

I look closer at the photo of Sasha in her soccer uniform, taken before she dyed her hair black and traded in her J.Crew–wear for torn jeans and tattered belly T's. Before she found out the truth.

Her skin is dark, like she just got back from someplace tropical; it brings out the golden-brown streaks in her hair and makes her blue eyes pop.

"Camelia?" Mom calls. She and Dad come into my room and stand behind me. "What are you looking at?" she asks.

"Sasha Beckerman," I say, still staring at the screen. "Do you know about her?"

"No," she says. The response comes as no surprise. Ever the hater of news stations, Mom has long claimed that their biased headlines, negative images, and politically slanted comments disturb her energy and clog her chakras.

I turn around to face them, focusing a moment on Dad: "Do *you* know about Sasha?"

He grunts out a yes. And in that single syllable, I can hear him make the connection.

"You're not planning to run away, are you?" His eyes widen.

"What do you want?" I ask, ignoring the question.

"We need you to hear us out," he says. "You know we love you, but you also have to understand that your mother and I made a conscious decision not to tell you the truth until we felt you were ready. I'm sorry if you don't agree, and I'm sorry for the way you found out, but I'm not sorry about our decision."

"Does Aunt Alexia know that I'm her daughter?" I ask, feeling stupid for posing such a question. I mean, how could someone possibly forget childbirth?

"I *think* she knows," Mom says, twirling the mood ring around on her finger. The color has turned a murky brown. "On some level, at least. But that was a particularly difficult time for her. She was barely twenty-two, staying at an assisted-living home that was overcrowded and run by the state. There were way too many patients and not nearly enough staff."

"It was the first facility she'd stayed at since moving out of her mother's house," Dad adds.

"I hadn't even known she was pregnant." Mom gives her ring a full twirl. "One of the facility's staff members just dropped her off at our house one day, saying she was due in a couple weeks, and asking if we could care for her."

"How could you not have known she was pregnant?" I ask. "Hadn't you visited her? Hadn't you tried to keep in touch?"

"That's the weird thing," Mom says. "Because I'd had lunch with her a month prior, and we'd spoken on the phone several times since then. . . . But she'd been keeping her pregnancy a secret. Not just from me—from everyone. Even the staff members said so. They said she'd been wearing lots of layers, keeping a low profile, and always toting around extra-large items to cover up her belly: her portfolio case, a giant purse, a couple of extra coats."

I sink back in my seat, imagining what that must've been like for Aunt Alexia: feeling so alone, so insecure, that she'd had to resort to keeping such a big thing secret.

"Anyway," Mom continues, "she stayed with your dad and me during the weeks leading up to the delivery. And then she asked me to be there at the birth. You were so beautiful." Mom smiles at the memory. "Just waiting to be loved."

"Because nobody loved me yet," I say, without even thinking.

"That's just it." She shakes her head. "We all love you. Alexia loved you so much that she wanted your father and me to raise you as our own. She knew she wasn't stable enough to care for you in the way she wanted. She wanted you to have a chance."

"Did she want me to know the truth?"

"Honestly," she sighs, "I don't know. She never wanted to talk about *you* as being *hers*. Once she'd placed you into my arms at the hospital, that was it. It was as if she'd already crossed over, which is why I'm not even sure what she remembers."

"Or what she blocked out," Dad says. "We'd invite her to family dinners, birthday parties, holiday celebrations. We'd tell her about various recitals you'd be in, softball games you were playing at, spelling bees you took part in. . . . We never wanted to exclude her from anything, but I think, even though she seemed to want to watch you from afar, the idea of most of that stuff was too difficult for her."

Mom continues to toy nervously with her ring. Dad notices and takes her hand to give it a reassuring squeeze.

"There's something else I need to know," I tell them. "Who's my father?"

Dad shifts uneasily. "It was someone at the halfway house."

"Another patient?"

"A med student," he explains. "He was an intern, working at the facility. After it happened, he was fired and kicked out of his college. But Alexia made us promise not to press charges."

"Did she love him, at least?" I ask, able to hear the anxiety in my voice. "Or was it just . . ." My voice trails off. I can't finish the thought: the idea that he might've taken advantage of her, that I might've been conceived out of something so horrible.

"She said she loved him," Mom says. "She said their relationship was consensual."

"Where is he now?"

"We're not sure," Dad says.

"Did he ever maybe ask about me?" I venture. "To know who I am or to find out how I'm doing? Did he ever want to see me after the birth?"

Dad keeps staring back at me—his dark brown eyes are wide and unblinking—silently telling me the truth. My birth father never wanted to know me.

"I think I need a moment," I tell them.

"Of course," Mom says, already standing up. She mutters something about a pot of tea and quickly leaves the room.

Meanwhile, Dad moves to take my hand, and once again I crumple into the strength of his embrace, unable to resist his affection, unable to stop my tears.

DAM COMES TO PICK ME UP as soon as he gets out of work. Dressed in cargo jeans and a bright white T that shows off his tan, he looks amazing, and he smells like vanilla-bean soap.

I tell my parents that I'm heading out for a while. Mom actually thinks it's a good idea. "Fresh air, fresh mind," she says, with her jar of almond butter in one hand and a giant spoon in the other.

But Dad is reluctant to let me go, perhaps fearing that I may never come back. "Don't be late," he says.

I intercept Adam on the front walk, before he can even get to the door. "Hey," he says, greeting me with a kiss.

"Hey." I give him a peck.

He leads me to his car, a '70s Bronco that looks pretty cool but that perpetually smells like eau de gas station. "So, what's wrong?" he asks, opening the passenger-side door for me.

"Please, let's just go."

Adam climbs behind the wheel and drives us around for a while before finally pulling in to the parking lot behind my high school.

"As if I didn't spend enough time here during the school year," I say, hating the tone of my voice, knowing that I sound ungrateful.

"Well, we have to talk somewhere, and it looks pretty private. Do you want to go for a walk?" He nods toward the area behind the parking lot, where the Tree Huggers Society has created a sanctuary of sorts. A circle of pine trees surrounds a bunch of granite-slab benches.

But the sanctuary reminds me too much of Ben. Of the time when I followed him along the path between the trees, sat beside him on a bench, and allowed him to run his fingers over my skin and to sense my biggest fears.

Even the parking lot reminds me of Ben. The first time I ever saw him, it was here. The first time he ever saved my life, it was here. For months afterward, he watched me from afar, sitting on his motorcycle on the opposite side of the lot.

Here.

I take a deep breath, trying my best to stay in the moment, but then Adam reaches out to take my hand. And again I'm reminded of Ben.

"Tell me what's going on," Adam says.

"I just found out that my parents aren't really my parents. My biological parents, I should say."

"Wait, *what*?"

I gaze out the window at the Tree Huggers' sanctuary, almost wishing there could be some other way to make him know the truth without my actually having to say the words.

But there isn't. And so I tell him everything.

"Whoa," he says, combing his fingers through his shaggy dark hair. "I'm not even sure what to say to that."

"Well, maybe we don't need to say anything." I turn to him, hungry for his affection—for him to take me in his arms and tell me that it'll all work out fine.

But unfortunately, he doesn't hold me at all. Instead, his face brightens. "I think I know something that'll make you feel better," he says.

He puts the Bronco in drive and moves out onto the main road, eventually crossing over into the town of Hayden. Is he taking me to his apartment to talk? Is there something he wants to show me at the college he attends?

There's a Ferris wheel in the distance. I'm assuming we're going to drive past it, but Adam pulls into the parking lot of the carnival.

A proud smile sits on his lips, as if bringing me here is the best idea he's had in a while. "No way anyone can stay upset at a carnival, right?"

I want to tell him that I'm not up for it, but I'm too emotionally drained to argue. Plus, he seems so excited by the idea that I don't have the heart to tell him that bringing me to a carnival isn't remotely close to what I need right now. And so I suck it up and pretend to enjoy the ride.

*A*DAM PULLS UP in front of my house to drop me off. We stayed at the carnival for about an hour, during which I tried to have fun. I went on a couple of rides, ate some cotton candy, and fed a few of the petting-zoo goats. But, as hard as I tried, I was way too distracted to enjoy myself.

Adam turns from the wheel to look at me. "I'm sorry if that was a lame idea. I just thought . . . how can anyone stay sad while hanging upside down on the Twirl-'n'-Spin, right?"

"Except I don't do upside down," I remind him, hating myself for sounding so deflated.

"And now I know," he says, still trying to keep things light. "From now on, it'll be nothing but right-side up between us."

"You're very sweet, you know that?" I smile, the first smile on my face all day, and it actually feels pretty good.

I lean in to kiss him good-bye, grateful for his attempt to cheer me up. "I'll call you later?"

"I hope so."

I kiss him again, feeling guilty for my lackluster mood, but I can't fake what I'm feeling.

Inside the house, to my surprise, I find Kimmie sitting perched on the living room sofa awaiting my arrival. In a sleeveless dress with a gargoyle-esque creature adorning the front, she looks more than slightly agitated, as evidenced by the way her arms are folded, the scowl on her face, and the bloodstained tongue of the aforementioned gargoyle. "Your. Bedroom. *Now*," she demands, before I even utter a hello.

I lead her into my room, relieved to finally be able to tell her stuff.

She closes the door behind us. "So, um, what's going on?" Her arms still folded, she taps the toe of her stiletto against the floor. "Because you were acting totally freakish on the phone earlier, and I'm not the only one who thought so."

"Have you been talking to Wes?"

"He said you sounded like a mental patient, and from what he told me, I couldn't have agreed more."

"Maybe 'mental patient' isn't one of the most appropriate analogies to make with me these days," I say, considering the fact that it was only months ago that doctors wanted to lock me up in a mental ward for hearing voices and talking about my premonitions.

"Since when am I appropriate about anything?" she asks, motioning to the front of her dress; there's a plastic fork stuck in the gargoyle's bloodshot eye. "Did you not have suicidal fantasies earlier today?"

"Excuse me?" I ask, wondering what Wes told her.

"So, you didn't threaten to jump out the window?"

"Okay, yes, but not in the way you think. Plus, my room's on the ground floor, in case you've forgotten. What's the worst damage I could do? A sprained ankle?"

"Just tell me," she says. "Is something weird going on with you? More voices? Mysterious phone calls? Are you having premonitions about some heinous murder that's yet to happen? Hence my dress, FYI. I had to block all the evil energy *somehow*."

"Except my energy is hardly evil."

"No, but some of the stuff you sense *is* evil."

Instead of reminding her that my premonitions have in fact helped saved lives, I sit down on my bed and tell her about the past couple of days.

"And I'm just hearing all of this *now*?" Her sparkly, gold-outlined eyes seem to double in size.

"I'm sorry," I say, feeling horrible for keeping secrets. "I mean, I was going to tell you earlier, but the last thing I wanted was to burst your Bonnie Jensen bubble with my depressing parental drama."

"Screw bubbles and Jensen. I'm your best friend first, remember?" Kimmie holds me for several moments—the way I wish that Adam had. "So what do we do now?" she asks.

"I don't know." I shrug, breaking the embrace. "I mean, I feel like such a mess."

"A little soap and water might help fix that," she says, not even joking.

"You have to understand." I wipe beneath my eyes with a tissue, which comes away with a smudge of residual eye makeup. "It's one thing when you learn that your aunt is suicidal and that she could possibly be schizophrenic. But it's another thing altogether when you find out that she's actually your mother, especially when you have dark thoughts, too."

"Oh, puh-leeze, Camelia." She rolls her eyes. "The darkest you get is hot cocoa without the marshmallows." She stands up to assess her hair in the dresser mirror. She's growing it out, inspired by 1920s flapper girls and has dyed it a bright shade of red. "You don't believe that your parents were just trying to protect you?"

"I don't know what to believe, and what makes matters worse is that I'd planned to visit my aunt at the hospital this weekend. Now, I don't even feel like I can face her."

"So, maybe you *shouldn't* visit." She turns back to me again. "Maybe you should give yourself some time, Camelia. You're human. You're allowed to react."

"Plus," I continue, trying to fill her in, "as if things couldn't get more convoluted, my parents aren't even sure if Alexia knows that she's my mother."

"Does she not remember lying spread-eagled on a delivery table and pushing a basketball-size baby out of a ping-pong-ball-size hole?"

"I don't know." I smirk. "You'll have to ask her."

"And I shall, in due time." She gives me a sinister grin.

We continue talking for a while—until I'm so over the drama with my family that I want to switch gears. I try asking Kimmie for more info about her Bonnie Jensen internship, but she isn't having any of it.

"No way," she says. "We'll have gobs of time to talk about how I'm gonna rock the Big Bad Bonnie Apple this summer. But for now, what do you say we head on over to Brain Freeze? I have a sneaking suspicion that there's a peanut-butter barrel with our names all over it."

"Sounds perfect," I say, giving her a squeeze.

# LESSON NUMBER THREE:
## *IF YOU'RE GOING TO PLAY THE GAME, YOU HAD BETTER PLAY IT WELL.*

I slam my back against the steel door of the cell, wishing that I had the power to knock it down. My legs ache from kicking at it. My hands hurt from clawing, smacking, prying, scraping, trying to tear my way out.

I'm just so incredibly dumb.

When nothing breaks, I let out a scream. It's loud and shrill, and it scares even me. My heart pounding, I try to catch my breath. It's at least several seconds before I'm able to settle down, realizing that the hour must be up and that he'll be returning soon, I finally hit RECORD.

"What I love," I mumble into the mic. "Nothing much anymore.

"What I hate: myself, you, the fact that my friend lied to me that night, the fact that I've hurt my parents.

"What scares me most: you; not getting out of here; not seeing my family again; the sound of your footsteps

47

coming toward me; having to see your face again; or worse, having you leave me here to die."

I press STOP and then REWIND, knowing that talk like this isn't going to get me out of here. I have to play along. I try again several more times, pausing when my emotions get the better of me. Finally, I shut off my flashlight so that I can get deeper inside my head. I channel Sandy Dumbrowski from *Grease*, one of the most idealistic characters that I've ever played. "I love the stars at night," I say into the mic, trying to make my voice sound dreamy, like Sandy's, "and caramel sundaes, hot-air balloon rides, and spending time with my friends.

"I don't like being by myself, which is probably the most challenging part about being here. It'd be great to have someone to talk to. I also hate books and movies with cliff-hanger endings. I need to know, without question, what happens at the end of every story.

"Including this one—me being here, I mean. What will the ending of this story be? What happens next? And can I help you to write the next couple of chapters or acts?"

I push PAUSE and replay my words, thinking myself so cunning. I hate caramel and have never actually been on a hot-air balloon. I never took much notice of the stars at night, either. Of course, now I really miss them: I miss the ability to simply look up and see something other than a steel roof.

The truth is, he has no right to know me. My character is the one and only thing that I can keep from him right now. And that, in this moment, gives me the strength to keep from screaming again, from smashing my head against these cinder-block walls and chucking the litter box toward the hole.

My list of dislikes is equally deceptive. I've never minded alone time, but I'm hoping that he'll feel sorry for me and offer to talk. I read once that if perpetrators see their victims as real people with real problems and real insecurities, they start to think of them in a new light, which is why I mentioned that part about cliff-hanger endings. I want him to know that I'm insecure about what happens next. Maybe then he'll actually be able to relate to me, to see me as a friend, or at the very least, as human.

Still in my role, I mentally prepare my list of fears before pushing the record button again. "I fear not being able to know why I'm really here," I say into the mic. "I mean, I thought you liked me and that we had a lot in common. I guess I'm really confused."

Only part of this is true. I *am* confused, but I couldn't care less if he liked me or not. And I'm pretty sure now that he didn't like me at all—not really. Because why else would I be here?

I turn on my flashlight, feeling emotional all over again just thinking about how stupid I was. While all the other partiers were living it up—dancing, drinking, smoking, laughing—he was sitting by himself, watching it all. That should've been a big tip-off, but in spite of it, I made a beeline for him.

I remember thinking that he looked a whole lot older than I was (ten years, at least), but there was a degree of comfort in that, in talking to someone more mature, less into the whole show—someone who didn't care so much about keg stands or hookups.

I asked him his name and he responded by telling me that labels were unimportant. I couldn't have agreed more. And so we talked about music, and I lied about loving anything by Twisted Monger and Island of Fowl, thinking that both bands were so much more exciting and sophisticated than my actual favorites: Lily Locklin and Tiffany Heaven.

I also remember that he seemed a bit preoccupied, always looking around even when I was talking, and that he insisted on buying me a drink.

A second later, I hear it: the sound of a key turning in the lock outside. My heart tightens. He's back and he wants the tape.

With jittery fingers, I push the tape recorder toward the hole and retreat into the faraway corner.

9

THE FOLLOWING MORNING, after a night spent
tossing and turning, I call Dr. Tylyn and ask her if
I can see her right away. Luckily, she agrees.

I emerge from my room. Mom and Dad are out on the
back patio having breakfast. The sound of a woman moaning comes from Mom's iPod. I'm sure the music is meant
to be soothing, but it sounds more like someone's bout
with stomach flu.

"Good morning," Mom says, spotting me standing in
the patio doorway. "Sprouted-wheat ginger-pear scone?"

"Maybe later. I have an appointment."

"This early?" The corners of Dad's mouth turn down.

"It's with Dr. Tylyn," I explain. "I told her it was an
emergency."

"Are you planning to tell her everything?" Mom asks,
perhaps intentionally being vague; perhaps the words are
too toxic for her to say.

"Is that a problem?"

She takes a thoughtful bite of scone and makes me wait while she chews it. It must have the consistency of hay, because I feel like it takes her five minutes to swallow. "No problem," she says, though her worried expression tells me otherwise. Still, she allows me to borrow her car.

About twenty minutes later, I pull in to the parking lot of Hayden Community College, where Dr. Tylyn has her office. I climb the steps to the second floor. Her door is already open.

"Good morning," she says, standing up at her desk to greet me. Her short dark hair is pulled back in a clip, showing off her rounded cheeks. "Can I get you some tea?"

"No, thanks," I say, noticing the smell of vanilla in the air. A cone of incense smokes from the bookcase, a couple of shelves above her collection of voodoo dolls.

We take a seat on her leather sofa, and I proceed to fill her in. Dr. Tylyn's eyes never leave my face as she listens to every word I say without showing so much as a speck of surprise.

"So," I say, after a pause. "What do you think?"

She takes a sip of her steaming tea. "What do *you* think?"

"You didn't already know this information, did you?" I ask, surprised that she doesn't seem more alarmed.

"Tell me what you're feeling." Dr. Tylyn says.

"Betrayal, for one. I mean, they lied to me. They let me take for granted something that wasn't true."

"Do you think they had good reason?"

"I honestly don't care what their reasons were. I deserved to know the truth, especially about something so big. I mean, this changes everything for me."

"In what way?"

"In the way that my *real* mother has spent the majority of her life fighting for her sanity. In the way that we both hear voices and have this psychometric power . . ."

"Yes, but you knew those things before. You just thought it was your aunt with whom you shared them."

"And now it's my mother, one degree closer. I mean, haven't you heard . . . the apple doesn't fall far from the tree?"

"Do you really believe that?"

"Why not?" I shrug. "Everyone else seems to."

"Are you *everyone else*? It seems we've been down this road before. Just because you have this lineage doesn't mean you have to follow the same path."

I look down at my hands, less than convinced.

"You have choices, Camelia. Remember? So, make a detour. Choose a different path. Talk about your problems. Accept the fact that you have this power and that sometimes it's apt to knock you on your ass. But don't choose to be alone. You have the resources. It'd be a shame not to use them when Alexia didn't have that option."

I nod, knowing that we've indeed been down this road. But it feels good to go down it again—to be reminded that it's not too late for me. Not yet, at least. "I guess that's why I called you."

"And I'm so glad that you did."

I manage a polite smile suddenly remembering that I didn't call Wes or Adam back last night; they've been great resources, too. "I still feel betrayed, though," I continue. "It's like I can't get over this anger."

"Why do you think you're angry?"

"Because I count on my dad to be honest with me. Because both of them said they were going to tell me the truth when I turned twelve, and then when I turned sixteen, but now I'm seventeen, and they still kept it a secret. I had to find out by accident."

"Nothing is accidental, Camelia. It was the right time for you to know." She takes another sip of tea. "But one thing I think we should explore—you seem very concerned about age: how old you currently are versus how old your parents said you needed to be in order for them to tell you, for example."

"I just don't get why they kept it a secret at all. Some kids are told right from the get-go that they're adopted. There isn't some big unveiling."

"And some kids don't know until much later," she explains. "The point is that there's no steadfast rule. Your parents had a choice, too. And, whether or not you agree with that choice, you have to accept that they made it. It's done. No one can go back and change it."

"So, then, what do I do with this anger?"

"Talk to them. Spend some time trying to understand why they made the choices they did. And then ask yourself if you're truly angry at them or instead just fearful of the fact that Alexia's your maternal mother."

"Thank you," I say, grateful for her help, but also anxious to get some air. "You've given me a lot to think about."

"Of course." She winks at me over her mug of tea. "That's what I'm here for."

# 10

*A*FTER MY SESSION WITH DR. TYLYN, I head to Knead in lieu of going home. Spencer seems happy to see me—or at least, happy for the diversion. Now that he's finished sculpting his life-size ballerina—which is currently displayed in the front store window instead of in the Met in New York; I mean, the thing is a museumworthy masterpiece—he's decided to switch gears (and media) to sculpt a bust.

Of himself.

"I'm not trying to be narcissistic or anything," he says of the mirror propped up against the wall, "but I need a demo for the class I'll be teaching this summer."

"So it has nothing to do with the fact that you enjoy looking at yourself in the mirror?"

"That's just an added perk." He pushes back his Fabio-like hair. "So, what brings you here on this bright, sunny morning?"

"Same as you. I'm here to work." I lift the tarp off my work-in-progress: a vaselike bowl. I started it around the time that Ben and I broke up, and I've been toiling away at it ever since.

When I first began the bowl, I imagined entwined limbs; sides that curved inward like the small of a woman's back; and a curvy base. I even took a figure-drawing class, in view of all the "body" in my bowl—to try to get the piece where it needed to be. But now that Ben's gone— or perhaps *because* he is—it seems I've lost my inspiration.

"Still stuck?" Spencer asks.

"It's so weird," I tell him. "I mean, I started this project to get over Ben, but now that he's gone, it's like I need him back to finish."

"Basically, a clear-cut case of out of sight, out of mind."

"*Basically*, or literally?"

"But, then again, Ben hasn't exactly *left* your mind, has he?"

"Am I that transparent?"

"I have eyes," he says, adding a bit of squint to the eyes of his sculpture. "And I'm also an artist. We artists can smell love loss from a mile away."

"Are you sure you aren't merely smelling your own body odor?" I joke, peeking at the sweat stains under the arms of his T-shirt. "Besides, I have Adam, remember? Or are you starting to forget things in your old age?"

"Feisty today, aren't we?"

"I guess you have that effect on me." I run my fingers over the sides of my bowl, at a complete loss.

"You know what you need?"

"A dose of inspiration and for people to simply be straight with me?"

"Trouble in platonic paradise? Am I to assume that you and Adam are having issues?"

"Who says I was talking about Adam?"

"Oh, I didn't realize." He looks up from shaping a pair of clay nostrils. "Is there some other screwed-up drama going on in your life that I'm currently unaware of?"

"What makes you think that my relationship with Adam is platonic?" I ask.

Spencer lets out a laugh, as if the answer were completely obvious. "Can you honestly tell me that things between you and Adam are ache-until-your-loins-sweat hot?"

"Okay, totally inappropriate conversation . . . Plus, FYI, love isn't supposed to ache."

"Are you kidding? There's *only* heartache with love. Everything else is just hokey-pokey."

"I don't even want to know what that means," I say. "But for the record, things between Adam and me *aren't* exactly platonic."

Spencer waves my words away, as if they had zero meaning. "What you need is some time away." He nods toward my pathetic sculpture and then reminds me that his recent trip to Nice was just what the doctor ordered in terms of getting his mojo back. "How do you think I was finally able to finish Monica?" he asks, referring to his ballerina sculpture.

"And where do you suppose I go?"

"Well, for starters, what's your plan this summer?"

"Work here, be depressed, eat obscene amounts of ice cream to ward off said depression." Unfortunately, I'm only half joking.

"You know what you should do?"

"Get a gallon of fudge ripple and an extra-large spoon?"

"Check out some of the summer intensives being offered at various colleges—something in sculpture theory or an abstract design course that will help inform your work. It could give you a real advantage when applying to schools next year."

"I suppose," I say, thinking about Kimmie's internship at Bonnie Jensen. Despite all the family drama involving her parents' separation, she's still pursuing what she wants.

"I don't need to tell you that both Savannah and RISD have top-notch programs. And, since I'm an alum of both programs"—he pauses to pat himself on the back—"I may be inclined to provide a bit of pull. For a reasonable fee, anyway." He winks.

We spend the next several minutes discussing the idea more, including the pros and cons of various programs, as well as their geographical benefits (i.e., powdery beach sand versus being close enough that Adam can visit).

"Do you think your parents will be supportive?" Spencer asks.

"Honestly, they have no right not to be." For all I know, they may actually welcome the idea of my being away. It might actually benefit us all.

"Anything you want to talk about?" Spencer asks. "No more bouts of temporary insanity, I hope."

"No," I say, fully aware that he's alluding to what happened at the studio a few months back. While working on a sculpture here, I had a major psychometric premonition that included both visions and voices. The result wasn't pretty, and involved my being pinned to the floor by a group of EMTs and jabbed in the leg with a sedative.

Spencer saw the whole thing. But oddly enough, we haven't really talked about it, so he thinks it was just a seizure.

"So here's what I need you to do for me today," Spencer begins.

"I kind of thought I was here to fix my project."

"Yeah, right." He laughs, looking down at my pathetic sculpture. "Give me a hand—literally." He plops a wad of clay in front of me. "In addition to busts, I need various body parts for this class. Think you can mold me one?"

"No sweat," I say, happy to abandon my work-in-progress—for now, anyway.

While Spencer goes into his office to make a phone call, I wedge out my clay, taking note of my knuckles and joints in preparation for my sculpture. And then I begin to form the shape, beginning with the wrist.

A couple of seconds later, I'm interrupted by the sound of my cell phone ringing in my bag. I'm tempted to pick it up, suspecting it may be Adam, but since my fingers are thoroughly saturated with clay, I decide to let it go to voice mail.

I close my eyes, trying my best to concentrate, even though part of me fears that I may have a psychometric episode (since I'm here at Knead rather than at home in the privacy of my own studio). I continue to work anyway, reassuring myself that my pottery has been premonition-free lately, and so have my dreams. The clay is silky-smooth against my waterlogged fingertips. I run my palms over the mound, thinking about Spencer's suggestion that I get away.

But then I hear someone crying.

I look toward Spencer's office, but the door is closed. Spencer's in the kiln room. I can see him loading the kiln with pieces ready for firing. Still, the crying persists. (A female; I'm almost sure of it.) I close my eyes again and concentrate on my sculpture, assuming that the voice is in my head, and that this in fact is part of a premonition, but with each breath the crying gets softer and less urgent.

"How's it coming?" Spencer asks, stepping out of the kiln room.

"Did you just hear something?" I ask.

"Something like me loading the kiln with a bunch of tacky garden trolls?"

"I guess," I say, unwilling to get into it. Instead I look back down at my hand-in-progress, expecting to see a partially formed wrist.

But instead I see the shape of the letter *t*: two intersecting tubes of clay stare up at me, confusing me, shocking me, making my heart beat fast.

"Is everything okay?" Spencer asks. "No chance I'll find you writhing around on the floor and moaning like a wounded cat?"

I shake my head and roll the *t* up into a ball before he has a chance to see it. "I'll be fine." I do my best to form fingers from the mound of clay, but I can't think straight. Meanwhile, the faraway whimper continues to play in my mind.

# II

*L*ATER, AT HOME, still shaken up about the voice I heard at the pottery studio, I log on to my computer and do a search for the word *psychometry*, remembering a blog I cyberstumbled upon a few months back called Psychometrically Suzy.

On her blog, Suzy talked about an incident in which she heard her father's voice, long after he'd passed away, while touching an old hat that had belonged to him. There were a couple of similar entries—instances where she was able to touch an item and smell, see, or hear something from the past—but unfortunately, in none of the posts did she discuss how she coped or dealt with what was happening or how having a touch power affected her life and relationships.

And right now I kind of need that. I need someone I can talk to, or at least read about, who understands, firsthand, what I'm going through, especially since Ben isn't here.

Not so surprisingly, there still isn't too much else online about psychometry. I find a couple of sites dedicated to defining what it is, a site to help people develop their own touch powers, and another that says that those who possess extrasensory powers are doomed to the depths of hell. As if I needed hell on my plate in addition to everything else.

I click on a blog entitled Touched, written by someone named Neal Moche. Since there are no pictures, nor any details about the author, my first thought is that it's going to be a dud, but even so, I identify with it right away.

There are pages and pages of entries. Some of them are locked, but a few are open, for anyone to read. And so I start with the one that was written yesterday.

● FOLLOW MY BLOG　　● RSS FEED　　● ARCHIVE

## From the Journal of Neal Moche

He's here again, at the park. Three days in a row now. This is obviously his routine. He likes to come here on his coffee breaks, have a bite and get a smoke, and then go back to work two streets over.

It feels weird keeping tabs on someone I don't even know, some guy I've never met before, but psychometry does that to you. It gets you up close and personal in other people's business whether you want it to or not.

So far, I know what this guy drives (a Ford pickup with a dented fender); where he likes to hang out (here, Tidy's Bar, and Village Billiards); and that he works in construction doing odd jobs.

I almost wish that I didn't know any of it, almost wish that I'd never made a pit stop here as I was passing through town, that I'd never accidentally brushed up against him in line that day and gotten that sudden shock. For the record, I haven't sensed something that intense in months.

We'd been standing in line at the pretzel cart. He stumbled back as he fished in his pocket. In doing so, he bumped into me, which isn't easy. I always keep a good distance from people; I like my personal space and then some. But he managed to collide with me anyway, stepping right on my feet.

That's when I got dizzy. It's also when I sensed his plans for later that day and found myself struggling to stay upright.

He was going to head home, drink some more, and then smack his girlfriend across the face. I could see his finger marks on her skin. The image was fleeting, but I was able to see that she had blond hair, brown eyes, and a tattoo of a cross on her neck. Quite a bit of detail, but still not nearly enough to know who she was, or where to find her.

After the guy stumbled, he looked at me and slurred out a "Sorry," but an apology was the last thing on my mind, because there was so much more going on than what I'd sensed about his girlfriend.

It's hard to explain. I mean, I sense stuff all the time. As much as I try to avoid colliding with people, it happens. And every time I do, I see stuff that I'd rather not know about.

But this was different—like a bolt of lightning striking inside my head, nearly knocking me to the ground. My pulse started racing and I felt my face flash hot, and in that moment, as screwed-up as it may sound, I almost felt as if we were supposed to bump into each other, as if it might somehow impact my life.

"Don't do it," I told him, referring to his afternoon plans for his girlfriend. The response was more impulsive than smart.

"Huh?" he asked. A goofy grin crossed his face.

I didn't know what to say, so I walked away, which got me a night full of restless sleep, unable to blot out those finger marks, and unable to stop myself from guessing the reason his touch had made me feel like that.

I sink back in my seat, feeling chills run over my skin. The author of this blog seems to know exactly how I feel—haunted, confused, alone, responsible. I search the page, curious about Neal's contact info—if there might be a link to e-mail him or post a comment. But I don't see either option.

"Hey, there," Dad says, poking his head into my room. "Do you have a minute?"

I go offline just as he walks in.

"Kimmie phoned while you were out," he says, without waiting for my response. "She said she'd tried to get you on your cell, but that you didn't pick up."

"Oh, right." I nod, remembering the missed call at the studio. "I need to call her back." As well as Adam and Wes. "Did she happen to also mention her internship in New York this summer?" I ask, wondering if I should broach the topic about going away.

Dad barely shakes his head before taking a seat on my bed. "How did your appointment with Dr. Tylyn go?" he asks.

"Fine. I mean, helpful. But, she didn't seem at all surprised by the news."

"A good therapist never shows surprise."

"I guess," I say, still suspecting there may be more to it than just a good poker face.

"So, your mom and I have been discussing everything, and—"

"Where is she?" I ask, cutting him off.

"That's sort of what I wanted to talk to you about. She's at the hospital, visiting with Aunt Alexia."

"She isn't going to tell her, is she?" I ask, trying to imagine what it might be like if Aunt Alexia knew that I knew the truth. How would it change things between us?

"No. And we'd prefer it if you didn't say anything to her, either. Your mom thinks it'd be too hard for Alexia, especially if she *has* somehow blocked it out."

"Too hard for *her*?" I ask, wondering how—or if—I even factor in to the equation.

"It's hard for us, too," he says, looking down into his hands, perhaps wishing, like me, that things could go back to the way they were. "Anyway, it's good that Dr. Tylyn knows the truth now. She'll know what to do—how to use the information to help us get through this." He looks up from his hands and gives me a tiny smile, but there's zero happiness behind it. His eyes look strained and tired.

I want to tell him that none of this even matters and that things will eventually return to normal. But I'm not sure if either of these things is true, which somehow feels worse than finding out about my birth.

After he leaves the room, I start searching for summer intensive pottery programs, grateful for the distraction.

Several pop up right away. I'm just about to check out the one at Savannah College of Art, remembering that Spencer recommended it. But something else catches my eye: the words *Renowned Master Potter Chase DeLande to Lecture at Sumner's Summer Intensive*. I click on it and Sumner College's pretty New England campus sprawls across the screen in full, sweeping color with the heading SUMMER INTENSIVES FOR HIGH SCHOOL STUDENTS. I open up another browser window to do a separate Google search on the town of Peachtree, Rhode Island, where the college is located.

A bunch of links pop up: news reports, cultural info, and event happenings. Both Peachtree and the program at Sumner appear to be rich in art and opportunity. But surprisingly, the link that catches my interest the most involves Sasha Beckerman, the girl who's been missing.

# 12

*A*CCORDING TO EVERYTHING I've researched online, Sasha was given up by her biological mother shortly after birth and adopted by the Beckerman family. Two parents, one cat, and thirteen built-in cousins.

One particular Web site maps out Sasha's life from childhood to present. She grew up the only child of John and Tracey, in a warm and loving home in Peachtree. Good in school, voted most valuable player in soccer, and a loyal member of the art club and contributor to the literary magazine, Sasha kept a tight network of friends. But once she reached her fifteenth birthday and learned the truth about her parents (like me, she discovered it by accident, when she found her birth certificate in her mother's keepsake box), everything fell to pieces, including her picture-perfect life.

I move my cursor up to the menu bar and click on

the About Me link. It brings me to the bio page of the person who maintains the site. I recognize her right away: Sasha's adoptive mother. I plug in my earbuds and click on a YouTube video Mrs. Beckerman has made, where she sits in front of the camera, urging anyone with details about the case to contact either her or the authorities. I stare into her pale blue eyes, wanting to know why she and her husband never told Sasha the truth about her birth. Were they concerned that Sasha wouldn't love them anymore, or afraid that she'd want to find her biological parents?

Mrs. Beckerman continues to speak to the camera, trying her best to be strong: "Please know that Sasha wasn't some reckless teen who acted out in school or went to underground parties. She was angry at her father and me, which caused her to behave in a way that was out of character. Sasha distanced herself from family and friends, abandoned her studies, and went to places she normally wouldn't have—and with people we didn't know. Her father and I understand that anger, and we will have to live with the choices we made on her behalf."

I wonder if she thinks that Sasha's already gone—if that's why she speaks about her in the past tense. I grab a Twinkie from my stash in the drawer, flashing back to what Dr. Tylyn said earlier: that there's no steadfast rule for when to tell your child that he or she's been adopted.

But does there ever come a point when it's *too* late to tell them—when the truth is a legitimate betrayal?

I spend the next hour eating junk food and learning more about Sasha, until she almost feels like a friend . . . or at least someone I already know. I read about the night that she disappeared. The people she was with claim to have been drinking. Supposedly, they don't remember if she'd left the party with anyone, or what the guy she'd been talking to looked like. Why aren't more people talking about him? Why is everyone just assuming that she ran off on her own?

As if in reply, the answer pops up in a small-town newspaper article, the writer of which interviewed the two friends that Sasha went to the party with, both of whom agree that Sasha had been threatening to run away for weeks and had even boasted about having a bag packed. The suitcase the investigators found in her bedroom closet contained a couple of sweaters, some old books, a few pairs of sweats, and a handful of travel products.

But if she *really* ran away, then why didn't she take that suitcase?

I play Mrs. Beckerman's video again, muted this time, because I don't want to be influenced by her words, by the cracking of her voice, or by the part at the end where she gets so emotional that her speech becomes almost too muddled to understand.

Mrs. Beckerman's face is creased with worry. There are times when she can't even look at the camera—like she's hiding something, or ashamed. By the end of the video, her arms are crossed over her chest and she's huddling forward, curled up on the chair. She looks more like a little girl than like a parent.

I glance at the clock again, startled to find that I've

been researching Sasha's case for more than two hours now. Clearly, what started out as a harmless distraction has turned into a time-sucking obsession, but that doesn't stop me from wanting to know more.

I decide to head down to my studio in the basement, hopeful that I might have a Sasha-infused premonition. I know it's a long shot. I know I'd probably need to go to her house and be among her surroundings to actually sense something significant. But still, I have to give my power a try.

# 13

I'M ABOUT TO GO down to the basement when my phone rings. It's Adam. "Hey," I say, picking up right away.

"Hey, stranger," he answers back.

"It's good to hear your voice."

"Well, I've missed yours."

"I know. I'm sorry for not calling you last night, but I'm a total train wreck, complete with lack of sleep and junk-food binges."

"Just wait until your mom finds out," he says.

My mom is a hater of any food that hasn't been picked from a tree, vine, or the earth. She's therefore made it her mission in life to rid the world of junk food, one whoopie pie at a time. During freshman year, she started a petition at my school against the cafeteria's serving of any foods that contained artificial additives, preservatives, sweeteners, or food colorings, or that were bleached, overly processed (according to her standards), or genetically modified. The petition stated that those who signed would be more than happy to pay extra (up to double) for lunch in exchange for "whole food." The idea was a flop; she got only seventeen signatures.

"Are you going to tell her about my stash of Oreos?" I ask him.

"Only if you aren't nice to me."

"Okay, but don't feel *too* excluded, because I didn't call Wes back, either."

"So, you're an equal-opportunity callback offender."

"Something like that." I smile.

"Anyway, I was thinking that maybe we could go to that drive-in movie place over in Lawston. We had such a great time there the last time we went. I mean, I know it's no carnival," he attempts to joke. "But it still might be fun, unless you'd rather . . ." His voice trails off. He seems slightly nervous.

I honestly can't say I blame him, because my gut reaction is to give him a big fat no. I don't want to pretend everything's okay. I don't want to have another carnival disaster.

"Camelia?"

It was just about a month ago that we went to that drive-in. It was John Hughes night, we saw a double feature of *The Breakfast Club* and *Sixteen Candles*, and Adam did the best impression of Long Duk Dong I'd ever heard. I laughed so hard I snorted out my root beer. Without a doubt, it was the funniest and grossest night I'd had in a long time. But still . . . "I don't think that's such a good idea," I tell him. "Only because we had so much fun the last time we went to that drive-in . . . I wouldn't want to ruin the memory with my depressing present state."

"I just thought it might be good to take your mind off stuff."

"Maybe we could get takeout and talk instead?"

"Sure," he says. "I'll call you later and we'll make a plan."

"Sounds great," I tell him, glad that he seems to understand. We say our good-byes. I hang up and then check my phone for messages. I have three: one from Wes, another from Kimmie, and a final one from Adam. They must've called while I was researching Sasha's case, while I had my earbuds in.

I make a promise to myself to call Wes and Kimmie later, and then I go downstairs, still inspired by Sasha's story. In the basement, I light a pumpkin-scented candle to mask the musty smell, all the while picturing Mrs. Beckerman in her video and replaying in my mind what she said. For just a moment, I wonder if it was her crying voice I heard while sculpting at Knead yesterday, but I quickly remind myself that the crying at Knead was different—quieter and more subdued.

I slice myself a thick hunk of clay and wedge it out against my board, focusing on Sasha—on the photos I saw, the articles I read, and a couple of YouTube videos that she was in (a Lady Macbeth monologue and a clip from the musical *Grease*). After several minutes, once again, a *t* pops into my head, but this time in more detail. I close my eyes to concentrate, and I see that it's black, with sharp edges, and about six inches long.

I start to sculpt it, at first thinking that I'm wasting my time by replicating a piece I've already made, but then I hear the girl's crying again: the soft whimper I heard at Knead. As I continue to sculpt, the crying gets louder and more distinct, and it almost sounds like she has the hiccups. I keep working, running my fingers over the *t*, perfecting the borders, and making the corners more defined. But soon the crying is too much to bear. And suddenly I find that I'm crying, too.

After a couple of deep breaths and a few final touches, I decide that the piece looks pretty finished. But now a new image surfaces in my mind, and I feel like I have to sculpt it, too.

I smooth out a slab of clay, and then I grab a scalpel to cut petals out of it—eight of them—as well as a disk. I put them all together, forming a stemless daisy.

My tears drip onto the sculpture. The crying in my head is so loud that I can't hear anything else. I drop the scalpel, but it makes no noise. I bump my work board, but there's no sound as it hits the table.

"Please," I whisper, but I can't hear my own voice. The crying sound is too loud, too big, too overpowering. I take a step back and pull my hands from my work.

After several moments, the crying seems to dissipate, becoming a slight whimper inside my head. I wipe my hands on a rag and cover the clues with a tarp.

Then I hear something else. A whisper. A word. I can't tell for sure, but I think she just called out, "Mom." The possibility of that—that she might be trying to communicate through me—compels me to go upstairs. I hurry into my room, check the computer screen for Mrs. Beckerman's contact info, and grab my phone. With trembling fingers, I block my number and dial hers.

Mrs. Beckerman picks up right away; I recognize her voice from TV and from her video. "Hello?" she repeats. "Is someone there?"

My mind is racing; I have no idea what to say, or if I should simply hang up. "Is this Tracey Beckerman?" I ask, playing for time, all out of breath.

"Yes. Who's *this*?"

"I can't really tell you who I am, but I have reason to believe that your daughter Sasha is still alive." *At least, I think she is. At least I think it's her voice I heard crying, and that I still hear crying now.*

"Who is this?" she demands again.

"Is there a plus sign?" I ask. "Or a *t* shape, or something with the letter *t* that might be a clue to her disappearance?"

"Excuse me?"

"Does Sasha like daisies?" I ask, aware of how little sense I'm making.

But it must make sense, because the other end of the lines goes church silent.

"Hello?" I ask, still able to hear the distant crying inside my head. I close my eyes and cover my free ear, trying to block it out.

"Please, tell me who this is," she says.

"Is there a special daisy, or a daisy charm . . . ? Were daisies her favorite flower?" I continue.

"Do you know where my daughter is?" Her voice quavers.

"No. I'm sorry." My voice is shaking, too. "But I believe she's still alive. I mean, I can't say for sure, but—"

"Where is she?" she snaps. "Have you seen her? Did you call the police? Is there something that I need to know?"

"I don't . . . I mean, I'm not—"

"Is it money you want?"

My heart hammers and my mouth turns dry. "No. I mean, I'm just . . ."

"Can I speak with her?" she continues. "Can you please just tell me if she's okay?"

I'm tempted to hang up, but now I feel like I'm involved—like I've almost made things worse.

"Tell me!" she shouts.

My mouth trembles. I'm at a loss for words.

"Camelia?" Dad asks, sneaking up behind me.

Startled, I turn off the phone, wondering what he heard, and hoping that Mrs. Beckerman didn't hear my name.

"What is it?" he asks, studying my face: the tears running down my cheeks, the blanching of my skin, the redness of my eyes.

"I have to go away for a while," I tell him.

He glances at the phone, probably wondering what just happened. I'm wondering the very same thing.

"For a few weeks," I say, correcting myself. "I want to do a summer art program. Spencer says it'll help get me into college. I've already done the research."

"Where?" he asks, somewhat taken aback.

"At Sumner College," I tell him. "In Peachtree, Rhode Island."

SPEND THE NEXT FEW DAYS filling out the paperwork for the program in Rhode Island, helping
Kimmie pack, and learning more about Sasha
Beckerman. Her crying voice continues in my mind, like
an incessant ringing in my ear—one that won't go away,
even when I'm asleep.

In my room, I sit down at my computer just as Mom
raps on my door.

"Camelia?" She walks in carrying a large white envelope in one hand and a candle in the other. "Blood orange,"
she says, referring to the candle. "Care to help me break
it in?" Without waiting for my response, she grabs a pottery dish off my shelf and sits down in the middle of the
floor. "Come join me." She sets the candle on the dish and
lights the wick.

I sit across from her with the candle between us, noticing that her henna-red hair is just a couple of shades darker

than the wax. "So, your dad told me all about this summer program you want to attend . . . in Rhode Island."

"Spencer says it'll look good on my résumé."

Mom reaches out to take my hand. "I assume that's not the only reason you want to go."

"You assume correctly," I tell her. "I need some space to figure things out. Plus, the program sounds pretty interesting—a three-hour studio in the morning, using an array of sculptural media, and then a theory class in the afternoon."

Mom looks down at our hands. They're clasped together in an awkward position; my pinkie finger's left out of her grip. "There's something I want to show you," she says, breaking the clasp to open the envelope. She pulls out a piece of paper and hands it to me.

It's a copy of my birth certificate.

"Dad said you were asking to see this," she says.

I gaze down at my name, just below Alexia's, feeling a slight chill. The space for the father's name has been left blank. "It's really real," I say, like there was any question.

"Definitely real and definitely empowering—that is, if you choose to see it that way."

"Did Aunt Alexia name me, then?"

"No. *I* did. That was never a lie. As soon as I held you, I could feel your strength. It emanated from your soul. Like a chameleon, I knew you'd have good survival instincts and that you'd be able to adapt to your surroundings."

Because I needed to adapt to them.

Mom hands me another document. "Here's the amended

birth certificate." It's dated six months after the original, when she and Dad officially adopted me.

"Wow," I say, feeling the hairs stand up along the back of my neck. It's one thing to hear about the details of my birth, but it's another thing to see the proof.

"Just one more piece to this puzzle," Mom says, reaching into the envelope again. She takes out a photograph and holds it up in the candlelight. "It's a little murky. . . ."

It takes me a second to process what I see: a picture of Aunt Alexia in a hospital bed, holding a baby. Holding me. The flickering of the candle casts a shadow on Alexia's face, highlighting her curious expression: a half smile, as if for an instant she might've been almost happy.

"So, now you can see for yourself," Mom continues. "We can have a clean slate. There are no longer any secrets." She grins like this is all a good thing.

But I'm not quite so sure. With the photo pressed between my fingers, I assume Aunt Alexia is oblivious to its existence. "Did she happen to mention that I didn't show up to visit her this past weekend?"

Mom shakes her head. "Alexia's so focused on her therapy these days. She had a progress check recently, and all the doctors agree that she's been so much happier and more alert lately—so much more at peace with herself, despite being cooped up in a hospital."

When I first found out that one of Dr. Tylyn's specialties was the existence and nature of extrasensory powers, I knew that I wanted her to work with me *and* my aunt. I knew that my aunt's therapy up until that point had mainly consisted of hopping around from mental institution to mental institution, and lots of prescription meds. Clearly it wasn't working for her, as evidenced by her attempts at suicide. And, as talented as some of her previous doctors might have been, none of them had ever explored the possibility that maybe her symptoms weren't simply psychotic—that maybe she was psychometric.

"Dr. Tylyn has truly been a godsend," Mom says. "Your father and I are so grateful to her. Not only has she been instrumental in your aunt's healing process, she's been great for all of us. I've grown closer to my sister, and now I'm working to move past my resentment for my mother. . . ." Mom closes her eyes, places her hands together in a prayer position, and takes a full breath, as if thanking the therapy gods and goddesses, the ones who sent Dr. Tylyn our way.

"And speaking of your mother," I start to segue, "did you ever end up calling her back?"

Mom meets my eyes again, but she doesn't speak.

"I'll take that as a yes?" I say, when she hesitates.

She shrugs, like the call was no big deal, but I can see otherwise. Red splotches appear on her chest. "She said she'd heard that Aunt Alexia was staying with us."

"That's it?" I ask, suspecting a lot more.

Mom swallows hard, clearly reluctant to tell me. "My mother wanted to make sure that Alexia was all set financially—that your father and I wouldn't be looking for any monetary help or support, because your grandmother doesn't want to give any." Mom studies my face, checking for my reaction. "I'm sorry to have to tell you, but there's power in honesty, right? I need to be mindful of that."

"Does that mean you regret not telling me the truth about my birth?"

"No regrets," she says, pressing her eyes shut. "I agree with your dad that we did the right thing by not telling you when you were young, especially considering Aunt Alexia's shaky path. And then this past year, when we were planning to tell you, I wasn't quite prepared, having almost lost my sister, not to mention everything that you were going through. But, at the same time, I feel that your emotions are valid, and so there must've been some other way to handle this—to prepare you for the news, or to give it to you in pieces. In any case, life is about learning lessons, and I obviously needed to learn that one . . . even if it was the hard way. And so I'm grateful for it—for what I've learned."

"Wait, *what*?" I ask, repelled by her yogaspeak. I don't want her to feel grateful for betraying my trust, for distorting my world.

"Tell me more about this summer art program," she continues. Her Zen attitude makes me want to scream. When did this become about her? About *her* lesson? About *her* growth?

I breathe in the blood orange scent of the candle. Meanwhile, the crying in my head gets louder. "I think I need some air," I say, hoping she gets the message and leaves.

But instead, she chatters on about how time and distance can give way to wisdom and perspective. "If all canals are open," she adds, "and you allow the water to ebb and flow—"

"Except my water has hit a dam."

"Water that flows *always* finds a way," she says, refusing to let my bitterness poison her peaceful mood. "Just give it a little time. . . . Which reminds me . . . Yikes!" She checks her watch. "I should probably get dinner ready. F-egg-salad sandwiches." She rubs her palms together as if fake-egg-salad sandwiches (scrambled tofu, mixed with turmeric) were a rare treat.

I muster a polite grin, relieved when she finally lets me be.

# LESSON NUMBER FOUR:
## *KNOW YOUR WEAKNESSES AND KEEP THEM TO YOURSELF.*

"Do you think I could have a new bandage?" I ask him, referring to the one on my wrist, in the same place where he's got his mark. I'm pretty sure I asked him about his mark that night, but I'm fairly certain I couldn't see it clearly. He might've had a wristband partially covering it, or maybe it was his sleeve. Or maybe I'm remembering wrong.

The edges of the bandage are tattered and black. I lift the tape to peek at my wound. Red, raw, and puffy, my skin burns as the air hits it and I wince. It looks as if I've been branded, like cattle—as if someone took a burning iron and seared it right into my skin. From one angle the mark appears to be an *x*. From another angle, it's more like a plus-sign.

"Please," I continue, curious to know how I really got this cut and if it has any significance. "I think it's infected." Is this how gangrene sets in? I vaguely recall a lecture in science class, when Mr. Manzo was talking about untreated surface abrasions.

"I'll be back," he says. "Hopefully by that time you'll know better than to talk unless spoken to."

I can see the heel of his work boot through the hole in the wall as he walks away.

"Please," I repeat; my voice is hoarse. My wound is throbbing. I venture to the front of the cell, angling my body so that I can stick my face into the hole. His lantern is still on the ground. It lights up the powdery dirt floor. The rest of the room appears as usual: concrete walls, wooden door, a pile of burlap bags in the corner.

He's whistling now. My words mean nothing. I watch as he picks up the lantern. He walks out of my field of vision and then I hear the sound of the door pulled shut.

15

*F*AST-FORWARD TWO FULL WEEKS. I've been officially accepted into the summer program at Sumner College, and I couldn't be more elated.

"I'm hoping that some time away will give me clarity and perspective," I tell Kimmie and Wes.

It's late afternoon, and we're sitting at the ice-cream counter at Brain Freeze, sharing a double-fudge peanut-butter barrel with extra whipped cream and chocolate syrup.

"Okay, but if you come back as annoyingly evolved as your mom, I'm seriously going to have to beat some misery into you," Wes says. "When I picked you up, she placed a crystal on my forehead and told me that my third eye was clogged."

"Don't mind her; she's all about chakra cleansing these days. It's almost like she's glad that I caught her in a lie, because it's given her an opportunity to become a better person."

"Sickening," he says.

"I know." I take a giant bite of ice cream.

"And how is Adam handling the news of your departure?" Kimmie asks.

"Okay, so I haven't exactly told him yet. We've only been out once since I got the green light from admissions, but we were so busy talking about my parental funkdom that by the time I was going to tell him, things somehow segued to an incident in third grade when he split his pants open . . . and something about a package of peanut butter. I was only half listening, which I know is all my fault, but he totally took it personally, even when I apologized, and then our night was over."

"Torn pants and peanut butter . . . It doesn't get any more mortifying than that." Wes shudders.

"Oh, really?" Kimmie raises an eyebrow. "Need I remind you of freshman year, Halloween dance, Wesley the Oscar Mayer wiener?"

"Need not," he says, unwilling to walk down memory lane.

"I'm going to tell Adam about Sumner tonight. I'm heading over there after this—that is, if you'll drive me . . ." I give Wes a pleading look.

"Why should I, Miss *I'm Deserting You Over Summer Break*? I mean, how am I supposed to survive swimsuit season with my dad without the two of you around? Did I mention he wants to feed me protein shakes, crack raw eggs into my mouth, and have me do weekly weigh-ins? He's also installing chin-up bars on all the doors."

"Well, at least you'll look pretty buff." Kimmie pinches his puny bicep.

He pauses in midlick (of syrup). "You do know that one can get salmonella poisoning from ingesting raw eggs, don't you?"

She rests her head against his shoulder. "I'm just trying to look on the bright side."

"Well, I have a better idea," he says. "Let me come with you. I haven't started the protein shakes yet, so I could probably still fit into your suitcase. . . ."

"Get in line behind my little brother Nate. He's already threatened to down a bottle of hot sauce if I leave."

"Because indigestion and stomach ulcers will keep you here?" Wes says, perking up.

"More like because hot sauce tastes like poison to him, and so he assumes it has the same effect," she says. "Now that Dad's got his new apartment and Mom's started working, Nate's been clingier with me than ever. He doesn't want to see me go. Seriously, it's hard being ecstatic about your future when just about everyone around you feels dismal."

I slip my arm around Wes's shoulder. "You can come visit me whenever you want," I tell him. "I'll only be a couple of hours away."

"Which leads me to my next question," Kimmie begins. "How did you even pick Sumner? I mean, don't they have pottery programs in places like Miami or South Beach?"

"Yes, but you have to remember that I decided to look

into this whole going-away idea a bit late in the game. I'm pretty sure that most of the other intensive programs were already filled by the time I started applying."

I have no idea if that's true, but I'm reluctant to tell them that though Sasha might not have been the original reason for my getaway, the fact that I'm sensing things about her now is the reason I ultimately chose the place.

Truth be told, I've almost caved at least a dozen times and told them about Sasha—about how the sound of what I assume is her voice has been keeping me up at night or about how stupid I was to call her mother. But I've felt as if Kimmie's head was so far into the Big Apple that she wouldn't be able to see my side. Not that that's a bad thing. She's really excited about her internship, and just as excited by the idea that her best friend may have a fantabulous opportunity lined up, too.

"I'm sure Sumner will still be amazing," she says. "Almost as amazing as five years from now, when the three of us will be sharing a loft in Manhattan. You, with your art exhibits at some of the trendiest galleries in town"—she smiles at me—"Wes, as a photographer, and me designing dresses for rock stars and tragic rebels."

I manage a nod, unable to break it to her that I haven't so much as thought about my future as a potter in weeks. It's like she sees us moving together in one distinct direction, whereas I feel like we're growing apart.

# 16

*A*FTER BRAIN FREEZE, I text Adam to say that I'm on my way, and Wes drives me over.

"Is he making you dinner?" Kimmie asks.

"I hope not," I say; I have just ingested what has to have been at least a quart of ice cream. "I think he might've mentioned something about a big game and making some team-themed munchies."

"Talk about romantic," Kimmie coos, clearly being snarky. She wishes me luck, and I climb out of Wes's car.

Adam is already waiting in the lobby. His face lights up as I come through the door. "Hey, you," he says, wrapping his arms around me. He holds me closer than he has in a long time. "I've missed you."

Even though it's only been a couple of days since we last saw each other, I hug him harder, knowing exactly what he means. "Yeah, I've missed you, too."

We climb the stairs and enter his apartment, and

already I can hear the sound of cheering coming from the big screen in his living room.

"Who's playing?" I ask, trying to sound interested.

"The Angels versus the Red Sox." Adam pulls on a Red Sox cap and gives me a matching one.

"Thanks," I say, putting it on. It seems that I have underestimated the value of this game.

"So, I made us some snacks." He takes my hand and leads me into the living room. The coffee table is set up with chips and guacamole, quesadilla wedges, buffalo wings, and bottles of lemon-lime soda. "Okay, so I didn't go the themed route, but I did make most of it myself."

"Wow," I say, utterly impressed.

"Hungry?"

"Sure," I lie.

We sit on the sofa and the TV blares. It's almost too loud to talk, and considering how excited he is about the game, not to mention all the trouble he went to with the snacks spread, I decide that our talk can wait.

Between bites of quesadilla and sips of soda, Adam snuggles close to me. It's been a while since I felt this secure with him, and I think he feels it, too. When a commercial comes on, he leans in closer and pulls off my hat to kiss me. "I've missed you," he says again.

"I know I haven't been the most ideal girlfriend lately," I admit. "My drama has pretty much taken center stage on most of our dates."

"Well, it isn't taking center stage now." He kisses me

again, and I try my best to kiss him back and relish the moment, but I can't help feeling disappointed that he doesn't acknowledge how hurt I've been or tell me that he'll be there for me no matter what.

Instead, he pushes me back against the couch; suddenly I feel a bit smothered. I pull away, putting an end to the kiss, and then sit back up.

"There's something I need to talk to you about," I tell him.

"Okay," he says, glancing at the TV. The game has come back on.

I grab the remote and click it off. "I'm going away for a while."

"Where?" He furrows his brow.

"I applied to a summer intensive program in Rhode Island . . . an art program . . . at Sumner College, about two hours away from here."

"Wow," he says, taking the news in. "I didn't even know that you were looking into that sort of thing."

"I wasn't. It was sort of Spencer's idea at first. But I think it'll be good for me for a number of reasons."

"The least of which concerns your art, I'm guessing."

"Is it so bad that I want some time away?"

"It's bad for *me* . . . for us. I miss you, Camelia," he says yet again, making me finally realize how much my drama has affected him.

"It'll only be for three weeks."

"Three weeks on top of the two that we just had."

"What do you mean?" I ask, though I already know. Things were so much better between us before I found out the truth.

"Look," he says, softening slightly, "if you were going away for your art, I'd totally get it. I'd be right there to support you. But you're running away because you learned something that you didn't like."

"There's more to it."

"Is there?" He gives me a pointed look. "I mean, life goes on, Camelia. People hear stuff all the time—stuff they don't like or would rather not know—but they don't just run away. They deal with it. They turn the page."

"I wish I could."

Adam takes my hands and pulls me closer. "What can I do to help you, to make it better?"

"That's just it. You can't."

"Why not? I mean, we've talked about this. We've discussed how your parents' secrecy affected you and how you feel like you've been betrayed. . . ."

"You have to understand," I tell him. "My aunt is my *mother* now. Do you know what that could mean? How much that terrifies me?"

"I do." He nods. "Because we've talked about that, too. We've been over this, Camelia. But you're not *her*, remember?"

"I realize that," I tell him. *But what if my premonitions get the best of me? What if I try to help someone and end up failing miserably? What if one day I feel so alone that I can't quite think straight?*

Adam lets out a breath, clearly frustrated and probably tired of trying to fix me.

"I should go," I say. My face feels hot. I'm holding back tears. I reach for my bag, hoping that Wes can pick me up.

"Don't go," Adam says, taking my hand. "Please . . ."

I rest my forehead against his chest.

"I'm sorry," he whispers, stroking my back. "I just want you to be happy. I just want everything to be great between us. You know I'd do anything for you."

I smother my sobs against his shirt, wishing that I could be stronger for him, hating the fact that I can't be stronger for myself.

# 17

*A*FTER ADAM DROPS ME OFF, I rush straight to my room. It's almost eleven, but I don't want to turn in just yet. And so I sit down in front of my computer and log in to my e-mail account. Ben's message from a few weeks ago is still sitting in my in-box. I read it over, hit RESPOND, and then tell him how much I miss him. *And not just being together as a couple,* I type, *but having someone who really gets me—who knows what I'm going through, and understands how complex this is . . . and how complex I can be.*

I lean back in my seat, relieved to have gotten it all out. But then I highlight the chunk of text, hit DELETE, and start again:

Dear Ben,

I'm glad to hear you had fun in D.C. I've been thinking a lot about you too, wondering where you are, if you're meeting new friends, and when you'll be done traveling. If by any chance you're still in D.C., be sure to check out the Botanic Garden—it puts the Tree Huggers' sanctuary to shame.

Miss you and thinking about you,

Love,
Camelia

I read my response over, worried that it may sound too needy.

The truth is that I'm happy he's enjoying so much of life, and I certainly wouldn't want to pull him back before he's ready. But I also miss the sense of connectedness we shared. We both understood each other in ways that no one else could. I can't help but wonder if he misses that, too.

I highlight the text and read it over several more times, afraid that I may be pushing the envelope with phrases like *Love, Camelia* and *Miss you*. But then I reassure myself that the suggestion to see the Botanic Garden and the question about friends counter any hint of how torn I feel without him.

I push SEND and navigate over to Neal Moche's blog to read another entry, still yearning for that sense of connection.

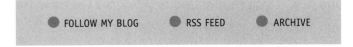

## From the Journal of Neal Moche

I've started following that guy around a bit, which is taking up a lot of my time, keeping me here longer than I'd wanted. He lives in a house with broken shutters, peeling paint, and stairs that have gaping holes. The house borders a wooded conservation lot, giving me lots of places to hide. I watch him come home at night and have dinner with his girlfriend. After that, it's lights-out, which is my cue to leave.

He spends most of his days working: painting houses (except his), doing construction, laying brick, and digging foundations.

I'm surprised he hasn't noticed me yet as I sit on curbs, lurk near bushes, and pretend to look at street maps. I almost think I'm wasting my time, especially since I've yet to figure out the reason I got that gnawing feeling when he bumped into me. But then I also can't stop this jittery sensation. I've been so jumpy inside, anticipating that something big is about to happen. I hate this part of my life—of having my power—but I know I'll hate things a whole lot more if I simply ignore what I'm sensing.

I close out of the blog, grateful to have this window into Neal's world—to know that I'm not the only one feeling haunted. Like Neal, who seems compelled to find out more about the guy from the park, I almost feel like I have no other choice but to go to Rhode Island and address this voice inside my head, so I can silence it once and for all.

# 18

$\mathcal{J}$T'S A WEEK LATER, and I'm packed and ready to go to Sumner. Mom's loading up the car with snacks and inspirational CDs for the drive, and Dad's printing out the MapQuest directions because he's yet to feel a need for GPS.

"Camelia?" Mom calls. "Don't forget to pack an extra toothbrush."

"Okay," I shout, grabbing the folder marked SUMMER ARTS PROGRAM off my desk. I've been keeping hard-copy info about Sasha's case inside it, including the address of her home and school. I stuff it into my backpack, knowing that Adam will be here any moment to wish me luck and say good-bye.

I zip up my suitcase and pinch my cheeks for color, noticing the dark gray circles beneath my eyes from lack of sleep—from Sasha's incessant crying. It now haunts me day and night.

"Best to not keep a boy waiting," Mom says, poking her head into my room to announce Adam's arrival. Have we suddenly turned the clocks back a hundred years?

I grab my bags and proceed to the living room, where Adam scoops me into his arms. "I'll miss you," I tell him.

"Camelia, we should probably get going," Dad says, checking his watch. "Orientation is only until three."

While Dad brings my bags out to the car, Adam continues to hold me. "Call me as soon as you get there," he says.

"Definitely." I nod, thinking how good this feels without the drama.

Once outside, Adam lingers in front of the house, watching as we pull out of the driveway. I wave to him out the window, feeling in some way lonelier than I have in a long time, because I'm separating from everyone I care about, but also more invigorated than ever before, because hopefully I'm getting closer to what I need.

After a couple of hours' driving (and a CD and a half of Dr. Wayne Dyer's inspirational musings), Dad pulls in to the Sumner College campus.

It's even more beautiful than the images online depicted it. High up on a cliff that overlooks the ocean, the campus has ivy-covered brownstone buildings scattered around a sprawling green lawn with flower beds that form the letters *SC*.

"So lovely," Mom says, pointing out an abstract sculpture that resembles a giant booger.

Dad drives around to the side of the main building,

where tents have been set up for summer-school orientation. Nearby, students are mingling. There's a volleyball game being played. And grills are smoking with "ground-up cow flesh and intestine-encased pig parts" (as Mom so eloquently dubs hamburgers and hot dogs).

As soon as we park the car, a couple of girls sporting Orientation Rocks! T-shirts come bounding over to us.

"Hey, there," the taller girl says, just as I step out of the car. Her superhigh ponytail and megawatt smile make me feel like I'm here to try out for the cheering squad. "I'm Carlie."

"And I'm Courtney," the other girl chirps.

"Put us together and we're C-squared," they sing in unison.

"Excuse me?" I ask, feeling as though I've just been bopped on the head with a couple of pom-poms.

"Carlie Sherman," the taller girl says, backtracking. She shakes my hand and then gestures to her friend. "And this is Courtney Porter."

"We like to call ourselves C-squared," Courtney insists on explaining, "which basically means that we're pretty inseparable."

"So, welcome to Sumner at summer," Carlie says. "Omigod, did I seriously just say that?"

"Only for the kagillionth time today." Courtney lets out a hyena laugh, as if what Carlie had just said were the funniest thing ever.

Meanwhile, I'm still trying to figure out if they chose to be inseparable because their names have the same first initial, or if it's simply because nobody else on campus can stand them.

"Anyway, welcome," Carlie continues. "To summer. At Sumner."

"Thanks," I say. "I'm Camelia."

"Omigosh," Courtney squeals. "You should totally hang with us. We could totally be C-cubed."

I look back at my parents. Dad's got my bags in both hands, and Mom's carrying a cooler loaded with snacks (some of her homemade fruit-and-nut bars).

"You can leave your bags over there," Carlie says, pointing to an area just beyond a water fountain. It appears that the area's been designated a drop-off depot for luggage.

"Could I bring them to Camelia's room?" Dad asks.

"We'd really love to see it," Mom adds. "And to help Camelia move in . . ."

"Well, that's the tricky part." Carlie grimaces. "Because we're sort of experiencing some technical difficulties of the sewage seepage kind." She twirls a strand of her short blond hair around her finger.

"But trust me when I say that we're doing you a favor," Courtney explains. "And the problem is being rectified as we speak. So, let's just hang out here for a while, shall we? We've got boccie, badminton, volleyball, and a dunk tank."

"Or maybe you want to get something to eat." Carlie nods toward the smoking grills.

I look out at the festivities, which are devoid of parents, and then back at Mom and Dad, standing just a couple of feet behind me now. "Do you want to go somewhere and come back?" I ask them. "Once it's okay to move in?"

"Nonsense," Mom says. "You go and have some fun, but call us when you're all settled in, okay?"

I lean in to give each of them a hug. While Mom's is tidy and quick (despite all that touchy-feely CD-listening), Dad pulls me against him, as if he doesn't want to let me go. When we end our embrace, his face is all red and blotchy.

Mom takes his hand. "You were like this on her first day of kindergarten, too," she reminds him. "But your little girl is growing up."

Dad nods and takes a step back, but it looks like someone just ripped out his heart.

After they leave, a jumble of emotion stirs inside my stomach: hopefulness, anguish, apprehension. I look at C-squared, who are playing a game of boccie now, and then toward the groupings of students meandering around munching on grilled food and getting to know one another.

And that's when I spot him. Sitting alone at one of the picnic tables, he stares in my direction, and it's all I can do not to cry out with glee.

Wes.

He gets up when he sees that I notice him and makes his way toward me. The smile on his face is every bit as beamy as mine is right now.

"What are you doing here?" I gush.

"Would you believe that I need to brush up on my painting skills?" he asks. "Pun intended."

"Excuse me?"

"You didn't think I'd let you go off by yourself in your time of need, did you?"

"You didn't seriously come here just for me."

"I didn't?" He blushes. "Well, it's actually for *me*, too. After you told me about the program, I may've been persuaded to check it out. And, I'll have to admit, their photography courses sound pretty swanky." He flashes me his temporary Sumner College ID card, which shows him sticking his tongue out and making the peace sign. "And let me assure you that it wasn't easy. I had to pull a few strings, talk to a few people, and tell my dad that I was in love with you and needed to follow my heart. . . ."

"And he bought that?"

"Are you kidding? He even gave me my allowance back."

I hug him. "You're the best, you know that?" I say, not quite sure if any of what he's saying about his dad is even remotely close to the truth. But right now, in this moment, I don't care if it is.

# 19

*I*NSTEAD OF PARTAKING in the BBQ-flavored orientation festivities, Wes and I sneak off to the booger sculpture to talk. We sit on the grass under a tree.

"So, what's the deal?" I ask him, already suspecting the real story, but wanting to hear him say it.

"The *deal*?"

"The main reason you came here, I mean."

"I already told you." He avoids my gaze, plucking at grass. "I thought you could use some company. I can sense a runaway situation when I smell one."

"Funny, but all I smell is old-man cologne," I joke.

"Are you kidding me?" He stops plucking to glare at me. "This stuff costs me a hundred and fifty bucks a bottle."

"Are you running away, too?"

"Could you blame me if I was?"

"No blaming here," I say.

"I just can't take it at home." Wes shrugs, more sullen than I've ever seen him before. "My dad told me that if I don't start becoming more of a man, he's going to disown me."

"And what does your mom say?"

"Mom's still his puppet, almost as afraid of him as I am."

"He doesn't hurt her in any way, does he?"

"Not physically," he says, now raking the grass with his fingers, "but he punches near her, on the wall. . . . He also pounds on doors. . . ."

"Does he ever hurt *you* physically?"

Wes shakes his head. "But sometimes I wish he *would*. I almost think that would be easier to take than his threats and put-downs—than him making me feel like pond scum all the time. Anyway, my mother's the one who insisted I come here—to follow you. She even paid the tuition out of her own allowance."

I bite my tongue to keep from asking why a full-grown woman has an allowance. "So, she wanted you to run away, too?"

"If she had it her way, she'd probably run with me."

"Does she know?" I ask, reluctant to say the words aloud, since he hasn't exactly stated them to me. "About your poetry journal, I mean?"

Wes looks up from the grass to study my face. His cheeks have gone slightly pink. "Well, she hasn't exactly read the journal, but I think she might suspect what's inside."

When I first read Wes's poetry journal, I wasn't exactly surprised that he was gay. More like relieved that he was finally letting someone (me) in. And so, upon returning it, I offered to talk, but Wes didn't want any part of a discussion.

"Anyway, here I am," he segues. "And it should be noted that I could just as easily have followed Kimmie to NYC."

"But instead I'm the chosen one?"

"Because I sensed that there was something else going on with you."

"Well, there is," I say, eager to open up about Sasha since he's being so open with me.

"Care to share over barbecued wieners?" He looks back toward the smoking grills. "They're smelling a little too yummy and overprocessed to resist."

"Sounds perfect," I say.

# LESSON NUMBER FIVE:
## *LISTEN, AND LISTEN WELL.*
## *YOUR LIFE MAY ONE DAY DEPEND ON IT.*

I wake up with a start, picturing his eyes. Light brown and almond-shaped, with long, curly lashes and deeply set lids. Eyes far too pretty for a boy's.

I remember that he looked at me almost as soon as I stepped through the door that night. He was sitting at the makeshift bar—what I imagined was once an old assembly-line table, because it spanned the length of the room. I figured he must've seen the scowl on my face and heard me snap at Jaden and Misery.

I remember glancing in his direction several more times, because I'd noticed that he'd noticed me. There was a certain power in doing something that Misery had warned me not to.

I hear him: the sound of locks opening, hinges creaking, and then his footsteps, moving across the dirt floor. I brace myself, hating his sounds.

I turn on my flashlight and aim it toward the hole, assuming he must've listened to the tape. The tape recorder is there again. He pushes it inside, following it with the microphone.

"Do it again," he says; his voice is tired and gruff. "But this time, tell me something honest."

"Why?" I ask, but as soon as I ask it, I want to take the question back, because I've spoken out of turn, and because the more he tells me, the more I'll know, and the less willing he may be to set me free.

"No questions," he snaps.

I hear him get up. I hear his breath as he lets out a tired sigh.

"Wait," I plead. My cut continues to throb. "Could I please just have a fresh bandage? And some more crackers and water?" I haven't eaten in what feels like days.

It's quiet for several seconds, as if he's considering the idea.

"Hello?" I call, when he doesn't answer. "My cut . . . It's burning. Could I at least have some fresh water to clean it?" I look down at the cross shape, still confused about what it means, but afraid to actually find out.

"Give me your flashlight," he says, finally.

I hesitate, fearing that I've pushed him too far, asked him too much.

"Give me your flashlight." His tone is cold and even.

My fingers trembling, I push my flashlight through the hole, hoping he's just going to replace the batteries.

He snatches it. His dirty fingers wrap themselves

around the handle. This time, I'm able to see his hand. Like mine, it looks as if it's been burned, as if he's been branded too. A muted red scar with a zigzag shape.

And then it's gone. And everything turns black. And I hear him start to walk away.

"Wait!" I shout. "Please, don't leave me alone. Don't leave me in the dark.

"Can you please just talk to me?" I continue. "Ask me questions. We don't need the tape recorder. I can tell you whatever it is you want to know."

But he doesn't answer. I hear the locks turn: *click*, *clang*, *snap*.

"Please!" I scream. The word tears at my throat. "Don't leave me like this," I whimper, knowing he no longer hears me, fearing that no one will ever be able to hear me again.

## 20

*I* WAKE UP TO THE CRYING VOICE inside my head, but this time there's actual speech. I'm sure of it. She's pleading to be heard.

"I *do* hear you," I whisper, without a thought, into my empty room.

Luckily, I got the single that I requested. The admissions person who read my application heeded my warning that having night tremors that involved waking up in the middle of the night and shouting at the top of my lungs would make me a lousy roommate. (Okay, so I might've lied on my paperwork.) They put me at the end of the hallway as a result, five doors down from any of the other students.

I place my hands over my ears, focusing harder on the voice. The crying sounds much more desperate than usual: a high-pitched wail that cuts through my core, urging me out of bed. I switch on the light and look at the clock. It's barely three a.m.

"Please," I whisper, plugging my ears with my fingers, but it almost sounds like the voice is outside my head now, coming from out in the hallway. I cross the room and open the door. The hallway is vacant and dim.

"I *do* hear you," I say again. The resident director's door is at the other end of the hallway. I move in that direction, pinching myself to make sure that I'm not asleep. The crying seems to get louder with each step. Is it possible that a student's crying—that the voice is indeed outside my head?

I'm about to knock on the resident director's door, but the crying sound is coming from above now, on the second floor. I follow it up the stairs, noticing an echoing sensation—it bounces off the bones of my skull, making my stomach lurch.

On Wes's floor now, I proceed toward his room, vaguely remembering having read somewhere that girls weren't allowed to be on the boys' floor—and vice versa—after eleven o'clock. But I knock on his door anyway.

He doesn't answer, and so I knock harder. Finally, he comes to the door. His eyes are bloodshot, and his normally coifed hair is matted and pillow-warped.

"Is there a fire?" he asks. Toothpaste residue lingers at one corner of his mouth.

"Do you hear that?" I ask him. "Did someone just hiccup?"

He furrows his brow. "Am I to assume that you're sleepwalking? Or perhaps you decided to party without me . . ." He tsk-tsks.

"Not sleepwalking. Definitely not partying." I shake my head.

"Okay, so then, your alarm clock must be on the fritz, because it's barely three a.m. And unless it's the day after Thanksgiving and you're getting in line early for some crazy holiday madness sale, for which I'm the lucky recipient, go back to bed."

"Is someone crying?" I ask.

He pokes his head out into the hallway and then looks at me like I'm full-on crazy.

"I need your help," I tell him, wishing I'd gotten around to filling him in about Sasha yesterday. I would have, but as soon as we got our food from the grill, a bunch of other students joined us at the table, and we all ended up chatting about art.

I peer over my shoulder, noticing how the crying seems to be moving further away now. I remember having read in Psychometrically Suzy's blog about the experience in which she touched her father's hat and heard his voice even though he'd already passed away. She followed the voice until it brought her to a photograph that he had evidently wanted her to see.

Maybe there's something that Sasha wants me to see. Maybe I need to go outside . . . or drive off campus.

"Can I borrow your car keys?" I ask.

"Not until you reveal a wide-open gash gushing with blood for which you need emergency medical attention. In which case, I'll drive you."

"Except you can't actually *see* my gash. It's inside my head, slowly driving me insane."

"Brain aneurysm?" He cocks his head, mock-sincere.

"Can I just come inside for a second?"

He opens the door to let me in. The setup of his room is basically like mine: an eight-by-eight-foot space furnished with a desk, a dresser, and bunk beds.

"Did you get a single room, too?" I ask. The upper bunk is vacant.

"No, but my roommate made a friend over boccie ball, and I guess the game went into overtime."

I take a seat on his rumpled bed and do my best to relax, but the crying seems more distant now, and I can't help worrying that I'm wasting critical time.

"I wish I had something flavorful to offer you," Wes says. "But how about a jug of water for now?" He gestures to the gallon jug on his dresser. "Don't mind the residual Nutella stains on the spout."

"I'm fine."

"So, what's up?" He plops down beside me on the bed. "Why the sudden urgency about my car?"

"I might need to go somewhere," I tell him, eyeing his car keys on the desk.

"Well, I could've *guessed* that. But I need way more information if I'm going to deem you Audi-worthy. Care to enlighten me as to what's going on inside that twisted mind of yours?"

And so I tell him. Everything. About Sasha, about how

she's the reason I ended up at Sumner, and how I believe that it's her crying that's been stuck inside my brain. At the end of it all, I almost expect him to bop me on the head to try to knock some sense into me, but instead he's surprisingly silent.

"Say something," I tell him, suddenly feeling self-conscious.

"I'm not sure where to begin. I mean, Sasha freaking Beckerman?"

"I assume you're familiar with the case."

"What makes you think you'll be able to find Sasha when the police haven't been able to?"

"I don't *know* that I'll find her, but maybe I can help in some other way. I mean, there's a reason I hear her voice, right?"

"And how are you so sure that it's *her* voice?"

"Because that's what my gut tells me."

"And what does your common sense say?"

"You really think this sounds crazy, don't you?"

"Okay," he says, "let's just say for argument's sake that it's indeed Sasha's voice inside your head. Why you? Why *your* head, I mean? It's not like you know the girl."

"No, but we have something very significant in common. We were both adopted."

"And you think that you two are the only ones that that's ever happened to? I mean, seriously, do you watch Maury Povich?"

"No, but when I was researching summer programs, I came across her case," I say, proceeding to fill him in on how I'd also seen it mentioned on the unsolved-mysteries show at the diner. "Anyway, I started to delve deeper, and then, when I was sculpting, the crying voice came to me."

"And so you just assumed that it was her?"

I shake my head and tell him about the *t*-shaped piece I sculpted. "It could've been the letter *t* or a plus sign."

"As in two plus two equals crazy?"

"As in I had no idea whose voice it was at first. But then one day, when I really focused on Sasha—on everything I'd been researching, including a video of her that I watched a kazillion times—the voice came to me again."

"When you were sculpting?"

I nod. "It was like I conjured it up, like I was definitely on to something big, because the voice got really loud, and I may've even heard her call out for her mother. I can't really say for sure." I sigh, realizing that I'm babbling. "Anyway, the voice has been in my head ever since. The crying, I mean. And it doesn't go away."

"Wow," he says, leaning back on his bed. He reaches for the Magic 8-Ball on his dresser, shakes it up, and flashes me the result: OUTLOOK NOT SO GOOD.

"Does that mean you won't help me?"

"Well, of course I'm going to help you, but do you think it can wait until dawn?"

"Not really. I mean, I hear her crying voice *now*. I want to see where it will lead me."

"You do realize how nutty that sounds, don't you? Okay, yes, I know it's *you*, that you're superpsychometrically talented and all, but where do you honestly intend to go at this hour? Denny's for a Moons Over My Hammy?"

"So, you won't let me take your car?"

Wes shakes the Magic 8-Ball again and flashes me the answer: *"Ask again later,"* he reads. "I need more sleep, and so do you. Trust me when I say that I'm doing this for your own good."

"Fine," I say, faking a smile, glad when he turns again to set the Magic 8-Ball back down—my cue to snatch his keys.

# 21

ES'S CAR KEYS gripped in my hand, I hurry downstairs, grab my cell phone from my room, and continue down to the lobby. No one's working the front desk, so I decide not to bother signing out. Instead, I plow through the doors, my adrenaline high, expecting the crying to be louder outside. But it's the same as it was in Wes's room: still there, yet somewhat distant and nowhere near as intense as it was just moments before, or when I could hear her actual words.

I proceed to his car anyway, hoping that I'm not too late—that the voice will intensify as soon as I get behind the wheel. Two campus security cars are parked on the other side of the soccer field. The fronts of the cars are pointed in opposite directions, but the driver's-side windows are lined up so they can chat. They don't seem to notice me—or if they do, they don't appear to care—as I disarm Wes's car alarm, slip inside, and start the ignition.

I pull out of the parking lot and circle the area, concentrating on the sound of Sasha's tears, but they're barely above a whimper now. I pull over and type the address of the Beckerman residence into Wes's GPS, hoping that seeing her house may help evoke her voice more.

The roads are mostly empty. Strips of light from the streetlamps reflect off the rain-soaked pavement. I take several turns, passing through the center of town, finally arriving at my destination, only five minutes from the campus.

The Beckerman house is like something straight out of a storybook: a grand Victorian-style home with multiple peaks. A pretty brick walkway leads to a stained-glass front door, illuminated by a porch light.

Other than the Beckerman house, none of the houses on the street have their outside lights on. The Beckermans must be keeping theirs on for a reason: maybe so that Sasha can find her way home.

I park out front and wait several seconds for something magical to happen. But the crying voice remains the same, making me feel both stupid and guilty. I never should've driven out here or taken Wes's keys. I reach for my phone, wanting to call him to apologize, but I'm reluctant to wake him again.

Just as I roll down the window to get some air, my cell phone rings. I pick it up, hoping it's Ben, that somehow he's sensing how lost I feel right now. But when I check the screen, I see that it's Wes.

"I'm sorry," I say, in lieu of a hello.

"You *do* know that grand-theft auto is a felony, don't you? Punishable by up to five years in prison?"

"So, do me a favor and have me arrested. I'll probably be better off."

"Hmm . . . tempting."

"I'm sorry," I repeat, shaking my head, hating myself for betraying his trust.

"Just tell me you're not sitting in front of the Beckerman residence right now, because that would, like, make you a crazy person for sure."

I look in the rearview mirror. "You're not spying on me, are you?"

"And how would I finagle that one? It's not like I have a car."

"Okay, so then you know me way too well."

"You're certifiable, Camelia."

"I know," I mutter, feeling a crumbling sensation inside my chest.

"Of course, you're *also* sleep-deprived and hearing voices," he continues. "So, I may have to give you a free pass—*this time*. Just get your thieving ass back here."

"Will do." I hang up and take one last look at the house, about to pull away. But someone inside has turned on a light. It's on the second floor, in what I'm guessing may be a bedroom.

I take off my seat belt, slide over to the passenger side, and search the window in question. A couple of sheer curtains hang at the sides, allowing me to see inside the room. The walls are yellow. There's a dresser with a mirror positioned over it, with what appear to be snapshots or cards of some sort tacked around the glass. It's Sasha's room; I'm sure of it.

The crying in my head gets louder, telling me that I need to go inside, but first I need a plan. A woman in the house crosses in front of the window. She doesn't seem to notice I'm there. Her hair is tied back, but I'd recognize her anywhere—Sasha's mother.

She moves in front of the window again, but this time she stops and looks out. Straight at me. My heart pounding, I scramble to get back behind the wheel and speed away as fast as I can.

## 22

*I* RAP LIGHTLY on Wes's door and he answers with his hand extended.

"Thanks for your keys," I whisper, depositing them into his palm. "I'm sorry again for taking them." I start to walk back down the hall, but he stops me.

"Hold on," he orders, stepping out into the hallway. "You don't seriously think you're going to wake me up in the middle of the night, steal my keys, and not give me details, do you?"

"It was kind of a bust, but I suppose that's what I get for not thinking things through."

"Feeling sorry for ourselves, are we?"

I shrug and turn away, wishing that I'd just listened to him in the first place and gone back to my room. "I'll tell you about it tomorrow."

\* \* \*

Even though it's four a.m., there's no way I can fall asleep. Back in my room, I bring my laptop over to my bed to check my e-mail. I scroll down past at least a dozen junk-mail messages until I find the message I was hoping would be there.

Dear Camelia,

I can't sleep tonight, can't get my brain to shut off. Sometimes I wish I could pick up the phone and call you, but I think that would make things confusing, and you don't need to be confused. Anyway, I hope all is well and that you're happy. You deserve all the happiness that life can bring you.

I'll be busy over the next few days, but I'll write again when I can.

Love,
Ben

I read his e-mail over and over and *over* again until my vision becomes slightly blurred. He sent the message less than thirty minutes ago, meaning he could still be awake.

I grab my cell phone, noticing that I have three missed calls—two from my parents, one from Adam—as well as a text from Kimmie ordering me to call her just as soon as I've settled in.

I search my phone's address book for Ben's number. My thumb hovers over the dial button for several seconds before I finally have the nerve to press it. After five rings, I assume my call will go to voice mail.

But then he actually answers: "Camelia."

The sound of his voice makes my whole world spin. "Were you sleeping?" I ask him.

"I wish."

"I got your e-mail."

"Sorry about that." He lets out a sigh. "After I hit SEND I wished that I could take it back. I don't want you worrying about my lack of sleep."

"I can't sleep, either," I tell him. "I mean, obviously, right?"

"Is there something on your mind?"

I pull the covers over me and stretch from head to toe, relishing the comfort of his voice. "I'm too restless, I suppose," I say, deciding not to tell him where I am.

"Yeah, I guess I'm feeling restless, too."

There's silence between us for several seconds—no doubt because neither one of us wants to reveal too much and become too vulnerable.

"Where are you, by the way?" I ask, wondering if he can hear the anguish in my voice.

"Not so far from home, actually."

"Are you headed back to Freetown?"

"Wouldn't that be nice?"

"Even though you sounded so happy on the road?"

"I guess I could use a little break from traveling. How's

everything going with Adam, by the way?"

"Do you and he still keep in touch?"

"I talk to him," he says. "All the time." The tone of his voice is strong and emphatic, as if he wants to drive the point home and have me read between the crooked lines: that he stays in regular contact with Adam for the sole purpose of keeping tabs on me and ensuring that I'm safe. "I probably always will," he continues.

His words stir an aching sensation inside my heart.

"But Adam keeps pretty tight-lipped where you and he are concerned," he adds.

I close my eyes, thinking about how I made a conscious decision to be with Adam—because I have fun with him, because he's good to me, because I always know where I stand with him—unlike the way I feel with Ben, where everything is always a mystery.

"I hope you and he always will keep in touch," I say, curious to know if he'll read between the lines, too—and if in turn he'll figure out what he is for me: the boy I will forever want but should never have.

"Adam's a really great guy," he reminds me. "And you deserve to be with someone great."

"I should probably go," I say, not wanting to discuss my love life with him.

"Not yet," Ben says. "I want to tell you about the Botanic Garden in D.C."

"You went there?" I ask.

"I'd love to say that it was because of your suggestion, but I actually visited it before I got your e-mail."

"And so, what did you think?"

"That's the weird part, because it reminded me of you."

The response hangs a question mark over my head. I mean, what is he trying to say?

He spends the next couple of minutes talking about how enchanting the garden is, with its varied species of trees and exotic breeds of ivy. And all the while, I can't help imagining him lying here beside me, the warmth of his chest against my back.

"Sorry about all my babbling," he says. "I should let you get some sleep."

"I miss you," I say without thinking, feeling my eyes well up.

"I miss you, too," he says, which makes everything so confusing, because it's not like him to tell me how he feels. "But I'll be in touch." He clears his throat, making me wonder if he's not getting choked up, too.

We hang up and I silence my phone, finally able to unleash my tears. They're accompanied by gut-wrenching sobs that surprise even me. How long have I been holding them back? How long have I been this unhappy?

I hug my pillow to my belly, feeling completely tormented, because Ben *isn't* good for me, because Adam's the one I'm supposed to want. But it's not just the loss of my relationship with Ben that I mourn; it's also the loss of our friendship. I want so badly to tell him things (about my aunt, about my parents, about where I am and what I'm doing here). But I can't, because of this palpable energy between us. An energy that's bound to suck me up and spit me out if I ever dare to open up to him again.

I roll over in bed and cry until I can barely breathe. Until I end up choking on my own tears.

Until Wes comes and crawls right in beside me.

Is it possible that I was crying so loud that he heard? Or maybe he couldn't wait until tomorrow to talk more? Did I leave my door open?

He doesn't ask what's wrong, and I'm not sure how much he heard of my phone conversation, if anything at all. Instead, he cradles me in his embrace and allows me to simply feel.

# 23

FTER ABOUT AN HOUR OR SO, when all my tears have dried up, I turn over to look at Wes. Still lying beside me on the bed, he's managed to nod off. His head rests against my pillow, and a string of drool drips from his mouth onto my bedsheet, creating a circle of spit.

I couldn't be more grateful for his friendship. Having him here also makes me miss Kimmie, the missing member of our tight little trio—so much so that I reach for my phone to send her a text: *Just wanted to let you know that I'm settling in okay and that I really miss you. I hope you're having a great time. Let's catch up soon.*

I push SEND, thinking once again about how things have really changed between us. Normally, I would've called her, regardless of the time. Normally, *she* would've been the one to come to my room, and offer a shoulder, and fall asleep on my pillow. And, as much as I love Wes, the fact that Kimmie's no longer that person makes my heart ache.

I get up, mindful of Wes's spit, and retreat over to my desk in search of a diversion. I open up my laptop and navigate to Neal Moche's blog.

FOLLOW MY BLOG     RSS FEED     ARCHIVE

### From the Journal of Neal Moche

Last night, after the lights had gone out at that guy's house, I decided to stick around and see if anything might happen after dark. My gut proved correct. After about an hour, a light inside the house went on.

Concealed by trees, I moved closer and crouched down behind some trash cans in the side yard. I could see his silhouette moving in the window of what I'd guessed was a mudroom. He was pulling on a pair of shoes and grabbing a jacket, getting ready to go somewhere, despite the fact that it was a little after midnight.

I leaned out a little farther, able to see him through the crack between the shade and the window.

That's when his girlfriend came into the room, startling him. The window was open, so I could hear some of what they were saying. She kept asking where he was going and if he thought she was stupid.

"Are you cheating on me?" she asked him. "Is that where you're going right now? To be with her?"

"You're speaking out of turn," he shouted, grabbing a lantern off a shelf. "Now go back to bed!"

I attempted to move a little closer, scurrying along the ground to hide behind a wheelbarrow, when I accidentally bumped against a trash-can cover. It fell with a crash.

I tried not to flinch, hoping they'd think the noise was from an animal trying to get into the garbage. Out of the corner of my eye, I saw the shade move and heard the window slam down. After that, the light switched back off. I kept still, fearing that one of them might take another peek toward the trash—toward me.

A second later, an outside light went on, illuminating the porch, only a few yards away from me. I heard a lock click, followed by the sound of a door creaking open. He was outside. I listened to the sound of his boots as he clomped down the stairs, catching his heel on one of the broken steps.

Holding my breath, I knew I wasn't completely concealed. I was pretty sure that my legs were visible under the wheelbarrow and that my feet were sticking out.

I could hear the jingling of keys. Was he going to drive somewhere? His pickup was parked at the front of the house, which meant he'd have to pass by me to get there. My head tucked down, I clenched my teeth, straining to hear something that might tell me his next move. Something dropped to the ground. The sound was followed by his footsteps.

He was moving away, toward the back of the house, using the lantern to guide him. I got up and started to follow him. He proceeded into the woods behind the house. I kept a good distance behind him so he wouldn't hear the snapping of twigs as I trampled over broken branches. But with no flashlight, I felt the woods closing in on me. With each step, it was getting harder to see my hand in front of my face, never mind follow a light that seemed to get farther and farther away.

The overgrowth was overwhelming, scratching at my face as I worked to navigate through the brush. The guy's lantern was no longer visible. I'd lost him.

By the time I get to the end of the entry, my adrenaline is pumping, and not just because of where Neal was and how he almost got caught, but also because of how much I can relate to him—chasing the unknown and going where he wouldn't otherwise venture, all because of what he senses, of what he needs to know.

*A*CLUNKING SOUND ROUSES ME. I whisper Ben's name and reach out to touch him, opening my eyes, startled to find Wes's sweatshirt scrunched up beside me. I've been using it as a pillow.

And that's when I realize that Ben isn't here. He was part of a dream. It was Wes who fell asleep in my bed last night, but now he's gone.

I roll over and start to sit up, hearing a gasp escape from my throat. Sitting across from me, at my desk, is Adam.

*Adam.*

"Am I still dreaming?" I ask, wondering how this can be real, if maybe he'll vanish in a couple of blinks.

"If I were part of a dream, don't you think I'd be wearing nicer clothes?"

I gaze at his long-sleeved T with tattered sleeves and his sweatpants with a hole in the knee.

Adam flashes me a tiny smile, and I want to smile back. But I'm too busy worrying he might've heard me whisper Ben's name just now.

"I left my apartment right after talking to Wes," he explains.

I glance at the clock; it's a little after one in the afternoon. I missed my studio class. Adam's missed his shift at work. If he doesn't leave soon, he'll miss his night classes as well.

And for what?

"Adam, I feel awful. You didn't have to come all this way. I mean, what did Wes *say* to you?"

Adam comes and sits beside me on the bed. "First of all, don't be mad at Wes. When I called this morning, he said that you were sleeping in because you'd had a rough night."

"And 'a rough night' brought you here?"

"Okay, so he might've also mentioned something about a nervous breakdown. But, like I said, don't be mad. It took a bit of prodding—not to mention some serious negotiating—to get the information out of him."

"Negotiating?"

"Kidding, of course." He smirks. "Wes can't be bribed."

"Well, thanks," I say, still feeling awkward. "For coming all this way, I mean."

"I must say, I was a bit surprised when Wes answered your phone." He raises an eyebrow at me. "I didn't even know he was doing this summer program with you, and then, when he admitted to having fallen asleep in your bed . . ."

"You can't honestly tell me you're jealous of Wes."

"Okay, so maybe not." He takes my hand. "But only because I *do* trust you. Completely."

"I can't even believe you came here," I say, shaking my head. His kindness is almost too much to bear.

"Are you kidding?" he says, squeezing my hand; his face is all aglow. "I'd drive cross-country for you."

I swallow hard and look away, not quite sure that I deserve his trust, and relieved that it doesn't seem he heard me whisper Ben's name.

"Let's go somewhere," he suggests. "I'll take you to lunch. Or, in this case"—he checks his watch—"how about breakfast?"

"I'm not really hungry," I say. "But maybe we could talk?"

"Sure."

"How much did Wes tell you?"

Adam reaches into his backpack and pulls out a bag from the Press & Grind. "Wes just said that you were probably homesick, which is why I thought I'd bring along a piece of home."

I peek inside the bag, spotting a triple-fudge brownie. "You're so sweet, you know that?"

"I have no doubt that you'd do the same for me."

I try to smile, thinking how unbelievably lucky I am.

"Do you want to talk about what's bothering you?" he

asks. "Because I have a feeling it's not just a campy case of homesickness, especially since you've barely been gone for twenty-four hours."

"Not just homesick," I admit.

"So, is it the whole adoption thing again? Or are you still feeling paranoid that you'll end up like your aunt?" His tone is soft, but his words hit hard.

*"Paranoid?"*

"You know what I mean." He flashes me a smile.

"I had another psychometric episode," I say, deciding to switch topics. "The stuff I've been sensing revolves around a girl named Sasha Beckerman. She's been missing for months now, and a lot of people think she ran away."

"Wait—is that the girl I've been hearing about on the news?"

"It is," I say, curious as to whether he knows that she's from Rhode Island.

"Why are you sensing stuff about *her?*"

"Because Sasha was adopted, too. . . . At least, I think that's why. As soon as I started researching her case, I felt an instant connection."

"Don't you feel you have enough going on without worrying about some girl that the FBI is already looking for?"

"And what if I'd had that same attitude a few months ago, when it was your life that was in danger?"

Adam lets out a giant breath. "Okay, so what can I do to help?"

"Let's talk about it later," I say, feeling slightly

reassured by his words, even though I can see the conflict in his eyes. I know he wants things to go back to the way they were before. What I wouldn't give for that, too.

I pull him a little closer, so that his face is within kissing distance. Adam's deep brown eyes are wide and unblinking as I press my lips against his mouth, hoping for a little normalcy.

My mouth smears against his as I silently remind myself how thoughtful he was to come all this way. Adam is everything any girl would ever want.

He starts to relax. His hands move over my hips as he leans back, pulling me on top of him.

I try to relax as well—to savor his kiss and enjoy the warmth of his touch. But I can't get my brain to shut off. I can't seem to stop asking myself questions and punishing myself for not being into the moment. And so I end up pulling away.

"Is something wrong?" Adam asks.

"I'm sorry," I say, hating myself. "I guess I'm a little distracted."

"You *guess*?" He sits up.

I shake my head, knowing he's right to feel frustrated. "I realize I'm sending mixed messages."

"Yes, but *why*?"

"There's just so much going on for me right now," I say, getting emotional all over again.

But this time, Adam doesn't ask me about it, and I can't really say I blame him. We remain seated on the bed, angled toward opposite sides of the room, not uttering a single word. If a psychologist were to come and evaluate our relationship based on our body language, we'd seriously be doomed.

"I should go," he says, after what feels like hours. "You'll probably want to get to class."

I nod, even though my theory class started an hour ago and I really don't feel like showing up late, especially since it meets for only ninety minutes.

I walk him to the door and we exchange a peck on the lips. I lean in for a hug, but I barely get a pat on the back. I want to tell him again how sorry I am, but I can't quite find the words. They all suddenly seem so inadequate.

"Thanks again for coming all this way," I tell him. "Are you sure you don't want to stay a bit, get some brunch, talk some more?"

"I'll call you later," he says, stepping out into the hallway. Understandably, he wants to leave.

And, as disappointed as I feel, part of me is relieved to see him go.

FTER ADAM LEAVES, I feel sick to my stomach, as if I've made a big mistake and I'm the most ungrateful person on the entire planet (not to mention the most stupid). I consider calling and asking him to come back, but instead I sink down to the floor, unsure of what I could possibly do or say that would make it all better. I can't pretend that I'm over the issues with my family and that everything is fine.

The phone vibrates against my desk, but I don't get up. I always thought that things between Adam and me would forever be black and white—the opposite of my experience with Ben. But in fact, I have no idea what just happened, or what it means, or what I'm going to do.

Meanwhile, the phone continues to vibrate. I force myself up to answer it.

"Where are you?" a male voice asks.

I check the caller ID. "Spencer?"

"You missed your classes, didn't you? And on the first day?" He tsk-tsks.

"Wait, how do you know that I missed them?" I peek out the window.

"Let's just say that I have my connections," he says, in a tone that's sharp and accusing. "And my connections tell me that you didn't show up."

"Were you checking up on me?" Spencer, as I'm learning more and more, is pretty well connected within the sculpture community. "Do you know one of the instructors here? Am I in big trouble?"

"Artists don't get mad, they get even."

"Excuse me?"

"Fix it," he snaps.

"How? I overslept."

"Don't you realize what an opportunity it is you're blowing? *Fix it*."

"And if I can't?"

"Then don't come back to work."

My mouth falls open; I'm completely taken aback. "You can't be serious."

"You're right." He sighs. His tone softens slightly, "I'm not. I need you for my boob mugs."

"Is that all I'm good for?" I attempt to joke. "Glazing and firing tacky pottery crap?"

"Don't blow this, Camelia. Promise me."

"I won't," I assure him.

"Good," he says, hanging up before I can say good-bye.

* * *

142

I splash some water on my face, leave a message for my parents that Wes is here and that I'm adapting as well as I can, and then head out to find the 3-D studio building where I was supposed to have my morning class.

When I get there and walk in, I discover it to be even more amazing than the photos online depicted it: high ceilings, pottery wheels galore, extruders and slab rollers, shelving packed with tons of tools, and not one but *three* kiln rooms. There are several students working inside the studio, a couple of whom I recognize from the orientation festivities.

"Hey," I say to one of them, hoping she can fill me in on what I missed. "I think I met you yesterday?"

"Right," she says, stepping away from her sculpture— a wide-rimmed bowl that looks like someone punched it at the base (but in a good way). The sides fold slightly inward, reminding me of ribbon candy. "I'm Ingrid." She extends her hand for a shake, but then realizes it's covered in clay, and ends up wiping it on the front of her apron instead.

"Camelia," I say, proceeding to explain that I overslept and missed the morning studio.

"And you don't have an alarm clock?" She gives me a pointed look. "Because you *do* realize you missed Chaste effing DeLande, don't you?"

"*Who?*" I ask. Maybe I didn't hear her right.

Ingrid looks at me as if I'm speaking another language, her amber eyes magnified behind a pair of square black glasses. "He's the master sculptor . . . the visiting artist," she explains. "*The Black Diamond Lady, Crystals in Winter Snow . . .*"

"Oh, right," I say, suddenly remembering having seen his name on the Sumner Intensive Web site. "And are those the names of his pieces?"

She pauses in disbelief. "His work sells for six figures in some of the most exclusive art galleries in the country . . . to people like the Obamas. He gets commissioned to do installations all over the world."

"Wow," I say, realizing how ignorant I must sound.

"His promise to make spontaneous visits to campus this summer quadrupled the number of sculpture applicants, you know. Anyway, bummer for you that you missed him."

"Yeah," I say, more eager than ever to redeem myself. "So, is that something from class you're working on?" I gaze at her piece again, trying to imagine what the assignment might've been . . . obviously, something on the wheel.

"This isn't high school, Caroline. You don't need to be told what to do."

"Camelia," I say, correcting her.

"Whatever." She rolls her eyes.

I turn my back, trying not to let her snooty attitude get the best of me.

Falling in line with the other students in the studio, who, like Ingrid, seem to have made themselves at home working on their various projects, I pick a spot in a corner of the room, slice myself a thick hunk of clay from the plethora of bagfuls, and wedge it out against my board.

Ingrid shoots me a dirty look with each thwack, bang, and slam of my clay, as if I'm disturbing her concentration. *Bonus*.

I glance around to see if I might be bothering any of the other students. But luckily, they seem too engrossed to care. Perhaps they missed the morning class, too, and are scrambling to catch up. Or, more likely, they're really into sculpture, as I'm supposed to be. As I've actually always been. But it's so much harder now that pottery—something I truly love—is tied to my touch power, which is something that's easy to hate.

I close my eyes, able to hear Sasha's whimper. It hasn't left me yet. Who knows if it ever will?

My clay all wedged out, I spend several minutes running my fingers over the mound and smoothing every crack. Images of all sorts start flying across my brain, but one particular image stands out brighter than the others. And so I start to sculpt it.

I concentrate as my fingers get to work, but with each stroke and pinch of clay, Sasha's crying gets louder and more insistent. I breathe through it, hoping her cries will dissipate, especially since I'm not alone.

But then I hear something else. A musical tune: a high-pitched chiming that I don't recognize.

I open my eyes and survey the other students to see if they've noticed how tormented I must look. One boy, sitting across from me, stares in my direction. His mouth is moving, but I can't hear what he's saying.

"What?" I ask, but I don't hear my own voice. The crying is shrill inside my head, creating a gnawing ache.

I stand up and take a step back. My forehead is sweating. My heart palpitates. I poke my clay-covered fingers deep inside my ears. Meanwhile, the music continues, too. It plays just behind the crying—a childlike tune with a repeating melody. I listen hard, trying to determine whether there's a message in the song.

But then I notice Ingrid. She's staring at me as if I'm a full-on freak. Her gaze travels upward, as though looking at someone behind me. I turn to find an older man—maybe in his sixties—standing there, shaking his head at the sight of my work. His lips are moving, but the only voice I hear is Sasha's. She's saying actual words again, wailing for me to hear her, for me to help her, for me to bring her out of the darkness.

"How?" I ask, without even thinking, still covering my ears, no longer able to hear the music.

The man continues to try to talk to me. The creases in his forehead deepen, and the corners of his mouth have turned downward.

My stomach lurches; bile burns at the back of my throat. I take a deep breath and tell the voice to quiet down, not sure if I've actually said the words out loud. Finally, I take my fingers out of my ears.

The man, most likely my instructor, points to the door, but I'm suddenly starting to feel better. Sasha's voice has weakened, and I'm able to hear other noises: the humming of overhead fans, someone mowing the lawn outside, and water dripping in the sink.

I look down at my sculpture, almost surprised by what I see: a clay frog, sitting inside a box. A rectangular slab, which I assume is the lid, lies beside it.

"Are you in need of medical attention?" the man asks.

"Professor Barnes?" I say, remembering the name on my schedule. "I mean, are you . . ." The remaining words in my mouth freeze, as does my entire body.

"Are you in need of medical attention?" he repeats, though his face shows irritation rather than concern.

"No. I just . . . I get a little carried away with my work sometimes."

"Carried away?" he says, clearly skeptical. "First you don't show up to class, and then you swagger in here at your leisure, and get *carried away* with the college's supplies. . . ."

I look back down at my sculpture, feeling my face flash hot. The boy across from me has paused at his work. Ingrid's vase looks even better than mere moments ago, the lips opening up like tulip petals. Another girl, sitting a few stations down, uses a hammer and chisel on a hunk of oak, sculpting what appears to be a seashell from the wood. Meanwhile, my pieces look like something from one of Spencer's small-fry classes.

"I'm sorry," I tell him, my voice barely above a whisper.

"With all due respect," he says, softening slightly, "this is a serious place with serious students. If you want theatrics, then I suggest you check out the drama department."

Ingrid laughs.

"I *am* serious," I say, knowing how ridiculous I must sound. But instead of fighting back harder, I merely walk out of the room, knowing that he's right. I *am* a distraction, and for that reason I don't belong here.

# LESSON NUMBER SIX:
## THE STORIES WE TELL OURSELVES ARE OFTEN THE MOST IMPORTANT.

After he took my flashlight, I ended up crying myself to sleep. Once I'm awake—Hours later? Minutes later? Is it the following day?—my eyes are caked with goo. They sting each time I blink. I wash them out in the basin, noticing that the water is only about an inch deep. I need more. My throat's parched. My lips feel swollen and sore.

I scramble for my cup, but I can't seem to find it now, and so I lean right in over the basin and lap up the dirty water. Pebbles slide down my throat, cutting into tissue. I wonder what would happen if I coughed . . . if I'd spit up blood. Is it possible to choke on your own blood in a heavy sleep? I almost wish that would happen.

I stop myself from crying again, but even when tears aren't pouring out, I feel like there's a continuous whimper inside me—one that I can't console, even with the stories that I tell myself in an effort to stay sane.

Story #1: This is all a practical joke, played by Jaden and Misery, who have a sick sense of humor. At any moment, one of them will poke her face through the hole and tell me it's time to go.

Story #2: My parents are teaching me to appreciate what I have and be more empathetic toward those less fortunate. They're in the process of redoing our house right now, and they want to surprise me with a brand-new bedroom: my prize for enduring all of this, and learning a valuable lesson.

Story #3: I'm being videotaped. Some executive from MTV saw one of my many YouTube videos and thought that I was really talented. He or she is preparing a pilot for a new TV show—one that I'll be the star of, that has the theme of survival.

I wonder if I'm going crazy. I think I read somewhere— or was it something I learned in psychology class?—that people often make up their own reality as a means of coping with what their brains can't possibly handle. The idea comforts me, because while no one else out there seems to be trying to protect or save me, at least maybe my brain is.

I fumble for the tape recorder, knowing that I need to give him what he wants if I am to move on to the next step, even if the next step is death. Death would be better than this purgatory.

I spend several minutes rehearsing what I might say, trying to be as vulnerable as Rizzo was in *Grease* when she sang "There Are Worse Things I Could Do." And then

I run my fingers over the controls, pushing the fourth button for RECORD.

"You say you want to know what makes me tick, so here it is: my heart. My heart ticks at triple its normal speed because of what I imagine: rats scurrying through the hole, nibbling at my ears as I sleep. Dying from this cut on my wrist. Never seeing my parents again, never getting to tell them how sorry I am.

"That's what this is all about. When I found out they'd lied to me, I decided to punish them for it. I started abandoning everything they loved about me, everything they'd made me into, everything I ever loved.

"Sounds like the perfect punishment, right? Give up what makes me happy as a way to get them back? Could anyone be more stupid?

"I threatened to run away. I even wrote a letter and packed a bag. My parents offered boarding school as a way to give me some space. But I guess you found me first.

"My biggest fear? They've assumed I found my own way of getting some space and aren't even looking for me now."

I push the third button on the recorder to stop it, surprisingly uplifted to have gotten all of that out. Sort of ironic, since my thoughts are going to him. The truth is, I had no real intention of running away. I think I just wanted to punish my parents and impress Misery at the same time. Sadly, I think I accomplished both.

I drag the recorder across my cell, feeling for the hole in the wall, confident that this type of honesty is exactly what he had in mind. Hopefully it'll earn me back my flashlight, as well as a fresh bandage and some water. And hopefully I'll soon be able to get out of here. Or maybe that's just another story I tell myself.

# 26

*A*FTER THE WHOLE mortifying debacle in the pottery studio, I head back to the dorm and go upstairs to Wes's room. Unfortunately, he isn't there, but fortunately the room's unlocked. I go inside and sit on his bed, not wanting to be alone; and somehow, being among all of his things, reminds me that I'm not. I grab his sock monkey just as my phone rings.

"Hello," I answer, still feeling shaken up inside.

"Hey, there." It's Mom. "I'm sorry I missed your call earlier. So, you're adapting okay. . . . How's your room?"

"Yes and fine."

"And Wes is there with you?"

"He is. It was a nice surprise," I tell her.

"Well, it's good to know that you have a friend there." She continues to chatter on about how having a solid support system can make all the difference.

"So, I'm kind of just getting used to this place," I say,

once she finally pauses for a breath. "But I'll give you and Dad a call in a few days; sound okay?"

"Is there anything we can do for you in the meantime? Do you have everything you need?"

"You and Dad allowed me to come here," I say, hugging the monkey to my stomach. "For now, some time away is all I can ask."

"Well, I'm not so sure Dad will be able to wait a few days until he speaks with you, but I'll tell him to be mindful of your need for space."

"Thanks," I say, glad that she totally gets it.

We say our good-byes, and then I call Wes to see where he is.

"I just got out of my theory class," he says. "I'm assuming yours is over as well. . . ."

"Probably."

"What's that supposed to mean? *Camelia?*" There's a fatherly tone in his voice.

"Where are you?" I ask him.

"In the café, sipping an iced mocha latte with some friends. And you?"

"In your room, hugging Mr. Sock Monkey."

"Gentle, he doesn't like it rough. Would you and Monkey like to come join us? My treat. I'll even throw in some extra foam."

"I actually think I should pay a visit to Mrs. Beckerman." Seeing that I've screwed up the majority of my day, I might as well be productive in at least one area.

"Wait, is Adam there with you?"

"No, and we can talk about him later. I need to borrow your car again."

"Why, what's the plan?"

"I haven't really thought that far."

"Which is part of your problem. You're too damned impulsive, Camelia. And acting on impulse is pretty much when every serial killer gets caught."

"Except I'm hardly a serial killer."

"Right, because if you were, I wouldn't be hanging with you."

"Glad you have your standards."

"You need a plan," he persists. "You didn't have one last night, and look at where it got you: stealing my car and breaking down in tears. And was it really worth it? Aside from getting me into your bed, that is. . . ." He snickers.

"I *have* a plan," I bluff. "I'm just going to knock on the Beckermans' door and tell them who I am, and that I believe Sasha's still alive."

"And when they probe further?"

"I have no problem telling anyone about my touch power."

"Even if they don't believe in that stuff and think you're crazy?"

"At least I'll know that I tried." I let out a giant breath, thinking about Neal Moche's blog—about how he also half believes that what he's doing is crazy. "So, can I borrow your car?"

"I'd prefer it if you waited for me."

"Can you come now?"

"Negative. I have a group assignment I need to work on."

"How about if I promise to text you the second I arrive and then the moment I leave?"

"Fine." He sighs. "My keys are on top of my mini-fridge, beneath the bag of fried pork rinds."

"Nice choice. No one would ever think to look there."

"Be careful, Camelia. I want a full report."

"Thanks," I say before hanging up. I grab his keys, along with a mozzarella stick from the fridge, and sit back on his bed. Heeding his advice, I spend some time going over what I plan to say and how I want things to play out, and trying to predict the toughest questions. Then I walk out the door.

# 27

*T*HE BECKERMAN HOUSE is even more inviting in the daylight, with pink and blue hydrangea bushes bordering the house and a wooden porch swing with a pergola-type roof.

I park in front, text Wes that I've arrived safely, and then get out of the car. Standing at the end of the Beckermans' walkway, I spot a book sitting on the swing. It's splayed open and facedown on the seat, as if someone had recently left it. There's also a minivan parked in the driveway.

I move up to the door and ring the doorbell. Mrs. Beckerman appears a couple of seconds later, standing behind the screen door.

"Can I help you?" she asks, smoothing her palms over her chocolate brown hair, as if I were anyone to impress.

In a lavender sundress, she's much tinier than I expected, much more petite than she appears on TV. The sundress hangs off her pale, freckled skin. She looks older than she did on TV. These past couple of months must've really aged her.

"I actually think that I'd like to try and help you," I say.

She squints and edges the screen door open. Her eyes are the color of the blue hydrangea bushes. "*How* can you help me?" she asks, giving me the once-over—from my clay-spattered T-shirt to my sweatpants.

"Is your husband home? Do you think I could come in and speak to you both?"

"You're the girl who called me," she says, "on the phone the other day."

I nod, feeling my mouth turn dry. "Please, can I come in?" I ask again.

Her face is full of questions, but she opens the door wider to let me in. "Do you know where my daughter is?"

Standing now in the entryway of her house, I notice that the interior smells like burned popcorn. "My name's Camelia Hammond." I fish inside my bag for my student ID and hand it to her as proof.

She takes her time reading it over, perhaps memorizing every word and digit.

"I'm participating in the summer arts program at Sumner," I continue. "You must know the campu—"

"Do you know where my daughter is?" she asks again. Her hand trembles in front of her mouth.

"I don't. But I can explain why I'm here."

She hands me back my student ID and I follow her into the living room. It's decorated in rich tones of violet and gold—too pretty for my T-shirt and sweatpants. I sit down on the edge of a sofa, eyeing a large black-and-white photo positioned over the fireplace: the Beckerman family on the beach.

"It was taken last summer," Mrs. Beckerman says, following my gaze. "Just before Sasha found out the truth. I assume you're familiar with the case . . . the reason she ran away to begin with?"

"Except I don't think that Sasha ran away."

She turns to face me again, her eyes glazed over with fear. "What do you know about my daughter?"

"Mostly what I've read online or heard about from TV. I have no real proof that she didn't run away. I just don't think that she did."

Her eyebrow rises in suspicion. "And you called me on the phone and came all the way here to tell me what you *think . . . ?*"

"It's actually more complicated than that."

Mrs. Beckerman sits down across from me and places her hands in her lap. Her fingernails are chewed down to the cuticles.

"I've been doing a lot of research on your daughter's case," I explain.

"Why?" Her eyes narrow. "Did you know her from someplace? Did you meet her at a party?"

I start to ramble about the unsolved-mysteries show and about my search for summer programs, and how the latter led me to a link concerning Sasha's case. "I clicked on it because of the show. It was sort of like what happens when you become interested in something; you start to notice it everywhere. . . ."

"And you were noticing Sasha everywhere?"

"Sort of," I say, trying to remain focused despite Mrs. Beckerman's intensity.

"And what about the daisy?"

"The daisy?" I ask, trying to catch up.

"You knew about it. You mentioned it on the phone."

"Right," I say, picturing the sculpture I did in my basement studio. "Did Sasha like daisies? Did she have a special daisy charm?"

"You also mentioned something about the letter. . . ."

I nod. "I didn't know if either of those things might be clues to her disappearance."

"What makes *you* think that they are?" she asks.

"I sense things," I tell her. "About the future, I mean. It's kind of confusing. I don't even fully understand it myself, but I have this power, and it's helping me to get clues about your daughter."

"A power?" she asks, her face scrunching up in confusion.

I pause to look back at the black-and-white photo. Sasha's smile is contagious. It almost appears as if she was caught in a laugh—as if she couldn't have been happier with her life. "It's really hard to explain," I continue, "but there were other clues, too."

"Well, I don't believe in superpowers." She stands up from the sofa.

But I remain where I am. "Was there a special box that Sasha kept?"

"I think you need to leave," she says.

"First, please hear me out."

"Leave now, or I'm calling the police." She pulls a cell phone from her pocket.

"I know it doesn't make sense," I blurt out, finally getting up. "I mean, I don't even know Sasha. I've never met her before. And up until a few weeks ago, I barely knew her name. But I've been hearing her crying inside my head—for weeks now; it hasn't stopped. It's how I know that she's still alive."

"I'm calling the police," she repeats, and starts to dial.

"Does your daughter have a frog?" I ask. "Does she keep that frog in a box with a lid? Was there some sort of music that played when the box was opened?" I rack my brain trying to remember the tune inside my head. I hum a couple of notes, frustrated that the crying voice kept me from hearing more.

Mrs. Beckerman's face goes white. "Who told you?" she asks. "How could you possibly know?"

"Like I said, I sense things," I tell her.

Visibly trembling, she reaches out to take my hand and leads me up the stairs. I follow her into the master bedroom. It has a four-poster bed and antique-looking furniture.

Mrs. Beckerman moves to her closet. From the top shelf, she pulls down a medium-size gift bag and hands it to me.

"What is it?" I ask, unable to help noticing how pretty the packaging is: a bright pink bag with shimmering purple tissue paper sticking out at the top. A matching purple ribbon ties the bag handles closed.

"It's a gift for Sasha," Mrs. Beckerman explains. "Go ahead and open it."

"Are you sure? Don't you want to save this for her?"

"I can easily rewrap it if I need to."

I look down at the bag and also take note of its ample weight. And then I reach in, through the tunnel of tissue paper, and feel a smooth, hard edge. I wrap my hand around it, pulling out a wooden box of some sort. I set the bag down and remove the lid from the box. A sterling-silver frog pendant sits inside the jewelry box's velvet-lined cavity.

My heart starts to pound as I realize my prediction was right and that I've finally convinced Mrs. Beckerman to listen to me.

"No one aside from Sasha's father and the jeweler I bought this from would've known about this gift," she says.

"But I was able to see it," I tell her. "Inside my head. The image came to me." I try to explain my power of psychometry and how this wasn't the first time I experienced it.

Mrs. Beckerman takes a seat on her bed, gripping the sides for stability. "And this supposed power that you're talking about . . ." she begins. "Is that also how you knew about Daisy?"

"*Daisy?*" I ask, completely confused. "I sculpted a

daisy . . . in my basement. It had the center part, with petals all around—"

"It was Sasha's name," she says, interrupting. "Before we adopted her and changed it, that is."

I bite my lip, feeling my blood churn. Chills run over my skin. "And what about the *t* shape?" I ask. "Two lines that intersect, like a plus sign?"

"I don't know." She shakes her head. "I guess I'd have to think about that one."

"But do you believe me?" I ask. "About my power, I mean? About how I know these things?"

Mrs. Beckerman doesn't answer, nor does she ask me to elaborate. Instead, she tells me about Sasha's love of frogs and how she's been collecting them since she was six years old. "Key chains, water bottles, fuzzy slippers . . . Come," she says, leading me out of the room and down the hall.

We stand in the doorway of Sasha's bedroom. It's painted a sunny yellow and the bed linens are all navy blue with tiny pink roses. It smells like roses, too.

"Look," she says, nodding toward the bed. It's loaded with stuffed animals—all of them frogs. There's also a frog-shaped pillow. A Kermit alarm clock sits on the bedside table.

I really want to go in, but Mrs. Beckerman pulls me back into the hall, closing the door. Sasha's room must be off limits.

"Shall we go back downstairs?" she asks. Without waiting for my answer, she starts down.

I reluctantly follow her, and we take seats back in the living room. To my surprise, I'm still holding the jewelry box. I run my palms over the sides, noticing a windup dial at the back. "May I?" I ask.

"Of course," she says.

I crank the dial all the way. Music begins to play. "From the *Nutcracker Suite*?" I ask, recognizing the tune as the same one that played in my head.

"It is. Sasha's father and I would take her every year."

I close my eyes and concentrate hard. Sasha's cry is a faraway whimper now. "I know this may sound weird," I venture, "but by any chance, when Sasha cries, does she sometimes get the hiccups?"

Mrs. Beckerman nods, and her eyes fill with tears. But I'm pretty sure they're happy tears, because I've managed to give her hope. She wraps her arms around my shoulders. "Thank you," she says.

"But I haven't done anything yet."

"You have indeed," she says, breaking the embrace. "You've given me hope that my daughter is still alive."

# 28

*A*S I LEAVE MRS. BECKERMAN'S HOUSE, I notice a car parked down the street: a dark green, beat-up Buick with a bashed-in taillight. It starts up just as soon I get inside Wes's car. At first, I don't think anything of it, but then it pulls away from the curb moments after I do, and follows me for four blocks, continuing behind me even when I take a turn.

I keep driving for another half mile, slowing down slightly to close the gap between our cars. I peek in the rearview mirror. The driver appears to be a girl; I catch a glimpse of her straight, dark hair whipping in the wind.

I slow down even more, searching for someplace to pull over. There's a farm stand in the near distance with a parking lot out front. I flick on my directional and turn in, eager to see if the Buick does the same. But it ends up swerving around me. The car speeds up—so fast that it jolts forward, the tires making a screeching sound—and

I'm not able to catch the license-plate number.

A second later, my phone rings. It's Kimmie. I consider calling her back later—after I finally catch my breath—but instead I pick it up.

"Hey, there, miss," she says. "How's college life treating you?" Her chipper voice reminds me of how far apart we really are, both emotionally and physically.

"It's certainly been an adventure."

"With Wes as your sidekick, I can only imagine."

"I miss you," I say, almost wanting to tell her what I'm up to. "We have a lot of catching up to do."

"You bet we do," she agrees. "Guess who's about to pull clothes for a photo shoot?"

"Hmm . . . *you*? So, I take it that things are going good?"

"Better than good, my dear. But I'll have to fill you in later, okay? My supervisor just walked in . . . fifteen minutes early, mind you," she says, lowering her voice. "Anyway, I can't wait to hear all about your room and classes and stuff."

We hang up and I drive back to campus, happy that Kimmie's enjoying this time. It kills me not to tell her what's going on with me, but I feel like that would distance us even more. And I'm not so sure I could handle that on top of everything else.

Back on campus, I park Wes's car exactly where he had it, and then I give him a call.

"I want details," he says, in lieu of a hello.

I arrange to meet him on Sumner's back lawn. When

I arrive, I find him sitting on one of the benches that overlook the ocean.

"Thanks," I say, handing him back his keys.

He moves his blue-tinted sunglasses to the top of his head. He looks better than I've ever seen him before. His dark brown hair is slightly sun-kissed, his face is Malibu tan, and his whole demeanor seems more relaxed, less tortured. "Can you stand it?" he asks. "I mean, could this day be any more perfect?"

I hadn't really noticed, but he's right. The sky is absolutely cloudless. There's a group playing volleyball in the distance, and the incoming tide crashes against the rocks below, creating a soothing sound. "I take it you had a good day?"

"Great new friends, stellar classes, and a resortlike campus . . . I'd say it's going pretty well. And you? Since you're still here, I'm assuming that all went swimmingly at the Beckerman residence?"

"Since I'm still here?"

"And not in jail for harassment and/or stalking, I mean."

"Ha-ha." I fake a laugh.

"Details, please. What happened? And don't leave anything out."

I take a deep breath, inhaling the cool, salty air. And then I begin by telling him about what happened today in the pottery studio, including how the frog-in-a-box sculpture turned out to be a premonition. I also tell him about the daisy clue and the fact that, according to Mrs.

166

Beckerman, Sasha often hiccups when she cries.

"And so, wait. Did the Beckermans actually believe you about everything?"

"It was just Mrs. Beckerman," I explain. "I'm pretty sure her husband was at work. But I think she believed me. I mean, it took some convincing, but the clues definitely helped."

"You do realize, however, that she's going to tell the police about your visit, and that they're going to want to know all about you, especially about how you discovered those clues."

"I already told Mrs. Beckerman about my touch power."

"And you really think the police are going to buy that? You may have Mrs. Beckerman convinced, but unless you're dealing with crystal-ball-loving coppers, they're going to be a lot more skeptical. They'll assume that either (a) you have an inside angle, one that they'll be eager to hear more about, or (b) you're actually involved in the disappearance or know the person who is."

"No one will think that," I say. "I didn't know the girl, and I'm not even from this area. Plus, how else could I have found out about the clues?"

"Well, for starters, *anyone* could've known about the frog-in-the-box gift. In the cops' eyes, someone probably told you."

"Except, no one else knew. Mrs. Beckerman said so herself."

"*Someone* knew. Even if it was just the salesperson. Or, how about the person who gift wrapped it? Then there are all the people hovering over the jewelry counter at the time of purchase. . . ."

"Okay, but what about the daisy clue—the fact that Sasha's name was originally Daisy? How else would I have known that?"

"Same way anybody else would." He yawns like this is all elementary. "The Beckermans could've shared the info with someone. Or, on second thought, maybe it was even the birth parents. Do you know who they are?"

"I do. . . . And there's not much of a story there. The mom's a church administrator. She lives in Seattle and has her own family. The father is an electrician, I think. They no longer keep in touch with each other, despite the fact that when the mom got pregnant, they were actually considering getting married and trying to make things work."

"Color me impressed," he says, referring to my investigative skills.

"It's actually not that impressive. Their lives became an open book as soon as Sasha went missing. Their info's been all over the Net."

"You're right." He yawns again. "That *isn't* so impressive. Where's the scandal?"

"No scandal: they were both completely cooperative with the police."

"So, if they've both been questioned, it wouldn't be unheard-of for old emotions to resurface," he says. "Ample reason for each of them to talk about the birth, the child they couldn't keep—a child who they named Daisy just before they decided to give her away."

"Okay, but then what about Sasha's crying?" I ask, hoping to stump him. "How else would I have known that she sometimes hiccups between sobs?"

"You don't seriously think you're the first person to ever hear Sasha's ugly cry, do you?" He raises his eyebrow at me.

I let out a sigh, more confused than ever.

"I'm just trying to play devil's advocate here, Camelia, because you can bet the police are going to be questioning this stuff, looking for some sort of logic. Not that your claim to have psychic powers won't be logical to them." He smirks. "No insight on the *t*-shaped clue yet, I take it."

"Not yet. And, by the way, you sound like one of the detectives on *CSI*."

"That's honestly one of the sweetest things you've ever said to me." He rests his head against my shoulder.

"Except I'm not exactly trying to be sweet. It's actually pretty annoying. But I'm not going to worry about the police right now, because the truth is that I have nothing to hide."

"Right." He sits up and stifles a laugh. "Because it's perfectly normal to have a history on your personal computer that shows hours and hours of case tracking of some girl that you *supposedly* don't know."

"I *don't* know her," I insist.

"Yes, but the police will be looking for some sort of connection."

"And when they can't find one . . ."

"I don't know." He shrugs. "Maybe they'll be too distracted by the fact that you moved to the victim's hometown and then stalked her primary residence."

"I came here to get away," I remind him.

"Right, right." He rolls his eyes. "And I'm sure they'll think it's purely coincidental that the school you decided to attend is practically in the victim's backyard. Of course, it probably doesn't help that you've also been the victim of a stalker in the past, as well as the stalker of a stalker."

"To which you were an accomplice."

"Then there's the whole psychiatric rap sheet," he continues, ignoring me, "which includes public fits and a suicidal aunt. And don't even get me started on the trail of injured parties you've left in your wake."

"Okay, it's settled, you officially suck."

"I know," he says, gloating over his criminal mind. "But just remember that my sucky self is here for you. And I'm willing to help every sucky step of the way." He smiles. His whole demeanor is nauseatingly neutral.

"I'm almost surprised you're not calling me crazy and suggesting that we head back home."

"Are you kidding? Head back to Freetown, population: negative lameness? I'm trying to figure out a way that we can graduate early and move here permanently." He nods to a row of students lounging on beach chairs, all of them wearing bathing suits and slathered in suntan oil. "If this is college, then sign me up."

"Hence your Zenful mood."

"You sound like Kimmie. She called me, by the way."

"Yeah, she called me, too."

"But you didn't tell her about all this Sasha business, did you?" he asks.

"It's better this way." I shrug. "I don't want my drama to put a damper on her New York state of mind."

"Justifying reasons for keeping secrets, are we?" He raises a suspicious eyebrow at me.

"What's that supposed to mean?" I ask, fairly certain that he's alluding to my parents—to the fact that they had their reasons for keeping secrets, too.

"You're a smart girl; you can figure it out. And, in the meantime"—he drops his keys into my lap—"take my wheels whenever you like."

"Seriously?"

"Why not?" he says, looking back over at the sunbathers.

"Thanks," I say, utterly grateful and more than a little surprised. "And speaking of wheels, after I left Mrs. Beckerman's house, a Buick started following me."

"Year and make?"

"I didn't notice."

"Male or female? License-plate number and state? Age of driver?"

"Female. I wasn't able to catch the plate number or state. And I'm assuming that she was young. I mean, her hair looked young."

"And tell me, oh, observant one, what does young hair look like?"

"What can I say? I did my best."

"Yes, but when a missing girl's life's at stake, you have to do *better* than your best. It could've been someone casing the house, someone following you, a reporter taking photos, or even a fan of *Open Cases*." He grabs his keys away from me. "Anyway, I take it back about the car. You need to go somewhere, you call me. Got it?"

"Got it," I say, relieved to have his help.

## 29

BACK IN MY ROOM, I glance at my suitcase, not yet unpacked. I still have to go through my orientation paperwork. Mom's cooler full of fruit and nut bars is sitting on my desk, unopened. It's like I'm only half here, half into my art, mostly because I'm half afraid of sculpting something new.

A few months back, Spencer advised me to give myself over to my sculpture, to form whatever it was my clump of clay wanted to be, and not to feel compelled to force it into any predetermined shape.

But what if the sole purpose of my clay is to reveal a clue about somebody else's future? What if I'm never able to sculpt normally again? Is wanting to do so selfish, especially since my premonitions have proven to be helpful?

After several moments of brooding, I force myself to unpack my suitcase. With each item that I place into a drawer or hang in the closet, I start to feel a little less sorry for myself, a little more in control.

That is, until I see my aunt's journal, the last thing I take out of the suitcase. The spine is all weathered and frayed, and there are pen-mark tracks etched into the cardboard. I flip it open and run my fingers over the pages—over her years of documented misery. Having it now—holding it, reading it, and seeing the way she wrote the words—takes on a whole new meaning, because she's no longer *just* my aunt, and if she'd succeeded in ending her life, I wouldn't even be here right now.

My cell phone rings. I get up to retrieve it from my bed, frustrated that the number is blocked. I answer it, thinking that it may be Mrs. Beckerman.

"Is this Camelia Hammond?" a female voice asks.

"Yes," I say. "Who's this?"

"We need to talk."

*"Who is this?"* I repeat.

"You need to go to the bakery at the end of Chansky Street. Look for the bright red mailbox at the side of the building. There will be something for you inside it."

"Wait, is this a joke?" I snap.

"That depends. Do you think Sasha Beckerman's life is a joke?"

My mouth opens, but no words come out.

"I didn't think so," she says, answering for me.

"Do you know where Sasha is?"

"Haven't you heard? She ran away. They found a note. They even found her packed bag."

174

"Then why are you calling me?"

She laughs. "You think you're pretty clever, don't you?"

"Are you the girl who was following me earlier . . . in the dark green Buick?"

"Don't listen to what the skeptics say," she says, skirting the question. "Just because Sasha left her bag behind doesn't mean that she didn't run away. Could be a million reasons why she didn't take it. Maybe wherever she was going, she knew she didn't need those things. Maybe opportunity knocked before she could get back home to retrieve any of her belongings. Or maybe the suitcase was staged—a cry for help, only no one answered that cry, and so she ended up leaving anyway. You know what a heartless bitch Mrs. Beckerman is, don't you? If she ever noticed that Sasha had her bag packed, I doubt she even cared. Maybe that's why Sasha left."

I shake my head, thinking about how tormented Mrs. Beckerman seemed. "Did Sasha and her mother not get along?" I ask, already knowing the answer. Media reports made it clear that they'd been fighting from the moment Sasha found out the truth about her birth parents.

"First, answer my questions," the girl continues. "Why do you even care about Sasha? Was she a friend of yours?"

"Was she a friend of *yours*? How do you know about me? And how did you get my number?"

"Go to the bakery," she insists.

"Will you be there? Can't you just tell me what you need to say over the phone?" I clutch the phone harder, as if that'll make more sense of this conversation.

"My advice to you, Camelia Hammond, is stay out of it. Walk away, before you get in over your head."

"And what if I don't?"

There's silence for several seconds, and then she finally hangs up.

# 30

*A*S SOON AS I CLICK THE PHONE OFF, I pocket my keys and hurry out of the room, eager to find Wes. I call his cell and he picks up right away. "Where are you?" I ask him.

"Currently? Taking photos of some girls dressed only in feathers."

"How much are you paying them?"

"Not a single cent," he says. "This is actually for an assignment—part of an anti-animal-product clothing campaign. Seriously, I love this place."

"Since when did you get all PETA-fied?"

"Since I started taking photos of girls dressed only in feathers."

"Okay, well, as much as I hate to interrupt you in your animal-rights obligations, I sort of need you."

"And so do these chicks," he says. "Pun intended."

Still holding the phone up to my ear, I race through

the lobby, spotting Ingrid, from the pottery studio. Sitting with a couple of friends, she stifles a laugh when she sees me.

I ignore her and step outside.

"Can I borrow your car, then?" I ask Wes. "Some girl just called and said she wants me to go to a bakery on Chansky Street. Apparently, she's leaving something for me in the mailbox there."

"Playing *CSI* without me, are you? I wouldn't recommend it."

"Well, then, what *would* you recommend?"

"Do you know who this girl is?" he asks. "Or how she got your number?"

"No," I say to both of his questions, wondering if Mrs. Beckerman has already told someone about me, or if maybe the girl got my information through one of the many online sites I visited. "Is it possible that one of the sites I was researching got hacked?"

"That depends. Did you tell anyone on the Web site that you were interested in Sasha's case?"

"No, but in order to enter a couple of the sites, I had to give my e-mail address."

"Which has your name."

"Yes, but I didn't get specific about anything. I didn't tell anyone what my plans were for this summer."

"It's actually not so hard to get that info. I mean, once they have your name, age, and state, everything else is a mere Google search and/or exercise in six-degrees-of-separation away."

"Great." I sigh.

"Hey, I gotta go," he says. "I've got a couple chicks clucking at me, saying their feathers are making them itchy. Give me ten minutes to finish up, and then meet me by my car."

"Are you sure?"

"Do chickens lay eggs?"

I hang up and make my way to the parking lot. Wes's car is there. I take a seat on the curb and cover my ears, focusing hard on Sasha's whimper, wishing that it would reveal a clue.

About fifteen minutes later, I spot Wes making his way toward me. "Hey," he says, donning a feather boa.

"Are you sure you're done with the assignment? Because I really don't want to hold you down. You're here for a reason, and accompanying me on a wild goose chase isn't it."

"Don't tempt me with more poultry products, or I may just have to peck you."

"You're nutty, you know that?" I stand up and give his boa a flick.

In the car, I fill Wes in on the details of the call.

"So, it doesn't sound like she was threatening you," he says. "More like she was trying to find out what you know and *why* you're getting involved."

"But she also made a point of mentioning the whole luggage mystery, justifying why Sasha might've run away, even though she left her bag behind."

"In other words, she *wants* you to believe that Sasha ran away."

"Or, she wants to see if I might argue with her—if I might have any theories of my own as to why the luggage was left behind."

"Because that *is* a really good question," Wes says, tapping his chin in thought. "Why *would* Sasha leave her bag behind if she was truly planning to bolt?"

"Or more importantly, why would she even pack a suitcase in the first place? Why not a backpack or a duffel bag—something easier to transport and a whole lot less obvious than an actual suitcase?"

"Sounds like she wanted to be obvious."

"Like maybe packing the suitcase was a cry for help." I nod. "Especially since what she packed was pretty bogus: a couple of old sweaters, some books, a few sweats, and a bunch of travel products you get in hotels."

"No essential jeans, or favorite clothes, or wads of cash for traveling," Wes says, totally getting it.

"Not at all," I say. "At least, from everything I read online. I should probably ask Mrs. Beckerman about it."

"And while you're at it, ask her if anyone had access to Sasha's room—any friends or frenemies—who might've staged the suitcase to look like Sasha ran away."

"Duly noted," I say, ever impressed by his suspicious mind.

Wes types the address of the bakery into his GPS and begins driving in that direction. After about twenty minutes, we pull in to Chansky Street. The bakery is a tiny shack of a place overlooking the harbor.

Wes parks a couple of stores down from it. "Puck's?" he

says, reading the sign out front. "And I'm assuming that's the mailbox in question?" He points to a bright red mailbox at the side of the building. Its flag is pointed upward.

"Must be," I say, wondering if the caller might be here, too. I look around, searching the cars parked in the lot and on the street, but there's only an older woman on her cell phone in a minivan, and a guy reading a newspaper in his pickup.

"No dark green Buick," Wes says, also peering around.

"Do you think I should go inside?"

"Not without me you won't." He pulls a pair of binoculars from the storage compartment in his door. "I'll bet you my right nut that someone's keeping a close eye on us right now."

"Okay, but I'm not really into nuts these days."

"Are you into Adam? You still haven't given me the dish about his visit, by the way. And, for the record, I had no idea he'd drop everything and come to your rescue. I mean, I only said that you'd had a bad day."

"We'll dish about it later," I say, opening the car door.

"Just to the mailbox," Wes orders. "And I'll be watching you the entire time. Here, take this." He digs around in the glove compartment and then hands me a broken CD case with a jagged edge—as if that's supposed to protect me.

Still, I take it and walk to the large, rusty mailbox. I look around to see if anyone's watching, but it appears that the coast is clear. My heart pounding, I pull the box's lever and peek inside, spotting a large envelope.

I pull it out and check the front, curious to see if it may simply be something for the bakery. But instead it has my name scribbled on it in ballpoint pen—and there's a return address in the corner.

I hurry back to Wes's car. Without a word, I lock the doors and tear at the envelope's flap. I tip the envelope over, dumping the contents out onto Wes's console.

A gold clip falls out.

"Hold on," Wes says, pulling a pair of latex gloves from the backseat, where he has a whole box of them. He puts them on and picks up the clip. "A money clip," he says, holding it up in the light.

I peek inside the envelope, searching for a note that might explain the clip. But there isn't anything.

"Any luck?" Wes asks.

I shake my head. "Just the return address. It has to be another clue."

Wes turns the clip over in his hand, and that's when we're able to see it. The letter *t*, engraved in cursive script and similar to the *t* that I sculpted.

"What do you think it stands for?" Wes asks.

"It's obviously someone's initial—someone connected to Sasha, most likely. Maybe the person who has her."

"Assuming that someone has her at all. We have no proof that she's being kept against her will."

I run my fingers over the return address. "The girl who left this definitely knows something."

"So, then, why not come out and say it? Why leave us such cryptic and tacky clues?" Wes attaches the money clip to his finger and wiggles it in the air at me.

"Maybe this girl's afraid. She told me not to get involved—that I'd be getting in over my head. Maybe she's already in way over hers."

"Or maybe she has something to hide." Wes grabs both a Sharpie and a Ziploc bag from his glove compartment.

"Do you think we should give this to the police?" I ask, noticing the scratches on the *t*.

"We *could*," he says. "I mean, it's probably the right thing to do, but if we give these clues to the police, then you can bet they'll want to know where they came from."

"And so I'll just tell them."

"Yes, but it's not that simple. What if they want to tap your phone, in case that girl calls you again? What if they trace all the calls that come in on your line and then listen to your conversations? They might also want to use you," he continues. "To have you act as bait to try and lure the mystery girl. Are you prepared for that kind of involvement?"

"Well, I already sort of *am* involved," I tell him.

"Yeah, I guess you are," he says. "Especially once Mrs. Beckerman informs the police about you, if she hasn't already."

"I should call Mrs. Beckerman," I tell him. "I need to know if she told someone about me. That could be our answer—as to who called me, I mean."

"Honestly," his face goes morgue serious, "I'd hold off from calling Beckerman, for now anyway. Because let's say that *she* was the one who told that girl about you. How much can we really trust her?"

"Maybe the girl who called me is friends with Sasha?" I say, thinking aloud. "Maybe she still keeps in touch with Sasha's mom?"

"Yes, but then why doesn't she give Sasha's mom the clue? Why give it to you—a complete stranger?"

"Unless whoever left me these clues didn't find out about me from Mrs. Beckerman?"

"I guess time will tell," he says, dropping the money clip into the plastic bag and then labeling the bag EXHIBIT A.

"It's like a crime lab in here," I say.

Wes shrugs, pulling off his gloves. "Dad says I need to grow up, that I should've gotten over my wannabe detective phase back in elementary school."

"And I say you're pretty amazing," I tell him. "Don't ever change, okay?"

"*Me? You're* the one who shouldn't change. All this stuff you sculpt that comes true? You're pretty freaking rock star, you know that? I mean, get a load of what you can do."

"Seriously?" I ask, feeling a smile creep onto my face, because I've never really thought of myself as having rockstar potential. Because Wes's version of me is so much better than the version I have of myself.

# 31

*W*ES AND I REMAIN IN HIS CAR for several more minutes, discussing whether we should go check out the address on the envelope or just drive back to campus.

"My thought is that we should wait to check it out," Wes begins. "Whoever left this clue *wants* you to go to this address. They probably even expect it."

"And how is that a bad thing? I mean, there's obviously more that they want me to know."

"Yes, but once again, my dear Chameleon, if things were that simple, this person would come right out and tell you. They're calling all the shots, sending you on a hunt."

"Yes, but I *am* on a hunt."

"So, let's continue that hunt tomorrow, when guards are down and we have a plan. Going right now wouldn't be smart. Plus, it's getting late."

I glance at my watch. It's a little after six. "Anxious for cafeteria food, are we?"

"Maybe I have plans," he says, pulling away from the curb.

"Is there another featherbrained photo shoot in your near future?"

"Cluck-cluck." He smirks.

We return to the Sumner campus and grab a quick bite in the student center—superchewy pizza and over-cooked broccoli smothered in a cheesy orange glaze. I'm just about to go pitch it in the trash when I spot Professor Barnes pouring himself a cup of coffee at the self-serve bar.

"I'll be right back," I tell Wes, before making my way over to Barnes.

Standing right beside the professor now, I look at the side of his face, waiting for him to acknowledge me. But instead he continues to stir cream into his coffee, as if trying to get the color just right.

"Excuse me," I say, but the words are barely audible. The cafeteria is loud. Someone's just dropped a stack of dishes. There's a band setting up (C-squared, featuring Carlie and Courtney from the orientation committee).

"Can I talk to you a moment?" I ask, louder now.

He stops stirring finally, to look at me. His face is absolutely deadpan.

"I'm sorry about what happened in the studio," I tell him. "And I'm sorry for missing class. I have a lot going on right now . . . not that that's any excuse. But if it's okay, I'd like to try to—"

"You know how lucky you are?" he asks, cutting me off.

"Lucky?"

"If it were up to me, you'd already be out. But *luckily* for you, a certain individual who's in your corner—one to whom I owe many a favor—plays by the three-strikes-out rule."

"Spencer," I say, eternally grateful.

"He assures me that you've got some talent, and so I'll try to forget what I witnessed earlier today."

"Thank you," I say, but I'm not even sure he hears me, because he's already turned away, and is headed for the exit.

Back in my room, I continue arranging things on my dresser, still trying to get into the idea of being here—and studying art. I set a couple of pieces of jewelry down on one of my pottery dishes, including a bracelet from Adam: a wide gold bangle with a dangling heart charm. I slip it on, remembering the night he gave it to me.

We were sitting on a bench in front of the duck pond at the park. Adam reached into his pocket and pulled out a purple box tied with a silver ribbon.

"These past couple months have been amazing," he told me.

"For me, too," I said.

"I'm glad." He motioned to the box, obviously eager for me to open it.

I took it, untied the ribbon, and lifted off the lid. "Adam, it's beautiful," I gushed. "Thank you so much." I leaned in and kissed his cheek before putting the bracelet on.

"Now you have my heart," he said. "So take good care of it, okay?"

I touch the dangling charm, thinking how happy we were when things were simple, and wondering if we'll ever be that way again.

I pick up my phone and dial his number. "Hey," I say, as soon as he answers.

"Hey," he says. "I'm glad you called. I feel like such an ass about earlier. I never should've bolted like that."

"Don't worry about it," I say, encouraged by his words. "It was my fault, too. I feel like such a mess—like I'm messing up everything."

"Well, life *is* messy," he tells me. "But it also goes on, right?"

"I guess I'm finding that whole rising-above-it thing to be a lot easier said than done. I need to figure things out first—not just for myself, but for Sasha, too."

"Sasha," he repeats, skepticism in his voice. "Have you talked to your shrink about her?" His tone tells me that he thinks I'm nuts.

"Look, I know that what I'm going through isn't the most ideal for our relationship—"

"I just want you to be happy," he says.

"I'll get there."

"But that's just it. You don't have to get there on your own. Your therapist can help you."

"I have to go," I say, frustrated that he's still looking for something (or someone) to fix me.

"Camelia, wait."

"Wes just showed up at my door," I lie. "I'll have to call you back."

"Sure," he says, but he sounds *un*sure. "Maybe we can get together this weekend. I can drive down again . . ."

"I'll call you," I repeat, thoroughly unsure as well.

I hang up, noticing how my bed linens smell like campfire—like the air outside, wafting in through my window. Someone must have a fire going on the beach. I look out the window. The sky is a bright shade of pink, making everything look warm and glowing, including the walls of my room.

I reach for my bag, eager to lose myself in work. I fish the envelope from the side pocket, take out the money clip, and focus hard on the engraved *t*. I close my eyes and try to picture the clip in someone's hands, but I can't seem to concentrate. There's a group of students outside on the terrace. They're laughing and talking, clearly enjoying the beautiful night, while reaffirming to me that mine sucks.

I'm almost tempted to venture out to join them, but instead I lie back on my bed, debating whether I should show the clip to the police or wait until tomorrow, after I visit the address on the envelope. I sit down at my laptop and type the address into Google. A restaurant pops up right away. The Blue Raven Pub. It's fifteen miles from campus.

I click on the link, but there isn't much on the site to help me—some menu highlights and the pub's hours. I forward the link to Wes and then check my e-mail. To my surprise, there's a message from Dad.

I open it, even more surprised to see that he's sent me a video.

"Hey, Camelia," Dad says, as soon as I click PLAY. He's sitting at the kitchen island, speaking directly into the camera. I spy Mom's jar of almond butter in the background. "Your mom said that I should respect your privacy. I do want to respect it, but I also want you to know that I'm thinking about you. When you have a chance, call me. I'd love to hear how you're doing. And in the meantime . . ." He pauses to open a bag from Taco King. He takes out a chicken chalupa and a basket of nacho chips drizzled in cheesy goodness. "Mom served dehydrated flaxseed sandwiches tonight. Need I say more?" He takes a bite and I can't help but laugh.

The video ends and so I play it again, missing our late-night junk-food excursions. And missing *him*. More than ever.

# LESSON NUMBER SEVEN:
## *NEVER LOSE HOPE.*
## *SOMETIMES IT'S ALL WE'VE GOT.*

He's here again. The door slams shut, a boom that jolts me awake. I feel like I've been sleeping for days. Without food, I've felt so weak.

At one point, hours ago, or maybe it was yesterday, I woke up and reached through the darkness for the area around the hole. The tape recorder was gone. I must've slept through one of his visits.

He moves closer, his feet scraping against the dirt floor, and suddenly I can see. The hole is illuminated by his lantern.

"Are you anxious to hear if I liked the tape?" he asks.

"Yes," I say; my voice is barely a whisper. I'm beyond hot, and yet I have the chills. I can feel goose bumps all over my skin.

A moment later, I see the tape recorder again. He's placed it down in front of the hole. The sight of it makes acid travel up my esophagus, burning the back of my throat.

He kicks the tape recorder into my cell, following it with the microphone.

I assume he's going to ask me to do the recording again, but instead he feeds some items through the hole: a flashlight, some bandages, a tube of antiseptic cream, a box of crackers, and a handful of granola bars. As if all of that weren't enough, he pushes through ten bottles of water.

"Wow," I say, almost beyond words. I actually catch myself in a smile. I hate that he can probably hear my happiness.

"Where's my thank-you?" he asks.

"Thank you," I say, taking the flashlight, opening a granola bar, reaching for a bottle of water. I try to open the water, but my hands aren't quite strong enough, and so I feed the granola bar into my mouth.

I turn on the flashlight and shine it over my wrist. My wound looks worse than I expected. The edges are crusty and dark and the skin is unrecognizable.

"I really liked your recording," he says.

"You did?" I ask, initially feeling proud to have pleased him—a gut reaction, as sick as that is.

"Enjoyed it *so* much," he continues, "that I'd like you to do another. Only this time, I want you to tell me why you're here."

"Why I'm here?" I ask, still eating. *I'm here because you*

*drugged me, because you took me, because I was too stupid to know what was good for me.*

"This was *your* choice, after all," he says. The sound of his voice gives me more chills. "You came here of your own free will. You wanted time on your own. I merely provided that."

"My own free will?" I ask, desperate to know what he's trying to say. Does he want me to make something up? To say that he did me a favor by taking me? Maybe then if he's caught, the police will think that I was happy here and not be able to arrest him?

"You know you wanted to come here. You remember begging me to take you, don't you?"

"Of course," I say, playing along. "I want to be here. I asked you to bring me. This whole experience has been really good for me."

"Exactly," he says; I can hear the smile in his voice. "But you can't just say the words. You have to make them believable. *Why* did you want to come?"

I nod, totally getting it. I need to pull off my biggest acting role yet. I grab the microphone and the box of crackers, feeling more excited than I have in a long time.

# 32

*A*FTER TOSSING AND TURNING for a couple of hours, I sit up, still able to hear the voices of students outside. It's hot in my room, even with the window open and the slight ocean breeze filtering in through the screen.

I get up and trade my sweats for a pair of shorts and my long-sleeved T for a tank top. Slipping on some flip-flops, I go downstairs and through the lobby, hoping that some fresh air will help me to relax.

Once outside, I notice that the sky is a deep purple color. I cross the back lawn to look out at the ocean. The moon paints a strip across the water. The waves ripple forward in glittering rows, spilling out over the rocks below, producing liquid gold. It's almost too beautiful to be real.

I start down the set of stairs that leads to the beach, and then I walk out to the water. The incoming tide rolls over my feet, bathing them in an iridescent glow. I spend

194

a few moments wading in the water before turning back and coming to a sudden halt.

I blink hard and shake my head, convinced that I must be seeing things. But he's there, descending the stairs, coming right toward me.

Ben.

My pulse races and my head starts to spin.

"What are you doing here?" I ask, feeling my face turn as pink as the sky was just hours ago.

Ben is dressed in torn jeans and a T-shirt. His hair is rumpled from the wind.

"How did you know where to find me?" I ask him.

He's standing right in front of me now, and it's almost too hard to breathe.

"I have my ways." His steel gray eyes focus right on mine, turning everything inside me into molten mush.

"I've missed you," he says, taking me in his arms, just like old times. He smells like charcoal and kindling wood.

I melt against him, drinking him in, cementing this moment in my mind forever. "You've been talking to Adam, haven't you? Is that how you knew where I was?"

He moves back to stare into my eyes again. "We have a lot of catching up to do, don't we?" Ben extends his hands to me, with the palms up.

My fingers trembling, I place my hands on top of his. He grips them tightly. His breathing is heavy. His eyes are closed. He's somewhere else entirely.

A few seconds later, I almost have to pull away, because his grip tightens. "Ben?" I ask, wondering what he senses.

I try to breathe through the stinging sensation, but he squeezes my hands harder. "Ben!" I shout, louder this time. My fingers are absolutely throbbing.

Finally, he releases me. "Why didn't you tell me about your aunt?" He opens his eyes; they look swollen and sorrowful. "How could you possibly have kept something like that from me?"

I stare at his lips, feeling my bones ache. "Maybe I was protecting myself from opening up too much and getting hurt all over again," I tell him. "I was protecting you, as well. You're the one who's always telling me how much better off I'll be without you. But maybe you're better off, too."

"My life will never be better off without you," he says.

Without another word, I move closer and press my lips against his mouth. He tastes like sea salt.

We stay on the beach kissing as the sky folds in all around us, changing from plum purple to smoky black. Ben's hands move over my waist and knead the small of my back.

As much as I'm into the moment, it isn't long before I'm overwhelmed by a sense of panic, knowing that I'm betraying Adam. I pull away, all out of breath.

"I'm sorry," I say, staring into his eyes, wondering if he can sense how much I want us to be together.

A second later, my cell phone rings. I check my pockets, startled to find that these shorts don't have any. And that I didn't bring a bag. So where is the ringing coming from? I look at Ben, figuring it must be his phone.

But he's gone now. Vanished. And still the phone continues to ring.

I sit up in bed, gasping for breath, realizing finally that it was a dream. I look at the clock. It's three a.m. The voices of students still linger outside. And the money clip remains clenched in my hand. I look at my fingers—at the impressions made from the metal tip.

Meanwhile, my phone continues to ring. A blocked call. I hesitate to answer it, still shaken up from the dream. On one hand, I'm disappointed it wasn't real. On the other hand, I'm completely relieved.

"Hello?" I say, finally answering.

"I saw that you went to the mailbox," she says. "And did you also go to the address?"

"Not yet."

"Why not? I was under the impression that you wanted to find Sasha."

"And going to the Blue Raven will help me do that?"

"It's a start," she says.

"And you want *me* to find her," I say. "If you're the one with all the clues, then how come you haven't been able to?"

She doesn't answer. Maybe she's thinking of what to say.

"You want her found," I continue, sensing that she does. "So, what's your deal in all of this?"

"Go to the Blue Raven."

"Is that where you got the money clip?" I persist. "Who does it belong to? And what does the *t* stand for?"

"It's obviously someone's initial."

"Do you know who that someone is?"

"I think you've asked me enough questions," she says.

"Should I take that as a yes? Is it a first initial? Or does it stand for a last name? Are you looking for Sasha, too?"

But unfortunately I've managed to push her too far. She responds by hanging up.

# 33

*U*NABLE TO GET BACK TO SLEEP after my dream—
not to mention the phone call—I go back to my
in-box to reply to Dad's video message when I
notice a new e-mail from Ben.

Dear Camelia,

I hope your summer is off to a great start or at
least that it's better than mine. I've sort of taken
a brief hiatus from traveling. Let's just say I'm
stuck in the same place for a bit, but I guess
that's life. We don't always get to go where we
want, and I suppose my priorities have shifted
a bit.

I miss you, as always. For the record, it's 2 a.m.
as I write this and I can't get to sleep. I had a

dream about you tonight, and I'm still trying to figure out what it means. Maybe you can help.

In the dream, we were both working on the same fifty-thousand-piece puzzle. The thing is, the puzzle was so big that we didn't even know that the other was working on it. It was like I was floating above the scene, looking down on us as we worked independently of each other, completely oblivious to the fact that we both had the same goal of putting all the pieces together.

Any ideas?

Love,
Ben

I reread his e-mail, thinking how surreal it is that we each dreamed about the other on the same night, and that neither of us can sleep as a result. I wonder why he's taken a hiatus from traveling and what he means by "stuck in the same place." I crawl back into bed, wanting to fall asleep, but my brain won't seem to shut off. I'm so wide awake that it almost hurts; my head feels like it could explode.

Wondering if Ben might still be awake, I reach for my phone and then notice a text from Dad. He tells me to check my e-mail for the video and that he loves me more than anything.

I reply with a simple thank-you, knowing that my brief response—not to mention my lack of an "I love you, too"—will probably sting. I push SEND, suddenly realizing that I'm more like Sasha than I thought. When Sasha found out the truth about her parents, she tried to punish them by acting out instead of communicating how she felt. And so I send Dad another text, thanking him for the video and telling him that it's the first laugh I've had in days.

Several hours later, I'm up, showered, and dressed for class. I call Wes to see if he'd like to join me for breakfast.

"Am I to assume that you're all geared up to go on this glorious day of redemption?" he asks.

"Something like that, which is why I'm off to partake in the most important meal of the day. Care to partake with me?"

"We're already partaking," he says; I can hear that his mouth is full.

"*We?*"

"Just some friends from class." He pauses to laugh at something one of his friends has said.

"Hello?"

"Come to the student union," he insists. "Waffles with whipped cream and strawberry drizzle: your mom's worst nightmare come true."

"Well, in that case, I'll be there in five."

## 34

*A*T BREAKFAST, Wes introduces me to his new posse—a trio of kids from his photography class: Doug, Leanna, and Rocky. They all seem nice and welcoming enough, but what I really want do is tell Wes that Mailbox Girl has called me again.

"Is everything okay?" he asks, picking up on my anxious vibe.

"Everything's great," I lie, forcing a sincere-looking smile as I take a bite of waffles, knowing that, frustrating as it is not being able to fill him in, I don't think I've ever seen him this happy—this relaxed and confident—with anyone aside from Kimmie and me. And so maybe my Mailbox Girl news can wait.

Thirty minutes later, in pottery class, Professor Barnes lectures us about form versus scale with respect to the integrity of a given artistic piece. He then gives us an hour to sculpt an example of form taking priority over scale.

The students, Ingrid included, get right to work on the assignment. I wedge out a hunk of clay, telling myself that I'm not going to have another psychometric episode—at least not in the next sixty minutes.

Ingrid appears to be sculpting a house of some sort, which makes perfect sense and seems perfectly simple: a model replica in which form takes priority over art.

I look at the clock. Forty more minutes. I've already managed to burn away twenty. The back of my neck is hot. Sweat trickles from my temples. And Sasha's cries seem louder than normal. The sound distracts me, psychs me out, and makes me feel like I don't belong here.

I gaze up at Barnes. He stares back at me. I have thirty minutes left.

I close my eyes and then sink my fingers a little deeper into the clay. Several moments of smoothing my palms over the mound and kneading the sides with my knuckles pass before an image finally flashes across my mind.

The crying inside my head gets louder. I breathe through it and begin to sculpt, mentally turning the volume down.

"Fifteen-minute warning," Barnes announces; I can hear the amusement in his voice.

I continue sculpting, unable to think about anything else, or even to consider fulfilling the assignment. I work fast, trying to get all the details just so, adding texture to the creases and carving into the top with my fingernail.

"Time's up," Barnes says, smacking his hand against the table.

I look at my sculpture, almost startled by how much it

resembles the image inside my head.

A hand, palm facing down. Its fingers are extended, as if reaching out. And there's a capital *W*—about two inches tall and wide—carved into the wrist.

A totally creepy piece. And totally outside the parameters of the assignment.

"So, shall we get started?" Professor Barnes asks, looking toward Ingrid's sculpture. He spends several moments pointing out its merits before moving around the room and assessing the other students' work.

And then he gets to mine.

He sits down beside me and cocks his head to one side as he examines my sculpture. Then he stifles a little laugh, as if enjoying every moment of my humiliation. "Care to explain how this satisfies the requirements of the assignment?" he asks.

"It doesn't," I say, shaking my head. Coming up with an excuse would only make things worse.

I look at my sculpture, noting that it actually has a lot of promise . . . or would have, if I had the time to finish the fingernails. Still, the detailing of the bones and the precision of the knuckles and joints almost make up for any weirdness. *Almost.*

"I guess I was sort of inspired by this hand," I tell him, hearing my voice crack. "I know that it was done to scale, which is the exact opposite of what you asked for. I mean, I *do* understand the whole point you're trying to make—"

"The point I'm *trying* to make?" His grin widens.

"I guess I just couldn't think of anything else," I say, which is actually pretty close to the truth.

"You thought of the *W*," he teases. "Any clues for us as to what it might stand for? Don't keep us in suspense, now."

I open my mouth, but no words come out, because I honestly don't have the answer. I glance past him at Ingrid. Even she appears to feel sorry for me. Her mouth twitches, and she looks down at her perfectly (and purposely) not-done-to-scale house, covering it with a tarp.

"I should go," I tell him.

"That would probably be wise, Ms. Hammond. I think you've wasted enough of our class's time."

I bite my lower lip, and then exit the classroom before he can see me cry.

## 35

$\mathcal{I}$N MY ROOM, still reeling from what just happened with Professor Barnes, I try calling Adam, but his phone just rings and rings. I'd pop up to Wes's room, but I know he's still in class. I go over every reason I shouldn't call Ben. But, desperate for someone to talk to, I dial his number anyway.

It goes right to voice mail. Still, it's good just to hear his recorded message—to hear the confidence in his tone and his promise to return the call. And so I call back again, after the beep, to hear his voice one more time. I sink down to the floor by my bed and begin a semicoherent ramble: "I'm sorry to be bothering you," I tell him, pausing to wipe my nose with a tissue. "I just feel like I'm screwing everything up here—*here* being Peachtree, by the way. I'm not sure if Adam told you, but I'm at a college in Rhode Island, trying to get away and take some classes. Only, my classes have been a failure—the one class that I've actually managed to attend, that is—because I'm sculpting things that don't make sense."

I stop to take a breath, sure that I sound like a flake. I purposely avoid mentioning Sasha's case, fearing that doing so might cause him to change his plans, wherever he is. Instead, I apologize again for calling him—for dumping my issues into his lap. "I just needed someone to talk to," I say, hearing the tears in my voice, and hoping he doesn't hear them, too. "Someone who really gets me." I shake my head, fully aware that I'm exposing way too much. "I should probably go," I say. "But maybe I'll talk to you—"

A loud beep cuts me off.

Still desperate for a connection, I grab my aunt's journal, flashing back to the last time I went to visit her at the hospital, just before I found out the news about my birth. We sat in the communal area, playing round after round of gin rummy and snacking on pretzel chips. It almost felt normal, as if we were sitting at her kitchen table, rather than in a mental health ward.

I spend the next couple of hours rereading pieces of her journal, reminded once again of how similar we are with respect to our art. But we're also very different. While Alexia is a victim of her powers, I'm trying my hardest not to be.

After a lunch of sprouted-seed granola bars, and feeling a bit more together, I go to my afternoon theory class, determined to salvage the day. The professor lectures us about Japanese Satsuma pottery and the work of ancient Greece. Normally I'd be totally engrossed, but I can't seem to concentrate, especially with Sasha's crying inside my ear. I excuse myself to go to the bathroom.

Out in the hallway, I check my phone for messages. There's a recent text from Wes: *Call me when ur free.*

I call him right away.

"Hey," he says, picking up.

"Did you get out of class early?"

"Imagine that. Have I mentioned how much I love college?"

"Except this is summer school for high school kids."

"Whatever," he says, like the distinction is no big deal. "How's redemption day?"

"Don't ask."

"Less than redeeming then, I take it? Well, are you busy? Do you want to go check out that creepy address?"

I consider going back to class, but the thought of sitting there for another half hour makes me want to cry right along with Sasha. "I'll meet you in ten minutes," I tell him.

Wes picks me up in front of the dorm, and we drive to the address on the envelope. It's a bit farther than I expected— in the next town over and about thirty minutes from the bakery where we got the money clip. On the way there, I tell Wes about the hand that I sculpted, as well as about my most recent phone call from Mailbox Girl.

"Despite her cryptic ways, I really think Mailbox Girl wants Sasha found," I tell him.

"Which probably means that Mailbox Girl is afraid for

Sasha. I mean, if Sasha truly ran away with some hot boy toy, Mailbox Girl probably wouldn't care."

"Right," I say, impressed by how quickly he catches on. "She wants her found, but for whatever reason, she's too afraid to say so or get involved."

"Because she may already *be* involved."

"Exactly my theory."

Wes takes a turn onto Farm Road and I peer out the window, looking for the Blue Raven Pub. It's a quiet street with only a few houses. The pub sits at the very end, bordering some woods. A sign outside says it's TWO-FOR-ONE CHRISTMAS MEAT LOAF NIGHT.

"Our lucky day," Wes jokes. "Except . . . what exactly *is* Christmas meat loaf? Meat loaf that's been kept in a freezer for seven months?"

"I actually think it means it's got red and green peppers in it."

"How festive," he says, pulling into the side lot.

We go inside, where it smells like cafeteria food. A bar shares the same space as the dining area, but people don't seem to mind. It's actually kind of homey, with a giant fireplace, plum-colored walls, and artwork hanging all around.

There's one loner guy sitting at the bar, eating something that looks suspiciously like the Christmas meat loaf. There's also a long table where at least ten people are seated, all of whom seem to be part of a book discussion group.

"I say we go talk to the bartender," Wes suggests, nodding toward a woman with a purple ponytail. "They always seem to have the answers."

He sidles up to the bar like a regular on two-for-one Christmas meat loaf night and takes a seat on one of the stools.

The woman smirks at his effort to fit in. "No milk on tap tonight," she tells him.

"We're hardly here for milk and cookies," he says, wielding his SpongeBob-adorned notepad. "What we're looking for is answers."

"Answers to what?" she asks, leaning over the bar. The silver feather in her hair matches the color of her lips.

Before Wes gets into it, he orders us a couple of root beers with cherries.

"You're going to get us thrown out," I say, as soon as the bartender turns away to get our drinks. I take a seat on the stool beside him, but he doesn't respond to my comment; he's far too busy jotting down today's date and time, and our present location.

A few seconds later, the bartender returns with our drinks, and then gives Wes a pointed look. "Now what?" she asks, scratching her nose, where she has a square hoop through one nostril.

I reach into my bag for Sasha's photo. "We're looking for our friend," I say, sliding the photo toward her. "Have you seen her?"

The bartender—Brooke, according to her name tag— picks up the photo, squinting at it. "Something tells me I might've seen this girl before," she says.

"Sasha Beckerman has been missing for a couple

months now," I explain. "Is it possible that you saw her photo on TV?"

"That's it!" Her face brightens. "And so why are you asking me? You think she hung out here or something?"

I shake my head. "We're not really sure."

"But we have a couple leads." Wes motions for me to show Brooke the money clip.

I pluck it out of the envelope—it's back in the plastic bag—and slide it across the bar toward her.

She takes it, turning the bag over in her hand looking closely at the engraving on the clip. "Where did you get this?"

"Have you seen it before?" I ask her.

"Do you have any idea what the *t* stands for?" Wes adds.

She turns away to polish the bar. "Don't you think the police know what they're doing?"

"Is that a rhetorical question?" Wes asks.

"Look," I begin, "if you have information about this clip—"

"It's Tommy's," she says, cutting me off. "He used to work here, in the kitchen, washing dishes."

"Do you know where he works now?" I ask. "Or where we might be able to find him?"

She shakes her head, still polishing. "Weird guy, though. I remember him pulling that thing out," she says, nodding toward the clip. "I didn't know people still used them. I remarked on it once and he got all pissy."

"So, if he worked here, then you must have all his

info," I say. "You must know where he lives and how to reach him."

"Hold on." She stops polishing and closes her eyes, as if all of this is going just a little too fast. "Why are you asking about Tommy? And why do you have his money clip? Is he dead or something? Is he involved in the Beckerman case?"

"We're not sure," I tell her. "But finding Sasha is really important to us, and we have reason to believe that Tommy might have some information."

"Have you told the police?" Brooke asks.

"Not yet," I say, taking a sip of root beer. "But it's definitely our next step, especially now that we know he worked here."

"Yeah, well, unfortunately, you'll be hard-pressed to find any info on him here. He got paid under the table—cash only—and said he didn't have a permanent address . . . always crashing at a different friend's place. He also claimed not to have a phone because he couldn't afford the monthly bill. It was all a pain, including his attitude, which was why he got canned."

"Are you seriously telling me that *nobody* who works here knows how to reach him?" Wes asks.

"Nobody," she says, staring right at him. "And to tell you the truth, it's been at least six months since Tommy worked here. I'm pretty sure that everyone who works here now came after that."

"Except you," Wes says, clearly suspicious.

"What can I say?" She rolls her eyes. "I'm a sucker for

crap pay and no benefits. But at least I get my weekends off." She gazes over her shoulder at the guy eating Christmas meat loaf.

"Can you tell us anything else?" I ask.

"Hold on," she says, turning her back to get Wes another root beer. "I *do* remember something. He'd wear his kitchen gloves everywhere. He said he had this hang-up about germs. But once I caught him with the gloves off."

"And?" I ask.

"And he had this really weird scar on his wrist. It almost looked like a burn. He must've been embarrassed about it, because he didn't want anyone to see it."

"Was it in the shape of a *W*?" I ask.

"Yeah," she says, tilting her head. "How did you know?"

"Did he say what the *W* stood for?" Wes asks, still taking notes.

"Not so fast," she says, looking directly at me. "How did you know what the scar looked like? Do you know Tommy already? Did he send you here to talk to me?"

"We should probably go," Wes says, getting up from the stool. "My hemorrhoids are starting to act up. If I don't get myself some anti-itch cream soon, there'll be no helping me. Camelia, can I borrow your hairbrush? My fingernails are still dull from my last flare-up." He drops a ten on the bar and then extends his hand to Brooke for a shake.

"Later," she says, leaving him hanging. And who can really blame her?

# 36

ON THE RIDE HOME, Wes and I dissect and discuss all the details of our visit to the pub, including the possibility that Brooke might've been either wrong or lying about nobody knowing of Tommy's whereabouts.

"Maybe we should go back to the pub when Brooke isn't working," Wes suggests. "We can ask somebody else."

"Definitely," I say, having thought the exact same thing.

Wes takes a turn onto the Sumner campus and pulls up in front of the dorm to drop me off. "Are you sure you don't want to come with?" he asks me. He and some friends are heading down to the beach for pizza by a fire.

"Maybe next time," I say.

"Well, call me if you change your mind."

"Will do, and thanks again." I give him a peck on the cheek.

Back in my room, I sit down in front of my laptop to read Neal Moche's latest blog entry.

## From the Journal of Neal Moche

I scoped out his house again. Yesterday, when I knew he was working, I knocked on his door, pretending to be advocating for the environment. I even brought along a clipboard for signatures and some literature about environmental causes.

His girlfriend answered the door, but only opened it a few inches. It was weird looking at her up close. I mean, I've seen her plenty from afar (through the window of their house as I peeked in from the outside, and getting in and out of her boyfriend's pickup truck), but there's nothing quite like seeing what you pictured in your mind—what you pictured as a result of touching someone, that is—standing right in front of you.

"Do you have a few moments?" I asked her, not even giving her the opportunity to answer. I started rambling on about global warming, regurgitating what'd I'd read in one of the pamphlets.

The girl, probably around nineteen or twenty, shook her head and started to close the door, but I held it open with my foot. Startled, she released her grip on the door, enabling me to nudge it open and peek inside the house.

But it was her neck that I couldn't quite get past. A pretty girl with long blond hair and big brown eyes, but with a massive scar. What I'd thought might be a tattoo of a religious cross (from the vision I had when I'd bumped into her boyfriend at the park) is actually a scar, with bubbled skin that's crusted over.

"Please, just give me a second," I told her. "Would you at least sign my petition?" I held out my clipboard, noticing the fear in her eyes. "Is there anyone at home who might like to show their support?" I peered past her, getting a good view of the house's interior: broken floor tiles and junk piled everywhere on the counter- tops. "Is your husband at home?" I asked, hoping she might say his name.

She shook her head. Her hands were trembling. All the color had drained from her face. It felt uncomfortable being there, pushing her, keeping the door open when I was obviously freaking her out.

"Would you like to add both of your names to support

the cause?" I continued, despite how shitty it felt. "After that, I promise to leave you alone." I tried to hand her the clipboard and a pen, but she refused to take either, and so I had to resort to something drastic.

I pretended to trip and tumbled forward so that she'd have to break my fall. And so that I could touch her. For just a second, my hand caught her forearm and I closed my eyes, trying to sense as much from her as I could. I saw a key ring, loaded with at least twenty different keys, but before I could sense anything else, she pulled away from me.

I wanted to grab her arm back, but her entire body began to quiver and twitch. "Sorry," I said, all out of breath. "I can be a real klutz sometimes."

Keeping her head down and her gaze toward the floor, she placed her hand on the door once more. Finally I allowed her to close it, feeling like crap for having scared her in the first place.

Honestly, the longer I'm here, the more desperate I feel and the lonelier I get. I'm still not sleeping much at night, and when I *do* sleep, I dream of being some-place else, instead of following around some guy that I don't even know, and terrifying his girlfriend.

By the time I get to the last line, my pulse is absolutely racing because of the way his words hit home—and how much I'm able to relate to his feeling of desperation and the lack of sleep that goes along with it.

Luckily for me, I have support, but I also know what it's like to feel alone. My aunt knew it all too well. And, from the sound of things, so does Neal Moche.

I start to reread the entry, wanting more than ever to contact him, but a knock on the door interrupts me. I get up from the bed, assuming it's Wes. But instead, when I open the door, a man and a woman flash their badges at me.

"Camelia Hammond?" the woman asks.

"Yes," I say, looking closer at her badge. Detective Susan Tanner.

Dressed in a plain black suit, she looks beyond me, into my room. "Can we talk to you for a few moments?"

I open the door wider to let them in, suddenly noticing the campus security officer standing just behind them. "What is this about?" I ask, though I'm pretty sure I know the answer.

Detective Tanner closes the door on the security guard, while her male colleague—twentysomething, with slick black hair and super-tanned skin—moves to stand at the back of my room, as if eager to take everything in.

"You paid a recent visit to Tracey Beckerman," Tanner says in a tone that tells me this isn't up for debate. She snags a notepad and pencil from inside her jacket. "Can you tell me about that?"

"What is it you'd like to know?" I ask, tugging nervously at my hair.

"How about why you went there, for starters?"

I swallow hard, noticing a sudden dryness in my mouth. I grab the day-old cup of water by my bed. There's a layer of dust on top, but I drink it anyway.

"Mrs. Beckerman mentioned that you knew Sasha's real name," Tanner continues when I don't answer quickly enough.

"Right," I say, proceeding to tell her about my interest in the case and how I stumbled upon Mrs. Beckerman's Web site while researching summer programs.

Detective Tanner scratches behind her ear with the pencil; her hair is the color of the graphite. "Yes, but *why* did the case interest you so much? Because it seems you put in a lot of effort to get here."

"I just found out that I was adopted, too." I glance at the other detective, who's standing between my closet and minifridge. His face is completely expressionless.

"So, if the fact that both you and Sasha were adopted is initially what got you interested in Sasha's case, what's keeping you interested now?" Detective Tanner stares at me, pencil to paper, ready to jot the answer down.

"I've been sensing things about Sasha," I say, feeling my heart hammer.

Her beady brown eyes narrow. "Sensing things?"

I nod and then tell her about my power of psychometry, how it comes to me when I'm doing my pottery, and how this isn't the first time I've experienced it. "I've used

219

my power in the past," I continue, "to help save my boy-friend's life. And then to save the sister of a girl I went to school with."

"Really?" she asks; a tiny smirk crosses her chalky lips.

"I'm not joking." My tone sharpens.

"Then what *are* you doing?" She raises an eyebrow.

"Getting frustrated," I snap, "that a detective who's been working on a missing-girl case for over two months isn't more open to the possibility that certain people may be able to see and know more than she does."

The male detective accidentally knocks a box of crack-ers off my fridge.

"I'm aware of people who *claim* to have psychic abil-ities," Tanner snaps back. "We've even consulted with psychics to get help with various cases."

"And so why not consult with *me?*" I ask. "Ask *me* about the daisy I sensed or the letter *t* that I sculpted. Maybe then I'll tell you about the girl who called me."

"What girl?" Tanner takes a step forward, clearly interested.

"She wouldn't give me her name, but she sent my friend and me on a wild-goose chase." I open my night table drawer and pull out the plastic bag with the money clip inside. I explain how Wes and I went to the Blue Raven Pub and found out that the initial *t* on the clip stands for Tommy. "And yet he supposedly has a *W* marked on his hand; it's either a scar or a burn."

Exactly like what I sculpted.

Detective Tanner writes everything down and then

snatches the money clip without so much as a thank-you.

"The thing is," I tell her, "I have no idea how the mystery girl who called me even knew about my interest in Sasha's case, never mind how she got my phone number."

"Did you tell anyone you were looking for Sasha? Anyone at all?"

"Just my friend Wes Mayer."

Tanner writes Wes's name in her notepad, then asks a slew of questions about him—where he's from, how old he is, if he knows Sasha, and why he followed me to Sumner.

"It wasn't Wes," I say.

"Well, it was *someone*," she says, closing her notepad. "And you can bet we'll find out who. But, rest assured, you've already been a great deal of help, even if this turns out to all be a hoax."

"*Hoax?*"

"You *have* heard of false leads, haven't you?" she asks. "What if the mystery girl who called you and the bartender at the Blue Raven Pub are actually working in cahoots? What if that's why the bartender didn't want you to question anyone else who works there?"

"So you believe me about my powers?" I ask.

"I make it a rule not to believe or disbelieve too much of anything—until all reasonable doubt is dissolved, that is. I wouldn't be a very good detective if I did otherwise." Surprisingly, she doesn't ask me anything more. Instead, she hands me her business card, shoots her mute partner an urgent look, and then leads him out the door.

# LESSON NUMBER EIGHT:
## *PHYSICAL AND MENTAL STRENGTH ARE EQUALLY ESSENTIAL.*

The tape recorder positioned in front of me, I finish writing my monologue in the dirt floor, using my finger as a pen. And then I close my eyes and channel Kathryn Merteuil from *Cruel Intentions*, one of my favorite manipulative characters.

I start my recording over at least a dozen times before I finally get the tone right. "I'm so glad he allowed me to tag along that night," I say into the microphone. "I know I must've been such a nag, asking him all kinds of questions about stupid stuff, like what kind of sports he liked to play and if he'd seen any good movies lately, trying to keep him talking. I figured the longer he talked, the longer I'd get to be with him. He was so sweet to me, too, even though I was a pest. Maybe it was his sweet side that caved and let me leave with him.

"I just didn't want to go home. I didn't want to face

my parents. I hated them for lying to me about being adopted. That's why I'd packed my suitcase. I'd planned to run away anyway, but this new friend gave me a quicker way out. He was older, so I figured he could take care of me, and he *has* taken care of me. It's been so great here, having this time away to think and to fully appreciate how lucky I've been. I have him to thank for that. He's been my teacher as well as my friend."

I press STOP and then lean back against the wall, hoping I've played the role convincingly. I slide the tape recorder and microphone through the hole, wondering if Misery's been questioned by the police yet.

I wash my wound and change the bandage for a third time, unable not to wonder if the burn mark might actually be the letter *t*, if it might stand for Tommy, the guy she'd wanted me to meet.

The guy who I think took me.

# 37

I'M ALONE IN MY ROOM, and the salty beach air filters in through the window, making me feel both restless and cold. I crawl into bed and pull the covers over me, suddenly realizing that I'm famished. I almost wish that my dad were here so that we could sneak out for chips and chalupas. I roll over, facing the window, thinking how adamant he was about defending his and Mom's decision to keep the truth about my birth a secret.

And as much as I hate to admit it, I can't help wondering what difference it would've made if he and Mom had told me the truth years earlier, when I was Sasha's age, perhaps.

Would I have ended up just like her?

The question haunts me, spinning around inside my head, colliding with all my other questions—like a video game gone awry. After at least an hour of trying to come up with answers, my thoughts start to dull and blur, and I begin to nod off.

A knock on the door startles me awake. I open my eyes and sit up in bed. It's a little after seven a.m. I get up, assuming it's Wes, that he wants me to join him for breakfast. I open the door, my eyes widening, unable to grasp who it is that's standing there, just inches from me.

I pinch my skin, noticing I have goose bumps. This isn't a dream. I'm not asleep. There's no way this is part of a hallucination.

"Ben." His name is like candy inside my mouth.

Without even thinking, I slide my arms around his waist and rest my head against his chest. He smells like bike fumes. "What are you doing here?" I ask, able to feel his heart beat fast beneath my cheek. "And how did you get in?"

"I came here," he says, wrapping his arms around me as well, "because this is where you said you were."

I get dizzy just holding him like this, just breathing him in.

Ben moves to take my hand. "Come on," he says, closing the door and leading me back inside my room. He sits me down on the bed. His skin is extra tan, most likely from riding around on his motorcycle and roaming the streets playing tourist all day. "I've missed you," he says, making my insides ignite.

Part of me wants to tell him how much I've missed

him, too. But I don't, because I don't want to get hurt. And I don't because of Adam. Instead, I squeeze his hand harder, hoping he can feel how much I've ached.

"I got your message," he says, pulling his hand away. Maybe the sensation is too intense. "So, tell me what's going on." His dark gray eyes never stray from my face.

I break down and tell him about my parents, how for years they kept a secret from me: "My dad isn't my real dad," I say. "And Aunt Alexia is actually my mother."

Ben's face doesn't show a speck of surprise, but then again it never really does. Maybe it's because of everything he's been through, everything he's already seen and heard. Or maybe it's because he doesn't *want* to show surprise and inflict his feelings on me.

"So, who *is* your real dad, then?" he asks.

"I don't know," I say, proceeding to tell him about the intern at the halfway house where Alexia once stayed, how he was kicked out of his college program as a result of violating the facility's code of ethics, and how he has his own life now.

"But he still might want you in it," Ben says. "Do you think you might want that, too?"

I shrug, unable to fathom the idea of a father who isn't the dad I know.

Ben asks me a few more questions—basically about whether my aunt's aware that I know the truth and how my parents are feeling as a result of my finding out. I answer everything, still uncertain about how to feel. But what's nice is that Ben doesn't tell me how to feel either. He doesn't try to fix things or provide any anecdotes. Instead, he simply cradles me against his chest and asks me to tell him more.

Lying face to face on my bed now, we spend the next two hours talking things out, only our hands touching. Ben slides his fingers up and down the length of mine. The motion itself seems innocent enough, but I couldn't feel more yearning.

"Can you tell what I'm thinking?" I ask, clasping his hand in mine. The warmth of his skin is intoxicating.

Ben blinks hard, as if he does indeed know, but his face remains completely serious. "Do you want to talk about what you've been sculpting?"

A stream of sunlight shines in through the window, illuminating his face, which glistens with perspiration. I gaze at his mouth, remembering having mentioned my mysterious (and disastrous) sculptures during my phone message to him.

"Are you searching for a girl?" he asks, gazing at my mouth now, too.

My cell phone rings before I can answer him. At first, I ignore it. But after four rings, Ben rolls onto his back and insists that I get it.

I reluctantly lean over him to answer the phone, pausing when I see Adam's name flash across the screen.

"Hi, Adam," I say, realizing that my voice sounds less than enthusiastic.

"Hey," he says, seemingly oblivious of my halfhearted tone. "Do you have a second? We need to talk."

"I agree. But I'm a little tied up at the moment. Can I call you back?"

"I'm actually in your lobby."

"*What?*"

"Would you mind calling down here to tell them that I'm safe?"

*What is it?* Ben mouths.

I hang up without thinking. "Adam's here," I say. "Downstairs. He's on his way up to my room."

"I should go," Ben says, getting up from the bed. "You two should have some time on your own."

"No," I say, getting up, too. "Don't go. Please. It's not like we have anything to hide here."

Standing right in front of me now, his eyes go slightly squinty, as if maybe my words have hurt him, and then he goes out the door.

## 38

*A*FTER BEN LEAVES, I call down to the lobby to tell the person working at the front desk that it's okay if Adam comes up. When he arrives at my door, I invite him inside, but he wants to take a walk instead.

"Why?" I ask, though I can see from the look on his face—his swollen eyes and the tenseness of his mouth—that something is definitely wrong. "I mean, what's going on? What are you doing here?"

"Let's go for a walk," he insists, as if he's planned it all out and being outdoors will somehow make what he has to say easier.

"Tell me what's going on," I say, my mind racing as I try to guess the reason for this impromptu visit.

He shuffles his feet and looks at the ground. "I really care about you," he says, stuffing the tips of his fingers into the pockets of his jeans. "But, I don't know. I feel like things were a lot easier before. I mean, I understand there's a lot going on with you right now, but I almost feel like what's going on is pulling us apart."

"It is." I close the door behind him and then sit down on my bed. "But only because you don't want to hear about my problems. You just want things to go back to normal."

"And why can't they?" he asks. "Why can't you deal with the news and move on? Why are you letting it dictate your life?"

"I have a right to feel what I'm feeling, Adam."

"Okay, but at what cost?" He comes and sits down beside me. "We had something really good, Camelia."

"Had or have?"

"That depends," he says, taking my hands. "I'm willing to talk about what's bothering you, but you have to be willing to help yourself."

"That's why I'm here," I say. "I wanted to get away, remember?"

"Yes, but being away means putting distance between us, too. I mean, if you were away and I felt secure about us, that would be one thing. But you keep sending me mixed messages, so I never know where we stand."

"So, wait, are you trying to say that you drove all the way out here just to tell me that our relationship isn't working?"

"Would you have preferred if I'd said it over the phone? I care for you too much, Camelia."

"I care about you, too," I say. "And you're right; our relationship *isn't* working, but I'm not the only one who sends mixed messages. You say you want me to tell you how I'm feeling, but can you honestly say that's true? You don't want to hear about the tough stuff. You just want me to be happy all the time."

"Is that so bad?"

"It's not bad," I tell him. "But it's also not realistic—at least, not all the time. Not everyone can simply blink their problems away."

"No one's asking you to blink them away, but it isn't healthy to dwell on them, either."

A breeze comes in through the window, sending shivers all over my skin. Should I be relieved that we're finally verbalizing what's obviously been on both our minds? Or heartbroken that our relationship has come to this?

"There's something else," Adam says, giving my hands a squeeze. "This isn't easy for me to tell you, so I'm just going to say it." He swallows hard and then takes a breath. "I lied about saving your life."

"Excuse me?"

"At that guy's apartment," he explains. "When you went to save Danica's sister . . ."

I nod, wincing at the memory of breaking into that psychopath's apartment four months ago, seeing Danica's sister tied up and gagged, and getting beaten up so badly that I blacked out.

I remember waking up, but still only half conscious, and seeing a blur of two guys fighting. Later, Ben told me that Adam and Jack (the psychopath) had fought and that Adam had saved the day. But I could tell even then—from the way Ben would barely look me in the eye, and from the way it seemed he was passing me off to Adam (the hero), trying to convince me what a great guy Adam was—that he wasn't telling the truth about the way things had played out.

"I hadn't intended on lying," Adam continues. "But when Ben said it—that I'd saved you—I kind of just went along with it. It didn't feel right, but I guess I liked the idea of being your hero."

I nod again, relieved to know the truth. Ben *was* the one who saved me that day.

"So why are you telling me this now?" I ask, suspecting that it might be his way of distancing us.

"I just thought that you should know." He lets go of my hands. "It's been bothering me for a while. And we promised not to keep secrets."

"I remember," I say, fully aware that I haven't been completely open about everything, either.

"Do you hate me?"

I slide the back of my hand against his cheek. The heart-shaped charm on the bracelet he gave me dangles against his chin. "I don't think I could ever hate you."

"So where does that leave us now?"

"I'm still going to be dealing with stuff," I tell him. "I mean, I want to move past this, but it's going to take some time."

"How *much* time?" He smirks.

"I'm not sure." I shake my head, almost amused that

he would ask, but unsurprised that he doesn't offer to wait. "This drama doesn't have an expiration date."

"In other words, it'll just fester inside you?"

"What can I say? I'm a festering kind of girl."

"A festering girl who needs some time on her own," he says, meeting my gaze.

I hug him—hard—until my arms ache.

"Call me for anything," he says. I know he thinks he means it.

"Ditto," I tell him, confident that I *do* mean it. I'd drop almost anything to be there for him. I give Adam one final kiss before he finally says good-bye.

## 39

*A*FTER ADAM LEAVES, I curl up on my bed, remembering that day in Jack's apartment: being only half conscious, feeling someone stroke the side of my face while he told me how much he loved me. I'd always thought it was part of a dream, but now I'm pretty sure that I was awake, and that the someone was definitely Ben.

I check the clock. It's after ten. My pottery class is already well under way. It's certainly tempting to skip it, but instead I grab my bag, reminding myself of why I'm here—or at least why I'm *supposed* to be here—and then I leave the room.

By the time I get to the pottery studio, I'm already an hour and a half late. The door is closed. The hallway is quiet. I try the knob, but the room is locked.

I peek through the vertical window that runs along

the door. There's a row of pottery wheels at the back of the studio. A different student works at each one, while other students await their turns. Professor Barnes looks on, pacing back and forth.

I knock on the door; Professor Barnes comes toward it and our eyes meet. He pauses for just a moment before resuming his pacing, as though I'm not even there.

I knock again, harder this time. Finally, he comes back to the door. He opens it a few inches and furrows his brow in annoyance. "Class has already started," he says.

"I'm sorry I'm late. I just—"

He holds up his hand to stop me from talking. "Not my concern."

"Well, can I still come in?" I ask. "I promise to follow along. You don't have to re-explain anything."

"You want to come to class, you need to get here on time. It doesn't get much simpler than that, Ms. Hammond." He closes the door and returns to the row of students.

In the hallway, I lean my back against the wall and sink down to the ground. I want to hate Barnes, but I know he's right. My priorities have shifted a bit. I'm not dedicated to my pottery—not the way I used to be.

My cell phone rings in my bag. I fish it out and check the screen. It's Ben. "Where are you?" I say when I answer.

"Still here, on campus. I didn't feel right leaving like that, and I saw Adam drive away. . . . I take it things didn't go so well?"

"They actually went exactly as they were supposed to,"

I say, confident that it's the truth, "but that doesn't make it any less hard."

"Can I come back up to your room?"

My heart pounds. I want to feel happy about talking to him, but I also can't stop this angst. It knots up in the center of my gut. "Meet me in the lobby," I tell him.

About ten minutes later, I walk through the lobby doors. Ben is already waiting for me. He's standing at the front desk.

"Hey," I say, feeling my insides heat up all over again, despite the hundred-odd reasons I should feel dismal. I sign him in—my fingers shaking—and then lead him upstairs.

Once inside my room, he takes my hand, forcing me to face him. His solemn expression tells me that he can sense the jumble of emotions inside me.

"I'm sorry," he says.

I wilt into his arms, eager for him to hold me and to feel this anxiety.

Ben leads me to my bed. "Everything will be fine," he whispers.

Tears of gratitude and sorrow run down my cheeks. I've never felt so loved and lost in all my life.

WHEN I WAKE UP, Ben is still here, lying beside me watching me sleep.

"How long have you been awake?" I ask him.

It's nighttime now, and the moonlight shines in through the window, casting a soft glow over his face, highlighting the paleness of his lips.

He moves a strand of hair from in front of my eyes. I want to reach out and touch him, too.

"I've been up for a little over an hour," he says.

"An hour," I repeat, nervous that I might have spoken in my sleep, or drooled on my pillow, or snored extra loud.

"How are you feeling about everything?" he asks.

"About Adam?" I say, untwisting the bedsheet from around my leg.

"For starters."

"Good and bad, I guess. I mean, Adam's a great guy, but I don't think that we belong together."

"And how do you feel about me?" he continues. "Being here, I mean?"

The question catches me by surprise and sends tingles straight down my spine. "I'm happy you're here," I tell him. "I wish you always would be—that you wouldn't always run off."

"Be careful what you wish for." His face is completely serious.

"Adam told me the truth," I say. "About Jack . . . about how you're the one who saved my life."

He nods and studies my face, perhaps trying to gauge if I'm upset that he lied. "Well, you saved my life, too," he says, finally. "I've done a lot of soul-searching these past few months, and you saved me in more ways than you'll ever know."

"How?"

He takes a deep breath; I watch the motion of his chest. "You helped me believe that I could actually have a somewhat normal life again."

"Because I trusted you."

"I hope you still *can* trust me, even though I haven't always given you reason to. I know I haven't been the most open, but it's only because I wanted to protect you."

I reach out to touch his face. The stubble is prickly against my fingers. I want to feel it against my cheek.

"I thought that Adam was better for you," he explains. "Safer, kinder, a lot less complex."

"Adam *is* all of that," I say, venturing to run my thumb over his lip. "But he's not the one I want."

Ben's lips part and his eyes widen, as if he can't quite believe my words. And so I kiss the truth right into him. His breath is hot and sweet against my mouth. At last I feel the scruff of his face against my cheek.

I feel the heat of his body as it pushes against mine.

I feel. Every. Single. Inch. Of my body. As he kisses me longer, deeper, and more intensely than ever before.

Lying beneath him, I slide my hands up the back of his shirt. His skin is warm to the touch.

"Camelia," he whispers, pulling away, and pausing to steady his breath. His whole body's sweating.

"You won't hurt me," I tell him.

"Well, I'd die if I ever did."

I lie beside him, resisting the urge to touch him again.

After several moments, he sits up, seemingly composed, as if having mentally splashed water onto his face. "You need to give yourself time," he says. "You just broke up with Adam."

"Is this really about Adam?"

"It really *should* be."

I know he's right, but I also know how I feel, how long I've waited, how he's the one I've been dreaming about.

"I don't want you to do something—in the heat of a rebound moment—that you might regret," he continues.

"Except you're hardly rebound material."

He shakes his head, refusing to argue, moving to sit on the edge of the bed. But I refuse to argue, too. I take his hand.

"Camelia . . ." He looks back at me.

"I know what I want," I tell him.

"Are you sure about that?"

"Really sure." I move closer to kiss him again.

"Camelia," he repeats. I can tell he's conflicted by the look in his eyes and by the tense grip he has on the bed.

I slide my palm over his thigh, where he has the chameleon tattoo; I'm reminded of how he got it before we even met—how everything about us seems to point to the fact that we belong together. "You could never hurt me," I tell him again.

"I love you," he whispers into my ear. The first time he's ever said it.

"I love you, too," I whisper back.

I pull his T-shirt over his head and toss it to the floor. He closes the window shade and then allows me to run my palms over his bare chest, to kiss his skin all over, and to pull him beneath the covers.

*B*EN GREETS ME the following morning with a cup of coffee and an array of pastries to choose from. Still lying in bed, I feel deliciously warm under the blankets.

"Thanks," I say, sitting up, feeling more awake than I have in a long time.

Ben grabs a sketch pad off my desk and uses it as a tray. "How are you doing this morning?" His tiny grin makes my face heat up.

"Okay." I grin back. "And you?"

"Pretty fantastic," he says, joining me on the bed.

Still tingling all over, I replay in my mind how he told me he loved me, noticing that my tank top smells like him.

"Can I get you anything else?" he asks.

I shake my head. "This is perfect," I say, grabbing a cinnamon scone.

"So, we should probably talk about the missing girl."

"Way to blow a perfectly romantic breakfast."

Ben leans across the tray of treats to kiss me. "Now can we talk about the missing girl?"

"Her name is Sasha Beckerman. Are you familiar with the case?"

"Vaguely, but I don't get too much news, being out on the road."

"Which brings me back to the question: what are you even doing here? I mean, I'm glad you came, but—"

"*You're* here," he says, interrupting me. "And when you called—when you left me that message—it sounded like you needed a friend."

"Okay, but you could've simply called me back. Did Adam tell you where I was?"

"You mentioned in your message that you were at a college in Peachtree. For the record, there's only one."

"When was the last time that you and Adam spoke?"

"Last week, but he never said anything about your going away. And sadly, neither did you."

"You know why I didn't."

"And *you* know why I couldn't stay away." His eyes lock on mine, making my heart swell, making every nerve in my body stand on end.

I'm half tempted to throw the tray to the side and crawl right into his lap. But instead, I lean over to kiss him again. He tastes like lemon pastry.

"Were you far away?" I ask.

"Not far at all," he says, leading me to assume that he was indeed on his way back to Freetown. "We have so much to talk about."

"I know," I admit. And so I proceed to fill him in on all my Sasha research and what I've been sculpting.

"Do you have any idea where she is or who she's with?"

"No, but I can hear her crying." I close my eyes and concentrate on her voice. "It's always in my ear, reminding me that she's still missing."

"And that she's still alive."

I nod, relieved that he wants to help.

"Well, for starters I think you should go back to the Beckerman house," he says. "See if you can get inside Sasha's room. Being in her space, among all her things, might help you sense more."

"You're right," I say, thinking about how simply researching Sasha's case enabled me to sculpt clues about her. I take a sip of coffee, on the verge of telling him about the money clip, but as soon as the idea pops into my mind, Ben gets up, moves the tray to my desk, and pitches his empty coffee cup.

"What's the rush?" I ask.

"No rush. But it might make sense to go to the Beckermans' place sooner rather than later."

"Did you sense something that I should know about?"

"I sensed a few things," he says, sitting back down. His forearm grazes my hip. "Mostly, the connection between you and Sasha. It's really strong."

"Definitely," I agree.

"I also sensed the responsibility you feel for Sasha's safety, and how disappointed you are that your parents kept your adoption a secret." He edges a little closer, his hip pressed against my thigh now. "But perhaps deep down you always knew there was something special between you and your aunt."

I nod, feeling a chill dance down my spine, amazed—once again—by how well he seems to know me. "Will you come with me to the Beckermans'?"

"I would, but I think it's better if you go alone, not even with Wes. I mean, think about it: you're asking to go into her daughter's room—a daughter that's been missing. That's sacred space. More than one person would be a party."

"Good point. And then what?"

"And then sculpt," he says, as if the answer were completely obvious.

"Except, I haven't exactly been welcome in the studio here." I look at the clock. The class started almost an hour ago. I'm already too late. "It's sort of a long story, but I wouldn't be surprised to find a picture of me outside the studio with a giant slash mark over my face."

"I know what you want, Camelia. . . . To be this amazing sculptor who has her own shop and whose works get commissioned all over the country. But you're already incredibly talented."

I swallow hard; my mouth feels parched even after the

coffee. I think about how Spencer, who subbed once for Ms. Mazur, singled me out in class. He said he'd never worked with anyone as young and talented as me.

"That talent won't ever change," he continues.

"But it already *has* changed. I'm no longer able to simply sit down and make a bowl. Now all of this other stuff gets in the way."

"Would you change it?" he asks. "When you really stop to consider the question . . ."

"I'm not sure," I say, thinking how I've already been able to help people with this power. What if I didn't have it?

Ben skims my hand and wrist with his fingertips. The hair on his forearm tickles my skin, sending heat straight to my thighs. "Sometimes we get this picture in our heads of the way things are supposed to be," he says. "But what if things *don't* turn out that way? What if they actually turn out better?"

Am I indeed better off with this power?

"It's a part of who you are," he reminds me, still touching my skin. "So what if you can't sculpt a bowl today? But what if you save a girl's life?"

I sit up and rest my head against his shoulder, remembering how Dr. Tylyn told me that I needed to embrace my power. How else am I going to live with it? How else am I going to accept myself? I may not always be able to control what I sculpt. But maybe I'm not supposed to.

"And what will you do while I'm at the Beckermans'?"

"Don't worry about me." He smirks. "I'm sure I'll be able to find something to keep myself occupied. But can I drive you?"

"No, thanks. I want to take a shower first, and I need to plan a strategy. I'll call Wes for a ride." I start to get up from the bed.

"Not so fast," Ben says, leaning in for one more kiss— a kiss that morphs into a full-on embrace. An embrace in which we end up melting against the bed, unable to resist each other's touch.

# 42

*I* FINALLY EMERGE from my room after what feels like days. To my surprise, Wes is at my door.

"Hey, stranger. I thought I might steal you away for lunch." He pauses to give me the once-over.

After Ben left, I took a shower and pulled on a T-shirt and a pair of jeans. My hair is swooped up in a ponytail.

"Don't you look particularly radiant today?" He grins. "Anything scandalous you want to tell me about?" He lowers his John Lennon glasses to inspect me over the rims (the gesture reminds me of Kimmie). "Might Adam have paid you another recent visit?"

"Yes, he did. But, no, it's not what you're thinking." At least, not exactly. "I'll fill you in, but first, can you give me a ride?"

"Hold on." He starts sniffing the air. "Ben was here, wasn't he?"

"You can smell him?"

"Okay, I might've also spotted his motorcycle in the parking lot. Care to dish?"

"What do you want me to say?" I can feel the embarrassment burning on my face.

"How, where, and for how long, for starters."

"You can't be serious."

"Judging from your resistance to making eye contact and your lightbulbworthy glow, I'd have to guess that it was a pretty good night. Am I right?"

"*Amazing* might be a better word. And how about you?" I ask, eager to change the subject as I take note of his spiffy attire. His T-shirt clings to his chest and the sleeves are tight around his biceps (I didn't even know that he had any). "Anything new with you and your band of photography buddies?"

"Just one buddy," he says with a wink. "And you're seriously going to have to drug me and then drag me from this campus if you think I'm going to willingly head back to Freetown. For the first time in my life, I feel like I can actually be me. Do you have any idea how liberating that feels?"

"I'm starting to," I tell him. "And I'm excited for you," I add, grateful to have been a part of his newfound happiness.

"So, what's on the agenda for today—aside from skipping your classes, that is?"

"How did you know I skipped?"

"That Ingrid girl in your class—the one with ginormous yellow teeth. Honestly, what is up with them?"

"I don't know. I didn't notice them."

"Are you kidding? They're like a flashing neon advertisement for teeth whitening. Anyway, she was looking for you and knows we're friends. . . ."

"Ingrid?" I ask, surprised to hear that she would've acknowledged my existence. "What did *she* want?"

"A really talented dental team; at least that's what she *should* want. Beyond that, she's a mystery to me, as are her gaucho pants and suspenders."

"Okay, *now* you sound like Kimmie."

"Who's doing phenomenally well, by the way. She loves her internship and they love her back. She's working on a fashion show and even collaborating on the design of a new pair of sunglasses. I told her it's all about polarization and blue-tinted lenses. Wouldn't you agree?"

"Sure . . . and **that's great**," I say, happy that my two best friends are doing so well, and that things are starting to look up for me, too, despite the fact that Sasha is still missing. "So, care to drive me to the Beckerman residence?"

"Is that all I'm good for? A cheap ride to a missing-person's-mother-of-a-could-be-slasher-victim's house? I thought we weren't going to tap that lead."

"We need to **tap every lead** we've got," I say, linking my arm through his, eager to get inside Sasha's room.

Per my request, Wes drops me off in front of the Beckerman house and agrees to pick me up as soon as I call him.

Mrs. Beckerman is working out in the front yard,

pulling weeds from the flower beds that border the porch. She stands up when she sees me.

"Can we talk?" I ask.

"Do you know something?" Her eyes widen with hope. "Did you find another clue?"

"I did." I nod, noticing the grass stains on the knees of her jeans. "But perhaps Detective Tanner already told you about some of them. I know you've been in touch."

"I assume she came to question you."

"Yes," I say, wondering what Tanner found out—if any of the clues proved helpful.

"Well, you can't blame me for telling her about you. You'd have done the same if it were your daughter missing."

"You're right. I would've. I'd do anything I could to find her, including telling one of her friends about my visit to you."

"What are you talking about?" She takes a step closer. A smear of dirt lingers on her cheek.

"A girl called me," I say, proceeding to fill her in about how Mailbox Girl sent me to find the money clip, and how I then learned about a guy by the name of Tommy, with a *W*-shaped scar on his wrist. "Apparently, he used to work at the Blue Raven Pub. It's in the next town over. Do you know the place?"

"I know *of* it," she says. "But my husband and I don't frequent it, and neither did my daughter."

"That you know of," I remind her. "We can't make any assumptions. Do you know who the mystery girl was who called me? And how she might've gotten my number?"

"Aside from Detective Tanner, I didn't tell anyone about your visit," she says a little too quickly, making me skeptical.

I look back toward the street, wondering if Mailbox Girl might've indeed been the one in the dark green Buick. But, then, how would she have gotten my phone number? "Do you suspect that any of Sasha's friends were involved in her disappearance?"

"I suspect everyone." Her jaw tightens. "I can't go anywhere anymore without thinking that the guy at the grocery store might have my daughter, that the teller at the bank could have locked her up in his basement, that the old man pumping gas might've already . . ." She covers her mouth, unable to finish the sentence.

"I'm only trying to help."

"I know." She forces a polite smile and then takes a sip from her bottle of water. "I wish my husband were here to meet you, but he's been working around the clock, putting in all kinds of overtime to keep himself busy. We all have our vices, I suppose." She nods toward her manicured garden. "Anyway, as for Sasha's so-called friends, the dregs she started spending all her time with after she found out the truth . . . I don't trust any one of them."

"Do you trust me?" I ask. "At least enough to go into Sasha's bedroom?"

"The police have already been through it," she says. "Numerous times."

"Yes, but maybe I'll be able to sense something."

Mrs. Beckerman studies my face as if trying to decide. "I think I should check with my husband first."

"We don't really have time."

"Do you know something more?"

"I know that Sasha's still missing, that the police have yet to find her, and that I can still hear Sasha's tears."

"Follow me," she says, leading me inside. She locks the door behind us and then takes me up the stairs.

43

$\mathcal{S}$ASHA'S BEDROOM couldn't look more perfect, right
down to the powder blue dust ruffle on her bed and
the vase of fresh roses on her night table (to match
the rose pattern of her bed linens).

"Did she always keep her room this neat?" I ask.

"Hardly. Most recently, after she found out the truth,
she was leaving her room a mess. Just another way to show
her anger, I suppose." Mrs. Beckerman points to a gallon
of paint by the door. "It's black," she explains. "Sasha had
said she was going to paint her room, but I suppose she
never got around to it."

"Can I see the suitcase she packed?"

"The police took it. They said they needed to study the
contents."

"I guess that makes sense," I say. "Is there any chance
someone could've staged the suitcase—someone aside from
Sasha, I mean—to make it look like she ran away?"

"The police asked the same thing, but her father and I are very strict. We only invite friends in that we approve of, certainly not the disrespectful clan she started to bring around, kids who smoked on my lawn and used my flower beds as ashtrays."

I take a seat on Sasha's bed. "Do you mind?"

Mrs. Beckerman turns away slightly, as if she does indeed mind, but I'm assuming she's willing to overlook it. I'm assuming her hope that I can sense something more trumps any irritation she may feel that I'm touching her daughter's things. And so I lean back on the bed and close my eyes. There's a sweet candy smell in the air, like I just walked into a chocolate shop. I pull Sasha's coverlet over me and grab one of her many stuffed frogs, trying to get inside her head. I spend several minutes rolling over from side to side and breathing into her pillow.

"Are you getting any vibes?" Mrs. Beckerman asks.

"My power doesn't work that way," I say, realizing how confident I sound. "I'm mostly here to get inspired, so that I can sculpt out a clue later." I get up and move over to Sasha's dresser. There's an empty jewelry dish sitting on top of it. I pick it up, feeling the smooth, glazed surface.

"Does she normally keep a watch in here?" I ask, picturing one inside my head. "Is it purple with an extra-long strap?"

"Yes," Mrs. Beckerman says. "Her father gave it to Sasha for her birthday. He had it engraved *To Sasha, with love*."

254

"She was wearing it that night, wasn't she?" I ask. "The night that she disappeared?"

"She hardly ever took it off." Mrs. Beckerman crosses the room to stand right in front of me. "Did you see her that night? Is that how you know about the watch?"

"You still don't trust me, do you?"

"Would *you*?" Her lower lip trembles. "If you were in my shoes, would you be able to trust anyone?"

"I'll only be another minute." I open the drawer of Sasha's night table, wishing that Mrs. Beckerman would leave me alone to concentrate.

There's a notepad sitting inside. I pull it out and flip through the pages. It seems to be a mishmash of stuff: lists of things she needed to do and some notes she jotted down for a project she'd been assigned in history class.

"Sasha was always writing something down," Mrs. Beckerman says.

I'm just about to put the notepad away when, flipping to the back page, I notice the name Tommy written across it. There's doodling all around it: butterflies, floating hearts, boxes, and a checkerboard grid.

I show the page to Mrs. Beckerman. "Tommy," I say. "That's the name we got from the bartender at the Blue Raven. Who is he?"

"I don't know." Mrs. Beckerman shakes her head and covers her mouth again. "But she liked to doodle when she was on the phone."

Meaning that Sasha possibly talked to him? Or maybe someone was talking to her about him? "Did you know the people that she went to the party with?" I ask, wondering if I should go to the abandoned sewing factory where it was held. There were pictures of it online. A sign carrying the plant's logo—a dressmaker's mannequin—still hangs outside.

"Sasha went with a girl named Misery, but Misery was already questioned and cleared by the police."

I nod, remembering having read that a lot of kids from that night were questioned. Misery claimed that Sasha was being difficult that night, angry at her for lying about the evening's festivities, and refusing to spend any time with Misery once she got to the party. Misery said that Sasha started talking to some loner guy sitting at the end of the bar. The next thing she knew, both Sasha and the guy were gone.

"Do you know Misery?" I ask. "Could you give me her phone number?"

Mrs. Beckerman reaches into her pocket for her cell phone, looks up Misery's phone number, then scribbles it across a page of the notebook. "I don't really know her. It wasn't until after Sasha's disappearance that we ever had a conversation."

"Can I take this notebook?" I ask, surprised that the police didn't spot it.

"Take whatever you want. Just bring my daughter back."

"I'll do my best," I say, about to leave the room, but she stops me.

"Wait," she says. Her face is moist with tears. "I need

to know why you're doing this. My husband thinks it's for money, but—"

"I feel a certain connection to Sasha," I explain. "Like I said before, she's in my head. . . . I hear her crying voice."

"Yes, but *why* do you feel a connection?"

"Because I was adopted, too," I tell her. "At least I think that's why. And, like Sasha, I found out by accident."

"I see," Mrs. Beckerman says, taking a moment to study my face, perhaps deciding whether or not to believe me.

"At first I was really heartbroken that my parents had kept the news a secret," I continue. "But now, having learned more about Sasha's story, I can't help but wonder what would've happened to me—what I would've done or how I would've reacted—if I'd have found out the news earlier."

"I see," she repeats, tears in her eyes. "You're glad you're not Sasha."

"I'm glad I'm able to help Sasha," I say.

"Well, parents are human, too, you know," she says between clenched teeth. "They have the same fears, the same insecurities. . . . There isn't a day that goes by that her father and I don't regret our decision not to raise her with the truth. Imagine having to live with the guilt that what you did—keeping a secret—is the reason your daughter disappeared."

"You didn't do this to her."

"No, but I drove her to it. Her father and I paved the way."

"You need to stop blaming yourself."

"Is that what you want your parents to do?" she asks, staring straight into my eyes.

I take a deep breath, considering the question, and thinking how, like Sasha, I wanted to run away. And in some respect, that's exactly what I've done.

"We were afraid to tell Sasha who her real parents were," she continues, "because her real parents didn't want any contact."

"You really don't need to expla—"

"Do you know who *your* real parents are?" she asks, cutting me off.

I nod.

"And can you understand why your parents kept the truth a secret?"

"I can now," I tell her, having finally come full circle. My parents didn't want to tell me that my real mother was suicidal, that she'd been in and out of mental institutions for most of her life, and that she'd never acknowledged my birth. How would I ever have been able to handle that truth at four, eight, or twelve years old, when I'm barely able to handle it now?

"We all have our reasons, don't we?" Mrs. Beckerman says. "All the ways we justify our lies." She moves over to Sasha's bed, crawls beneath the covers, and snuggles up against a frog-shaped pillow. She starts mumbling to herself about how short life is and that nothing else matters. Her voice sounds deflated, as if someone had cut a hole in her heart and drained out all the hope.

"Mrs. Beckerman?" I say, feeling awkward for standing there.

She doesn't answer, just continues to mumble. And so, notepad in hand, I decide to let myself out.

# LESSON NUMBER NINE:
## *SOMETIMES IT'S THE LITTLE THINGS THAT KEEP US SANE.*

I look down at my fingernails, where only a few chips of polish remain: navy blue, to match the dark mood I was in the night I was taken. My parents had told me to stay in. I responded by telling them they had no right to dictate my life. I slammed my bedroom door, snuck out the window, climbed down the trellis, and never looked back.

And now my nails are almost unrecognizable, cut up from picking at the walls, and soiled from clawing at the dirt.

One of the first times I tried to dig my way out of here, I came across a rock. I've been using it to write, etching my lessons into the concrete walls—all the things I've learned from being here. It gives me a sense of purpose, makes me feel like I have some control. And maybe someday my lessons will prove helpful to someone. But, then again, if someone else winds up in here, then she's probably already screwed.

# 44

I CALL WES TO PICK ME UP and we spend a half hour pulled over in front of the town post office discussing my visit with Mrs. Beckerman.

With the notepad flipped open to the page with Tommy's name on it, Wes holds it at different angles, trying to see if there's anything hidden in Sasha's doodles. "I'll bet she knew him," he says. "He was probably her secret boyfriend. They probably ran off together."

"But then why, on the night that she disappeared, did it seem like she didn't know the guy at all?"

"You're assuming that the guy she disappeared with was Tommy."

"You're right." I sigh. "It could've been anyone."

"On second thought, maybe she *didn't* know Tommy," Wes says. "Maybe she simply knew *of* him. You said that she doodled when she was on the phone, right? Maybe whoever she was talking to was merely telling her about him."

"Like, trying to fix her up."

"Or trying to warn her."

"Bottom line, we need to call this number," I say, pulling it from my pocket. "What are the odds that this is our mysterious Mailbox Girl?"

"I'll bet you my enviable collection of Pez dispensers that it is."

"And does that collection include Buffy the Vampire Pez? Because that would be way cool."

"No, but only because it doesn't exist. Now, call her," he insists.

I press ∗67 to block the call, and then I dial the number and set my phone to speaker mode. It rings twice before a recording says the line's been disconnected.

"So, what now?" I ask Wes.

"Perhaps you're forgetting who wears the psychic pants in this relationship. Go sculpt out some answers."

"Because it's totally that easy."

"Well, it'll be a hell of a lot easier if you bring this notebook with you," he says, tossing it into my lap. "It's sure to provide inspiration. Either that or creepy nightmares." He points to an evil-looking beetle (with devil horns and a pitchfork) drawn in the corner.

"You're right," I say, stuffing the notebook into my bag and thinking about the way my power of psychometry is still evolving. Why else would I have been able to picture Sasha's watch when I touched her jewelry dish? "Maybe I'll be able to sculpt something really telling."

"There's the attitude." He gives me a corny wink,

complete with an even cornier thumbs-up. "I have a sneaking suspicion that things are going to be turning around for you very soon."

"What do you know?"

Wes zips his lip and then pulls away from the curb. As he drives us back to campus, I check my cell phone for messages, noticing a couple of texts from Kimmie. Apparently, she spotted the most perfect Roller Derby outfit for me (as if I'd been on a desperate mission to find one). There's also a message from home and a missed call from my dad.

I play the message from home right away. It's from my mom. She tells me about being at the Tea Tree café, sitting by the water fountain, and trying to read her book. Only she couldn't stop reminiscing about our old Wednesday afternoon routine there, when she'd pick me up from school and we'd chat over cups of steaming chai.

"Is everything okay?" Wes asks, after I hang up.

"It will be," I say, confident that it's the truth.

A few minutes later, we arrive back on campus. Wes drops me off in front of the sculpture building. Before going in, I sit down on one of the benches and pull my cell phone back out.

I try calling my dad first, but it goes straight to voice mail. I text Kimmie that I'll need a stylish tote to go with my Roller Derby garb. And then I dial home.

Mom picks up right away. "How are you?" she asks. "Are you enjoying your classes?"

"I'm actually making a wreck of them," I say, opting

for honesty. "The professor absolutely hates me. I can't seem to make it to class on time."

"That doesn't sound like you, Camelia."

"I've been having more psychometric visions," I explain, "and so my work has been pretty disastrous. Meanwhile, the other kids are sculpting all this amazing stuff."

"Just be true to yourself, Camelia."

"Are you referring to my psychometric visions?" I ask, surprised if she's condoning them, never mind if she's acknowledging them.

"I'm referring to everything," she says. "How brave you are—always doing what you feel is right, despite how difficult it is. Don't let anyone take that away."

Her words give me goose bumps, because her approval means so much to me, and I haven't felt it in a long time. "Have you been talking to Dr. Tylyn?" I ask, suspicious that this new perspective may be the result of at least a couple of therapy sessions.

"I have, and she wanted me to remind you that you can call her whenever you want."

"I know," I say, grateful for Dr. Tylyn's support. "But I kind of want to figure things out on my own this time. I feel like I have all the tools."

"That's what it's all about," she agrees. "Learning more, evolving into a better person . . ."

I can picture Mom sitting in her sacred corner in the living room, with all her happy things: her yoga mat, her Buddha dolls, her embroidered pillows from India.

She takes one of her Kundalini breaths; I hear the familiar dog-panting sound. "You've been a real inspiration to me," she says, finally.

"Wow. I mean, I don't know what to say."

"Say that you'll continue to be true to yourself."

"I'll do my best," I say, at first disappointed that she doesn't ask about the psychometric episodes I've been having in sculpture class. But then I take a deep breath, too, and remind myself that Rome wasn't built in a day, and that Mom's accepting me for who I am is monumental on its own.

# 45

BEFORE HEADING into the sculpture building, I text
Ben to tell him I'm back from Mrs. Beckerman's
and will give him a call later.

Inside the pottery studio, there are a couple of students
working. One boy is carving into a tree stump, making a
bowl of sorts, reminding me of what I love so much about
sculpture: the possibilities are absolutely endless. There's
a girl using the extruder and someone else in the kiln
room. But there's no one I really recognize. Until Ingrid
walks in.

She spots me, too, and walks over.

"Hey," I say, remembering that she asked Wes about
me. I open up my bag of clay, pretending that her presence
doesn't affect me.

"So, you haven't really been around much," she says,
getting right down to it. "I haven't seen you since you got
booted by Barnes. I mean, what was up with that?"

"Which time?" I ask, using a wire to slice myself a thick hunk of clay. "I guess I've had a lot on my mind. My sculptures haven't exactly been coming out so great."

"Are you kidding?" Her mouth drops open, exposing her ginormous yellow teeth (as Wes so kindly called them). "People are still talking about that hand."

"Just call me the Queen of Creepy," I say, thinking about the *W* that I carved into the wrist.

"More like the Queen of effing Genius," she says, her eyes bugging out. "How is it possible that you're able to sculpt that much detail in under thirty minutes? I mean, you had freaking knuckle lines, for God's sake. The nails, the individual joints, the wrist bones . . . After class, a few of us flipped the hand over. The palm looked so eerily realistic you could've asked a palm reader to come in and tell a fortune."

"Wow," I say, surprised to see a side of Ingrid that isn't totally bitchy. "Thanks."

"Did you take lessons in figure drawing?"

"Actually, yes," I reply, perking up. Of course, I didn't exactly make it to all of those classes, either.

"I guessed, from all that detail. Anyway, Barnes is an idiot for not noticing, but word is he's a stickler for following directions, which is probably why he's a no-name," she says, lowering her voice. "I mean, hello, where's *his* six-figure art show?"

"Wow," I repeat, at an utter loss for words.

"So, can I just ask? Of course, you don't have to tell me. But what was with the *W*? Like . . . what does it stand for? A few of us were trying to guess. Someone said 'war.' Someone else thought 'warrior.'"

"It actually stood for 'winter,'" I say, playing along. "As in, the death of that which lives . . ."

"Whoa," she says, closing her eyes. "That's totally deep. Barnes has got you pegged totally wrong."

When Ingrid eventually goes off to pursue some work on the wheel, I wedge out my clay, slapping it against my board and pounding it with my fist. Sasha's notebook positioned in front of me for inspiration. I can't help thinking how surreal this is. I mean, just weeks ago, I'd barely even known her name. And now I've been in her house and taken something from her room.

I wet my mound of clay with a sponge and watch the drops slide down like tears. Then I close my eyes and listen for Sasha's voice—her crying—picturing her lounging in bed, talking on the phone, and doodling Tommy's name.

A series of images runs through my brain. And suddenly it feels like I'm holding a movie camera, like I'm flying high above the scene, getting footage of things below me. I see a tiny house with broken shutters and collapsing stairs. It borders a forest. On the opposite side of the forest is farmland—rows and rows of dead cornstalks and overgrown weeds. There's a tractor with missing wheels parked beside a dilapidated garage.

My mind's eye focuses harder, moving closer, behind the tractor, where there's a pile of brush, like someone was raking, trying to clean up the area. I zoom in even closer on the pile until I feel like I'm swimming in it. Leaves and sticks are kicked away; at the bottom of it all is a wooden slab. It takes me a second to realize that it's actually a trap-door. Someone grabs a metal handle. I can see a man's hand; it's stained with dirt, and it pulls the handle upward. I look to see if there's a *W* on his wrist, but there isn't.

My heart beats fast. Now it feels like I'm stuck in the scene—as if I'm in this man's skin. I start down a ladder able to hear it creak beneath my feet.

I'm now facing a wooden door; there's a series of locks surrounding the knob. I push the door open. It's already unlocked. I aim my flashlight beam inside the space. It's small, about ten feet by ten feet in size. There are dirt floors and dirt walls. And there's a separate room, too. A steel wall with a locked door cuts the room in half. I move a little closer, noticing a hole at the bottom of the steel door, just big enough to fit a soccer ball through. Is this a bunker of some sort? Or maybe a storage space?

I move toward the separate room, noticing a light coming from just behind it. A beam shines through the hole, making a path across the dirt floor. I crouch down. At the same moment, something hits me from behind on the crown of my head—and I grunt.

The next thing I know, the scene changes, and I'm inside a house, still stuck in someone else's body. Is it the same person? I can't at all tell. A rag is placed over my mouth. I gasp—a male voice—and feel my head go imme-diately woozy. My world starts to fade away.

Only half conscious, I'm dragged from behind. Across a floor. Cold kitchen tiles.

My eyes flutter open. I see someone—the blur of a figure. A mosaic of colors. The corner of a ceiling fan. A smile on someone's face.

"Surprise, surprise," a voice says.

Male or female? Older or younger?

Suddenly, the scene shifts again. I'm still in the same kitchen—still stuck inside a man's body—but now there are flames all around me, walls coming down all around me. A ceiling fan descends right on top of me. I'm burning up right along with the house. And it's too late to find my way out.

# 46

$S$UDDENLY, I FEEL myself being shaken. Ingrid is here. She sits me down on a stool, places her hand on my forehead, and then goes to get me a glass of water. I'm still in the pottery studio. The other two students are no longer here.

"Are you okay?" she asks.

I try to shrug it off—to look like I have everything under control, even though my heart is absolutely pounding.

"You were whimpering," she says, studying my face, noticing perhaps the trembling of my upper lip. "And flinching. Your whole body was, like, twitching—like you were having some sort of attack. And yet you kept right on working, so I wasn't sure if that was just part of your process: getting both physically and mentally into your work."

I attempt to drink the water, but it laps over the rim

of the glass. My hand quivers. A hiccup escapes from my throat. I get up from the stool. My legs feel like sticks of butter, mushy and unstable, like I could melt into the ground.

My sculpture is about six feet away now, partially obscured by my bag of clay. I move in front of it, startled by what I see.

A dressmaker's mannequin, exactly like the logo on the front of the sewing factory—the same factory where Sasha was on the evening that she went missing. Is it possible that Sasha's still there?

"What's wrong?" Ingrid asks.

"I think I just need to get something to eat," I lie.

"Oh, are you a diabetic? Because I think I might have some candy." She turns to fish inside her bag, and hands me a half-melted Kit Kat.

"Thanks," I say, sitting back down. I unwrap the candy and force myself to take a bite. "Just what the doctor ordered."

"Great," she says, finally returning to her work.

Meanwhile, I reach for my cell phone and dial Wes's number.

Wes picks me up from the pottery studio and we walk to the middle of the campus. He motions to an open spot on the lawn. "Think you can make it?" he asks, linking his arm through mine for support.

"I'm fine," I tell him. The sun shines down on my face and already I feel better.

272

"Have a seat," he says, pointing to a bench that's already partly occupied. A girl sits at the end of it with her back to us. Her hair is a couple of shades darker than her giant pink purse.

"Maybe over here," I suggest, moving toward one of the empty benches, relieved to be out in the fresh air.

"*What*, do I smell or something?" a voice snaps. I turn to look, surprised to find that it's the pink-haired girl talking to me. She swivels to face us, and that's when I see.

"Kimmie!" I say.

Her face brightens and she stands up from the bench.

I hug her, my eyes welling up. "I can't believe you're here." I take a step back to drink in her new look. Wearing a short purple dress and green rain boots, she still has a style that's all her own, but it's as if she's taken it to a brand-new level.

"And *I* can't believe you didn't tell me that you were having psychometric visions again." She folds her arms and glares at me.

I peek at Wes, curious as to what he told her, exactly, and suspecting it's why she's here. "I didn't want you to worry about me."

"Um, *hello*! You're my best friend. It's my job to worry. Did *you* not worry about *me* when my dad was stuck in a seventies time warp, complete with visible chest hair and gold medallion necklaces?"

"I guess."

"Well, I *know*," she says, flicking a pink and black striped hair extension over her shoulder for added effect.

"You look amazing, by the way," I say, noticing how her green eye shadow matches her boots.

"And *you* look like crap," she says, never one for beating around the bush.

I wipe my eyes, still trembling inside. Kimmie knows me like nobody else, even more than Ben, and so I can't help giving her another hug, pulling Wes into our hug as well, so grateful that they're both there.

IMMIE, WES, AND I move to the area by the edge of the lawn, where we can get a peek at the ocean below. We sit in a circle on the grass, as Kimmie explains that Wes filled her in on pretty much everything.

"I can't even believe that you didn't tell me." She gazes down at her shiny green nail polish, and I can see the hurt in her eyes.

"It's only because I didn't want to ruin your time in New York," I tell her. "And because I felt like you were so excited about the two of us doing things for our future— you with your internship and me taking classes here. I didn't want to break it to you that the classes were just an excuse for me. . . . That coming here really wasn't about my future at all."

"I *did* know that. At least, I did initially." She shrugs. "But I don't know. I think I was so psyched about my opportunity, I couldn't really see beyond it. Anyway, I'm sorry. You're my best friend—way more important than classes or internships."

I lean over to give her another hug. "And so are you," I tell her, "which is part of the reason why I never said anything about my visions. I mean, it wasn't as if my life was on the line, so why should you sacrifice an opportunity? And speaking of . . ." I segue, "shouldn't you be preparing for a fashion show as we speak?"

"For your information, I got special permission to extend my weekend a tad."

"Well, it means a lot to me that you're here. But you can't talk me out of helping Sasha. Doing this—helping people—it's become a part of who I am. I need to be true to myself," I say, surprised to hear my mom's words come out of my mouth.

"At the risk of your own dream?"

"I'll always love pottery," I tell her. "It'll always be a part of who I am. But what if dreams change? What if helping people is what I'm meant to do?"

"Do you really think you can help this Sasha girl?" she asks.

"I'm certainly trying. And, honestly, I wouldn't trade a pottery bowl for her safety."

"Wow," she says, reaching out to take my hands. There's a curious smile across her lips. "What's happened to you?"

"I'm just reprioritizing, I guess. People come first."

"Especially best friends." She gives my hands a squeeze.

"Which is precisely why we're all here," Wes says.

We continue to discuss the details of the case, including about how I feel that getting to know Mrs. Beckerman has really benefited me on a personal level. "It's like I've been given this rare opportunity to get a different perspective—to see things through the eyes of someone who blames her secrecy for the fact that her daughter is missing. It's helped me understand my own parents more."

"While that's superdeep and interesting and all," Wes says, "could we please get back to the fact that you looked like *Night of the Living Dead* coming out of the sculpture building?"

"You did look sort of zombieish," Kimmie agrees. "But I'd put you in the crack-addict category, with that pasty white face and those peaked eyes."

"Great," I say, proceeding to tell them about the out-of-body experience I had—how I hallucinated finding an underground room and then getting knocked over the head. "I blacked out," I tell them. "And then, when I came to, it was like I was someone else or someplace else . . . inside a house. Someone placed a rag over my mouth. It made me feel all woozy and disoriented."

"Probably chloroform," Wes suggests.

"Are we suddenly the resident expert on consciousness-altering drugs?" Kimmie raises an eyebrow at him.

"No comment." He smirks. "But chloroform usually renders people dizzy and confused, if not putting them out entirely."

"Was it *you* who got drugged?" Kimmie asks me. "In your hallucination, I mean."

"I'm pretty sure it was a man. I saw his hands. It was like I was in his body, feeling his anxiety."

"Anxiety about what?" she asks.

"I don't know." I shake my head, then tell them about the separate underground room and how it appeared as though someone was inside it.

"Someone like Sasha?" Wes asks.

I shrug, having suspected the same. "Anyway, the next thing I knew, I was being dragged across a kitchen floor and then burned to death. Someone had set the house on fire."

"Fabulous," Wes says. "And what were you saying before about this lethal stuff being much more fulfilling than your pottery?"

"Not more, just different," I say, clarifying.

"Wait, so some guy—whoever he is—is going to burn to death while only semiconscious?" Kimmie asks.

"Too out of it to save himself, but just alert enough to experience the whole thing," Wes explains.

"Okay, so someone's clearly pissed at him," Kimmie says. "Ever think that that someone could be Sasha? That maybe she's getting revenge on her captor?"

"Assuming that she's been kidnapped," Wes says. "Too bad you didn't see the guy's face, because now it seems there might actually be *two* people to save here." He folds his arms as if silently accusing me of not hallucinating better.

"Not to add pressure or anything," Kimmie adds.

"Anyway, while I was stuck in my hallucination, I was able to sculpt another clue. A dressmaker's mannequin," I explain. "It's the logo used on the abandoned sewing building where the underground party was held—where Sasha Beckerman went missing."

"So we need to go there," Wes says.

"Definitely," I agree.

"Not *you*," Kimmie snaps at me. "Your eyes are bloodshot, your hands keep trembling, and your face is still pasty-ass white."

"I'm fine," I assure her.

"But you'll be a whole lot *finer* with some rest," she insists. "Wes and I will go scope the place out. If we find anything, we'll call you, and we'll definitely call the police."

"Maybe that's where the underground room is," Wes suggests. "Is the sewing building surrounded by a forest?"

"It's actually on the outskirts of the city."

"So maybe there's a clue we need to find there." Kimmie taps her chin as she thinks. "But how will we get in?"

"With my skeleton key." Wes pulls a shiny dental-like instrument from the front pocket of his backpack.

"We'll call you once we're in," Kimmie says. "Now, get some rest." She stands up and checks the back of her dress for grass stains.

I get up, too. I feel dizzy, and Sasha's crying voice doesn't help. Meanwhile, Kimmie and Wes decide whose car to take. Kimmie has gotten a rental for the weekend, courtesy of one of her new Bonnie Jensen clients (her "B.J. clients," according to Wes). And Wes can't seem to find his car keys. He checks his pockets and searches the area, having apparently forgotten his keys in his room.

"In the B.J.-mobile we will go!" he cheers.

# LESSON NUMBER TEN:
## *EVEN IN MISERY,*
## *LOOK FOR AN OPEN DOOR.*

The locks turn. He's back for his tape. He takes the tape recorder and then slides a folded-up paper bag through the hole: my cue to empty the litter.

I unfold the bag, wishing I had a shovel. I tip the litter box, but it's too heavy to manage with one hand while trying to keep the bag open with the other. Once again, the gravel spills out onto the ground, making me want to hurl.

"What's the problem?" he asks.

"I could use a spoon, or even a cup." After the last time I changed the litter, I made a makeshift shovel out of an old box of crackers, but I can't seem to find it now.

"Hold on."

I hear him move toward the exterior door. I lower my head so that I can see through the hole. He's left the door wide open—most likely while he goes to search for something. I shine my flashlight into the doorway, able to see the set of stairs. It's so close and yet so far away.

ON MY WAY BACK TO THE DORM, I check my phone. There's a text from Dad, telling me that he's made another video. As soon I get into my room, I log on to my computer to check it out.

"Hey, Camelia," Dad says, waving to the camera. "Just thought I'd tell you that I was at the bookstore today. I passed by that book you liked when you were little . . . the one with the dancing chicken who wore mismatched socks. I think I must've read it to you at least a couple times a day for a full year. Anyway, I couldn't resist buying it." Dad pauses to pull the book out of a bag. "I thought I might read it to you again for old times' sake. So, here goes. . . ."

Watching Dad read one of my favorite children's books takes me back to when I was six years old, snuggling beside him with my stack of books, along with Miss Dream Baby, my favorite doll. I grab my phone and call him.

"Hey, there," he says, picking up on the first ring. "Did you get my latest video?"

"I did." I smile.

"Weird?" he asks.

"More like wonderful. I miss those days."

"Yeah," he says. "Me, too. So, how's everything going?"

"I'm learning a lot."

"Well, I'm happy for you," he says.

"Thanks," I tell him. "For everything."

"You don't have to thank me, Camelia."

"I love you, Dad," I say, without even thinking.

"I love you, too. More than anything."

We say our good-byes and I promise to call him in a few days, feeling more together than I have in a long time. I lie back on the bed, determined to get some rest, but when I close my eyes, I can still see the flames from my hallucination in the pottery studio. And I can still hear the man's screams. They drown out Sasha's voice.

I replay the scene inside my head: the ceiling fan toppling down; the support beams consumed by flames; the wall of fire growing closer, hotter, bigger, stronger. I take a deep breath and refocus, picturing the underground room and the wall of steel, flashing back to the moments before the man was hit over the head. He'd crouched down in front of the hole in the steel door as if inspecting it or checking things out, making me think that he wasn't Sasha's captor. I open my eyes, able to hear the grunt he uttered when he was hit over the head. As hard as I try to deny it—and as much as I try to come up with another explanation—the voice sounded a lot like Ben's.

I reach for my phone and call him, but it goes right to his voice mail. I roll over in bed, feeling my stomach churn, beyond nervous about where he might be. I check my e-mail, hoping to find a message from him, but there isn't one. And so I click over to Neal Moche's page, desperate for inspiration.

**From the Journal of Neal Moche**

I can't get that key ring out of my head—the one that I envisioned when I touched that guy's girlfriend. Tommy is his name; I know because I asked one of his coworkers, claiming that I thought we might've gone to middle school together. Why he has a *W* tattooed on his wrist (I spotted it that first time in the pretzel line) is just another mystery to me.

Maybe it stands for his last name; the coworker didn't seem to remember it.

Normally, I'd have walked away by now, especially since it doesn't seem like the stakes in this are particularly high. But since bumping into Tommy, I've been over-whelmed by this weird sense of duty—like I *have* to see this through, like my future somehow depends on it.

I know that that doesn't make any sense, but the sooner I solve this puzzle, the quicker I'll be able to move on to more important things.

Like my girlfriend. I went to see her recently, and I know more than anything now that we're meant to be together. There isn't a single doubt in my mind.

The crazy thing? I spent years trying to convince myself that my heart was bulletproof, that I was immune to emotion, that I didn't want to be—couldn't ever be—touched, never mind loved.

But then I met her, and touched her, and eventually let her into my heart. I was never able to look back after that, despite how hard I tried to push her away by keeping secrets or distancing myself by traveling around.

I recently visited her at the college where she's stay-ing, and we spent some serious time together. For the first time, I told her that I loved her, and she actually said it back.

I want to be with her, but I also need to solve this—to see what it means for me, what the bigger picture is. And so I'm going back to that guy's house to find the key that will unlock this puzzle once and for all.

## 49

MY HEART FEELS LIKE it's about to explode, because the similarities are too big to deny. The *W* on the guy's hand. The recent trip he made to see his girlfriend at a college. The secrecy that scared her away, not to mention the fear that kept him from getting close. And the scar on the girl's neck.

This blog is being written by Ben.

I scroll back through past entries, remembering having read something about the time he bumped into that guy at the park—how he pictured a cross-shaped tattoo. I reread the second-to-last entry, where he describes the visit to the guy's house, and sees that the cross tattoo on Tommy's girlfriend's neck is actually a scar—what sounds like a burn—just like the *W* on Tommy's hand.

Just like the *t* shape that I sculpted.

The cross must actually be the letter *t*. Ben and I are working on the same case—only, from two different angles. Were those *his* screams I heard in the fire? And is that where he is right now?

I close my eyes, picturing the man's hand from my most recent hallucination—when he lifted the trapdoor that led to the underground room. The idea that it could've been Ben is far too overwhelming.

I reread the last blog entry, noticing that it was written today. He must be there right now. I try his number again, but he still doesn't pick up. My fingers trembling, I fish Detective Tanner's card out of my desk drawer and dial her number.

To my surprise, she actually picks up. I tell her all about the blog and stress what I know about the letters *t* and *W*. "It was just like what I envisioned," I tell her, "when I sculpted the letter *t*. . . ."

"The money clip was actually reported stolen three months ago," she tells me. "We did a thorough analysis of it, including where the clip was purchased and made, the composition of the metal, the jeweler who designed it . . ."

"And?" I ask, trying to anticipate the outcome.

"The owner was an older man, eighty-six, who could barely get out of his apartment—not exactly the profile of the guy working at the Blue Raven."

"So, maybe the guy working at the Blue Raven stole it."

"Maybe." She sighs. "Only, I checked out your story. I talked to the bartender you spoke to."

"Brooke?" I ask, my pulse racing.

"She denied ever talking to you. She denied knowing anyone named Tommy. And when I asked the manager, he had no record of anyone named Tommy working there within the past two years."

"They're lying," I snap. "I had another vision. There was a fire. And someone got drugged. Please, you have to help me. You have to go there. I think my boyfriend might be in danger."

"Go where?" she asks.

"I don't know," I mutter. Tears roll down my cheeks. "There was a thick forest and an old tractor. It was underground somewhere, but there was also a house, and lots of barren farmland." My chest tightens until I can barely breathe. I know I'm not making any sense.

"It sounds like you need some rest," Tanner says. "Why don't I call you later, when I know you've gotten some sleep?"

"Didn't you check out my past?" I ask, noticing that I've thrown off my sheets in frustration.

There's a long pause, and then she promises to call me in a little while. "Would it make you feel better if I personally checked in on your boyfriend?"

"Please," I say, knowing that she won't be able to find him, but that at the very least she'll be looking.

"I'll call you in a bit," she says, before hanging up.

I hang up, too, realizing that she never even asked for my boyfriend's name, that she isn't taking me (or my powers) seriously, and that she has no intention whatsoever of helping me out.

ACCORDING TO BEN'S E-MAILS, he'd been in Washington, D.C., before he came to see me, and then he'd driven north. I'd assumed that he was on his way back home, but maybe he stopped in Rhode Island en route. Was that when he bumped into Tommy at the park? Is that what kept him in the area for longer than he'd wanted?

With no leads as to his whereabouts, I do a Google search on abandoned Rhode Island farms that border wooded lots. It doesn't take long before I find the old Strappley Farm. It's been closed for fifteen years. I do an image search, knowing that I'm probably grasping at straws. Hundreds of photos pop up, some of which show the Strappley Farm when it was bursting with cornstalks and apple trees.

But others reveal what's happened after years of neglect. Everything looks dead. A dilapidated garage sits at one corner of the property, and outside it is the broken-down tractor with missing wheels.

Exactly what I envisioned.

I scroll down to look at more of the images, trying to figure out where an underground room might be. And that's when I spot the house. A tiny shack of a place. It borders the same woods as the farm, but it's on the opposite side.

I scribble the address on my hand, pocket my cell phone, and then hurry to Wes's room. The door is locked, but luckily his roommate's there.

"Can I help you?" he asks, giving me the once-over.

I push past him to get to the minifridge. The keys are right on top, behind the half-eaten bag of pork rinds. "Thanks," I say, snatching the keys.

I run down the hall and plow down the stairs, bursting out the doors and scurrying across the parking lot to Wes's car. I get in and peel out, anticipating what awaits me at the farm, and hoping I'm not too late.

# 51

I TYPE THE ADDRESS of Strappley Farm into Wes's GPS and then I start out. It's drizzling. The streets are wet. The windshield wipers paint streaks across the glass, making it hard to see.

Why didn't I bring a weapon of some sort? Why don't I have a flashlight, for when it gets dark? I glance in the rearview mirror, checking to see what kind of spy gear Wes has stashed in the backseat. But surprisingly, it's empty.

My cell phone still clenched in my hand, I call Wes.

"We've hit the abductor's jackpot," he declares, his voice cranked up on adrenaline.

"Did you make it inside the sewing factory?"

"Better than that, my friend. We found a locked room in the basement of said factory. It's hidden beneath a stairway, behind an old soda machine."

I turn past the Blue Raven Pub, noting that it's on

Farm Road. I must be close. "I need help," I tell him. The GPS orders me to take the next right and then a sharp left. The area is becoming more remote. The streets aren't fully paved; I'm practically driving on gravel now.

"What's that?" he asks. "You're breaking up. Are you getting some rest? I was going to call you, but—" He cuts out.

"I need help," I insist, louder this time. Woods surround me on both sides of the road, but it seems I'm driving to Nowhere—just farther and farther away from town, away from everyone.

"I did call for help," he assures me. "Detective Tanner is on her way."

"No!" I shout. "*I* need help. I think I know where Sasha is."

"Camelia?" he asks. I can hear the panic in his voice. "Where are—?"

He cuts out again. The phone goes blank. I scream his name, but the call's been dropped.

A second later, I see it. At the end of the road. The house I envisioned. It's on fire.

I drop the phone and pull up in front. I tear out of the car, race up the stairs onto the porch, and run to the door. The knob scorches my hand. The surface of the door is almost too hot to touch. But I try anyway, using the fabric of my shirt as a buffer.

The door is locked. I pound at it, kick it, and slam against it with my shoulder.

The next thing I know, someone grabs me from behind.

I turn to look, startled to find a girl there: blond hair, pale face, maybe twenty years old. The letter *t* is tattooed on her neck.

I pull my arm away, noticing the tears welling up in her eyes.

"Are you one of them?" she asks.

I open my mouth, unsure how to respond, but there's no time to hear her out. I go for the window closest to the door, just a few feet away. But the girl grabs me by the arm and yanks me down the stairs. I fall backward against the pavement.

"I'm talking to you!" she shouts. Standing right over me, her mouth is puckered in disgust. "You're one of them, aren't you?" she asks. Drops of rain or tears stream down her cheeks.

Glass breaks somewhere above, somewhere inside. It's followed by a cracking sound that cuts through my core— the sound of floorboards splitting or beams coming down. More glass shatters. The house is bursting open from the inside.

"Listen to me!" she shouts.

I try to get up, but she kicks me back down. The heel of her boot plunges deep into my gut.

"You're one of them," she says, shaking her head, standing right over me. "Are you looking for his secret place?"

"Yes." I manage to nod.

"Bitch!" she screams, kicking my side.

A screech tears out of my throat.

"Somebody already broke in to his secret place," she continues, looking away toward the back of the house.

At the same moment, I get back up, climb the stairs, and try the window, but all I see is fire. Its brightness stings my eyes. "Where is he?" I ask her.

"It's too late," she says. "He's already gone."

The word is a mystery inside my head. *Gone* as in, he left? As in, I missed him? "Did he go to get some help?" I ask.

"He's dead," she explains. "I saw to it myself. I stayed inside too long. See, I got burned."

She shows me her arm: there's a patch of red skin. I stumble back, unable to grasp her words. There's a blurry haze all around me, and my mouth fills with bile. Still, I try to get past her, keeping an eye on Wes's car.

But she grabs me again. Her cold, wet fingers wrap themselves around my forearm. "You're not going anywhere," she says through clenched teeth. She starts to drag me back toward the house.

At first, I feel weak. But Sasha's crying inside my head grows deeper, louder, infusing me with strength. Finally, I'm able to pull away.

The girl gazes toward the fence; there's a shovel propped up against it. She starts moving in that direction, but I push her from behind—hard. Her head hits the corner of a barbecue grill, and she slips forward against the wet pavement, letting out a piercing shriek.

I hurry toward Wes's car, tears nearly blinding me. I fling the door open and grab my phone to dial 911, but I still don't have reception.

The house is completely engulfed in flames now, like something you'd see in a movie. I scream until my throat burns raw, knowing that I'm far too late—that Ben is already gone.

# 52

$\mathcal{I}$T TAKES ME A MOMENT to realize that my head is pressing against the steering wheel and that the horn is sounding. I'm still sitting there, in front of the house—still crying, screaming, seething.

I fish my key ring from my pocket and try to start the car. It won't turn over. I try again. Still no go. I look at the keys, realizing they're for my room. Wes's aren't in my pockets, nor are they on the seat or under the floor mat. What did I do with them after I parked?

Sasha's cries seem to grow louder by the minute, reminding me that she's still out there, still missing. And I'm still determined to find her.

I reach into the glove compartment. Thankfully, there's a flashlight and some rope. I stuff both into the waistband of my jeans, then hurry back outside. I can feel the heat from the fire on my skin. I move around to the side of the house, passing through the driveway.

The girl is no longer lying there. I grab the shovel and hold it like a bat, ready to strike if I have to. I cut through the forest behind the burning house, remembering my premonition, remembering the view from above. The farm was on the other side of a wooded lot.

I cut through the forest. The rain has dissipated. The sun peeks through the trees, making the woods look almost enchanting, like nothing ugly could ever come out of this place.

Running now, I use the shovel to push branches and brush from in front of my eyes, remembering the entry in the Neal Moche blog, where Ben tried to navigate here in the dark. It must've been nearly impossible.

A stick breaks, and I hear something fall; that's followed by a swishing sound. I stop. I turn back. "Who's there?" I shout, clicking on the flashlight.

No one answers and I don't see anything.

My heart pounding, I wait a few more seconds before beginning forward again. I quicken my pace and take a wrong turn, ending up in the thick of some bushes. At first, I think I can get through them, but they're taller than I am, bigger than I am, and I get trapped among their branches.

I start to backtrack, my pulse racing. A broken branch with a jagged tip rips through my skin. I touch the spot and feel blood.

Breathing hard, I maneuver out of the bushes entirely. Back on the path, I continue forward, coming to the end of the woods.

The farm is sprawled out in front of me. I close my eyes, conjuring up my premonition, able to picture the trapdoor that led underground. It didn't seem far from the garage. I move in that direction, past the tractor to the door at the rear of the garage.

And that's when I see it: the pile of debris. Broken sticks and mangled cornstalks are collected around a wooden slab. The pile's been kicked away, revealing the trapdoor.

I look behind me again to make sure I'm still alone. The sky is black with smoke. Burning embers fly into the sky, making the clouds appear to be ablaze, too. As I stand right over the slab now, my whole body's shaking. I want to be sick.

The metal handle is just like what I pictured: black and rusty. Keeping a firm grip on the shovel, I reach for the handle. The door is heavy and opens with a *thwack* against the ground.

A wooden stairway leads underground. I grab the edge of the trapdoor and pull it closed behind me as I descend the set of stairs.

My flashlight still on, I proceed downward, noticing another door at the bottom of the stairs. It's only slightly taller than I am, and there's a series of locks around the knob.

With jittery fingers, I push the door open. It's like stepping inside my hallucination: the dirt floors and the cinder-block walls. The entire space is probably about as big as my dorm room. This was probably once a root cellar, used for storing food.

A steel wall faces me, dividing the room in half. It almost reminds me of a prison cell with a steel frame attached to concrete walls. A solid door—with no bars—is secured with a padlock.

I scoot down for a better look, spotting a hole cut into the bottom of the door, a little bigger than a cantaloupe. "Sasha?" I call, still able to hear her crying.

The flashlight beam travels toward the hole. "Who's there?" she asks.

"Are you Sasha Beckerman?"

"Yes." Her voice trembles. "Who are you?"

"My name's Camelia, and I'm here to help you. I'm going to get you out of here."

"Is he coming back? Do you know where he is?"

"I'm going to get you out of here," I repeat, not wanting to tell her the truth: that I have no idea where Tommy is.

I pull at the padlock, but it's definitely secure.

"He's going to come back," she cries out.

I nod to myself, knowing she's right. Why else would the doors be open? Why else would this have been so easy? Maybe it's a trap.

I place my flashlight on the ground, angling it so that I can see, and then, holding the shovel above my head, I strike downward with the blade, smashing it against the lock.

But the lock doesn't break.

I try again—harder this time—using all of my weight. For an instant, I think the lock gives. There's a deep *plunk*

300

sound and my arms ache from the impact, but still the lock remains intact.

I take a step back, adjusting my grip, aiming the point of the blade at the lock's loop. But then I feel a yank on my hair from behind. I lose my footing, falling flat on my back. The shovel drops to the ground.

The girl with the tattoo on her neck is here. Holding a lantern, she keeps a firm grip on my hair, dragging me to the center of the room. I struggle to get away, reaching behind me, trying to swat at her hands.

Finally, she releases her grip, but it isn't because of my efforts. As she stands over me, there's an eerie grin playing across her lips. "Nobody replaces me," she says, setting the lantern down.

"I don't know what you're talking about," I tell her.

"Sure you do." She pulls a rag from her pocket and folds it. "You want to steal him away from me. You think you're so much better than me."

"No," I insist, shaking my head, remembering the rag from my premonition. It'd been doused with something that put me out.

"He didn't even care that I knew he was cheating," she continues, pouncing on my stomach, with her legs straddling my middle. I swipe at her face, but she leans back, avoiding my blows. Her grin broadens, as if she's enjoying my efforts. I keep moving, my legs flailing as I try to knee her or knock her off me. But nothing seems to work.

"What's happening?" I hear Sasha cry.

The girl looks away, reaching into her pocket again.

At the same moment, I thrust my pelvis forward, gaining leverage with my hips. Finally, I'm able to sit up and push her back. The girl falls against the ground. A tiny bottle tumbles from her grip.

I try to retrieve the shovel, scrambling on the ground to reach it.

"No!" the girl shouts, coming at me with the rag.

I struggle to my feet and lift the shovel high, feeling the muscles in my forearms stiffen. When she gets too close, I smash the blade against the crown of her head, and the shovel falls from my hands.

She lets out a wail, but still she tries to force the rag toward my face. I kick her in the shin. She stumbles back, but then comes at me again. I'm able to rip the rag out of her hand, toss it to the ground, and then shove her away. She trips over her own feet and falls onto her back.

I grab the shovel again. The next thing I know, she's got me in a headlock from behind. The rag is placed over my mouth, between my lips, against my tongue. I hold my breath and take a step back, digging my nails into the flesh of her forearms.

There's a loud cracking sound. It's followed by a high-pitched scream. The girl's grip on my neck loosens. And the rag falls away. I turn around to see what happened.

Ben is there. He's alive. It's almost too much for my brain to process.

It appears that he hit the girl from behind with a long steel pipe. Lying in the corner, she's definitely hurt but not out.

Ben motions to the rope sticking out of the waistband of my jeans. Still somewhat in shock, I toss it to him and then retrieve my flashlight, watching as he winds the rope around the girl's wrists, behind her back. Naturally, she fights him, trying to kick him and wriggle her body free, but she's no match for him.

Wearing gloves, Ben squeezes her legs together—tightly—securing the rope around her ankles.

I pick up the fallen bottle. "Chloroform," I say, reading the label. To put someone out. To make someone sleep.

"It's what I used on Tommy," she says. "Right after I found out that people like you were trying to take him from me."

"Where *is* he?" I ask her.

"By now, I'd have to say hell." She smirks.

"He was in the fire," I say, putting the pieces together. When she saw me trying to get into the burning house, she must've thought I was looking for him. He was the one she was referring to when she said that he was already dead. "Did you know about this?" I ask her, nodding toward the cell. "That he was keeping someone captive here?"

She looks up at the ceiling. The letter *t* on her neck moves up and down with her breath. "She's no replacement for me," she mutters. "And neither are you."

Ben slips the pipe into the padlock's loop and then pulls the pipe downward, breaking the lock entirely. He pulls the steel door open.

Sasha is there, crouched in the corner in a fetal position.

Her skin looks sallow, and I can tell that she's lost a lot of weight.

I approach her slowly, then scoot down. "My name's Camelia," I tell her again.

Sasha looks at me with haunted eyes. The tips of her fingers are cut up and bloody—most likely from picking at cement. And her wrist has a bandage on it. The skin around it is puffy and yellow. "It's been burned," she whispers, pulling the bandage back.

I try my best not to wince at the sight of it: the letter *t*, bright red and weeping with pus. Black, leathery skin curls up to frame it. Aside from the infection, it's exactly like what I sculpted.

"You're going to be okay," I say, beyond relieved to have found her, and finally no longer able to hear her tears. I take her hand, feeling her fingers clasp my own, grateful for the power of touch.

# 53

*A*s soon as Ben, Sasha, and I emerge from the root cellar, Ben runs off to get help. Meanwhile, Sasha can barely stand up straight. Her gait is slow, as if she's just learning to walk. She gazes around at where she is, her eyes struggling to take everything in. The sky must seem far too bright.

"Do you want to sit?" I ask, looking around for someplace comfortable.

She shakes her head. "It feels like I've been sitting forever."

"Your mom's really missed you," I tell her. "She loves you more than anything—both of your parents do."

She nods like she already knows—like maybe it took being locked away to figure it out. Tears fill her eyes and she lets out a tiny cry. It takes me a moment to realize that the sound is outside my head.

After only a couple of seconds of standing, she moves to

sit down anyway. I join her on the grass; it's still wet from the rain. If she notices, she doesn't seem to care. Instead she scoots a bit closer, as if eager for someone to hold her. I wrap my arm around her shoulder, and she rests her head against my chest.

About fifteen minutes later, sirens sound in the distance, and Sasha huddles closer against me.

"It's going to be okay," I assure her, but her cries deepen and intensify.

It isn't long before an ambulance and two police cars pull onto the long dirt road that leads to the farm. They drive right up, over the crabgrass.

"Sasha," I whisper, trying to get her to sit up. But her body's gone limp against me. Her lips are chalky white and her eyes have rolled back in their sockets.

The medics go right into action, lifting her onto a stretcher, bringing her into the ambulance, and hooking her up with a bag of fluids. A syringe is jabbed into her arm.

A male and a female police officer linger at the rear ambulance doors.

I move closer, too, anxious to see if Sasha's okay.

"She's coming around," I hear one of the medics say.

Her head's propped up on a pillow now, and her eyes flutter open; she's not looking at anything in particular.

"Your parents will meet you at the hospital," the male officer tells her. "We've already contacted them."

"Thank you," she says, but she's staring straight at me now.

"I'll come visit you," I promise her.

One of the medics closes the doors and gets behind the wheel. Once the ambulance leaves, with a police car following close behind, I turn to look for Ben, spotting him talking to the female officer. I join them, listening as Ben tells the officer that when he first went down to the root cellar, Tommy hit him over the head from behind. "It knocked me out, but only for a bit," he explains. "When I came to, Tommy was gone."

"Where did he go?" the officer asks.

Ben shrugs. "I'm assuming he went back to the house— probably to look for a weapon or some rope to secure me. That's when I ran out to find something that would break the lock."

"And you didn't see Tommy again after that?" she asks.

"No." Ben shakes his head.

Tommy's girlfriend must've found him instead. The thought of that gives me chills.

After Ben answers a couple more questions, the officer moves on to me. I give her my complete point of view, including how I knew where to look for Sasha, but she insists that Ben and I come down to the station.

"Need a lift?" Ben asks, once the officer gets inside her car.

I turn to him, still overwhelmed that he's actually here. "I thought I lost you." I press my forehead against his chest.

Ben lifts my chin to look into my eyes. "You'll never lose me—not if I can help it. I think it's fairly safe to say

307

we're pretty much connected on every level."

"Did you have any idea that we were working on the same case?"

He shakes his head. "Don't you think that if I had, we'd have reconnected a whole lot sooner? I'd do anything to protect you."

"I think you've proven that once or twice." I encircle his waist with my arms and breathe into his chest.

"The day I bumped into that Tommy guy at the park . . . It was totally by chance. I was on my way back to Freetown from D.C. I'd stopped in Connecticut, and then I needed to stop again in Rhode Island."

"You were headed back?" I ask, hoping that I might've been the inspiration.

"Being away helped me figure things out," he explains. "But I also felt like I was missing something."

"I can definitely relate."

"Good, because now that I think about it, it kind of makes sense that we were working on the same case. There was a reason I felt compelled to follow that guy."

"And a reason you felt compelled to write it all down and post it online?"

"Wait, *what*?" he asks. His face is a giant question mark.

"I saw the blog," I explain. "I read the entries. So, who's Neal Moche? And why are you using his name?"

Ben looks at me, his mouth hanging open, as if completely dumbfounded by the question. And that's when I suddenly realize that there's no way he could've possibly known that I'd found his blog, never mind that I'd figured out his identity.

"Neal Moche *is* you, *right?*" I say.

Ben proceeds to tell me that he's always kept a journal or blog of some sort, but it was only recently that he decided to keep some of the entries open. "And that was because of you," he explains. "Because of what you said before . . . how reading about other people's experiences with psychometry helped you with your own. I thought that keeping a blog might in some way—someday—help someone."

"Well, you were right," I say, wondering about the coincidence of it all—me finding the blog and Ben just happening to bump into Tommy that day in the park.

Or maybe nothing is a coincidence at all. Maybe it was all meant to be—all a part of what we created and made happen. I chose to help Sasha. And, at the same time, Ben chose to follow his instincts—instincts that brought him to me.

"And Neal Moche?" I ask.

"It's *Chameleon*," he says. "Scrambled up."

"Chameleon," I repeat, taking a moment to mentally unscramble the letters.

"It's you," he says, pulling me close, his hands at the small of my back. "It's always been you. Even before I met you—when you were just a hope inside my head."

I kiss him, hearing more sirens in the distance.

"So, how about that lift?" he asks, his gaze lingering on my lips.

"As long as you don't mind if we make a pit stop. I need to go save Wes's car. I also need to call him and Kimmie. They're probably freaking right about now."

We head away from the fire, through the dead cornstalks—what once must've been lush land—finally reaching Ben's motorcycle, parked on the road that the police and ambulance used.

"Shall we?" he asks, handing me his helmet.

I hop right on behind him, holding on tight, and we ride off into the sunset.

## 54

I T'S SATURDAY MORNING a week later, and Kimmie and Wes are sitting in my dorm room eating bagels and helping me pack. Kimmie went back to New York for the week, but then took the bus here last night.

"Thanks again for coming all this way," I tell her.

"You're paying me back, remember?"

"Right, and agreeing to walk in your fashion show ranks right up there with abandoning New York City two weekends in a row and breaking into an abandoned sewing factory to search for a missing girl."

"You're going to have to wear leather spikes and carry a whip," Wes reminds me.

"Okay, so maybe we *are* even," I joke.

Wes and I have agreed to be part of the fashion show that Kimmie is organizing as part of her internship.

"For your information"—she glares at him—"it's not a whip; it's a frilly cane."

"Silly me." He fakes a smile.

"Of course, breaking into that old sewing building *did* have its merits," Kimmie says. "I got to see the layout of what used to be one of the most productive sewing factories in the country. Plus, I snatched myself a swanky souvenir." She pulls a thimble from around her neck; it's attached to a leather rope. "I found this gem whilst trying to get into a locked closet. Wes had me convinced that Sasha Beckerman was tied up and gagged in there."

"What can I say?" He shrugs. "It was a kidnapper's dream: a padlocked room on the basement floor of an abandoned building, hidden behind an old soda machine. . . ."

"It was a closet," Kimmie reminds him. "And, FYI, Detective Tanner was less than impressed."

"Sorry we snagged her from you." Wes gives me a sheepish grin. "I mean, you were *supposed* to be getting some rest. Who knew you'd wind up at a burning house where the captor was being flame-broiled, and then down in a root cellar where you had to fend off his jealous girlfriend?"

"No worries. It wasn't like Tanner was willing to help me, anyway."

After Sasha was taken away in the ambulance, Ben and I went down to the police station to give a formal statement. I found out that most of what I'd assumed to be true had been. Ben had followed Tommy that day, and watched him at the farm. When Tommy stepped away from the cellar, leaving the trapdoor wide open, Ben went down to investigate, never having imagined that there would be someone held captive inside.

Tommy returned to the cellar after only a few minutes, most likely shocked to find Ben. He struck him from behind, knocking him unconscious, and then went back to the house for some rope.

That's when Tommy's girlfriend (Darcy, for the record) decided to get her revenge on Tommy. She'd been suspecting that Tommy was cheating on her. And apparently, when he came back to the house for the rope, he was muttering about how someone had found his secret place and how they wanted to steal his girl.

Enraged, she drugged him—just enough so that he'd be semiconscious—and then burned the house down with him inside.

"So, the *t* on Darcy's neck stood for 'Tommy'?" Wes asks.

I nod. "Because she belonged to him. Just like there was a *t* on Sasha's wrist, because Sasha was his as well—or at least, that's what he thought."

"And the *W* on Tommy's wrist?" Kimmie asks.

"It stood for Wendy, his stepmom," I explain. "Because, apparently, growing up, she treated him like a possession."

"*Issues,*" Wes sings.

And unfortunately, the issues don't exactly end there. After talking to Sasha, the police again questioned Misery, who turned out to be Mailbox Girl. Misery knew Tommy. They'd first met at the Blue Raven and had been acquaintances ever since.

Misery confessed that Tommy had paid her a thousand dollars to set him up with someone who could be described as "lost," someone who didn't get along with her parents and could have used some time on her own.

According to Misery, Sasha had seemed to be the perfect candidate, always bragging about running away. "I didn't think he'd go all abductor," Misery argued to the police. "I mean, yeah, he was a little off, but I never imagined he'd just keep her like that—for two whole months."

"The weird part," I say, "is that Misery didn't seem too surprised that Tommy took Sasha, only that he took her for *so long*."

"Translation: Misery knew what she was getting into," Wes says, "but then she freaked out at the thought of being named an accomplice."

"Because she *was* an accomplice," I say, thinking about the doodling I found in Sasha's bedroom—how Sasha had written Tommy's name. According to Sasha's statement, Misery had originally told Sasha that there was a good-looking guy named Tommy that she'd wanted her to meet. But then, once Misery had collected her money from Tommy and arranged for both Tommy and Sasha to be at that party, she'd started having second thoughts about the arrangement, which was why she told Sasha to keep a distance from him.

But that only made Sasha want to meet him more.

"My vote is that Misery, postpayment, somehow developed a conscience," Wes says, taking a big bite of bagel.

"How did Misery even know about you?" Kimmie asks me. "I mean, if Mrs. Beckerman supposedly didn't fill her in . . ."

"She'd been watching the Beckerman house," I say,

"feeling guilty for her part in Sasha's disappearance . . . or so she recently confessed to the police. She saw me leave the Beckerman house that first day and decided to follow me. When I pulled over, I thought that was it—that she was gone—but she'd merely turned on to a side road, waiting for me to drive past, so that she could continue following. At Sumner campus, she asked people about me—who I was, where I was from, which dorm I was staying in. Once she got all that information, it wasn't hard for her to get my phone number."

"What's going to happen to her now?" Wes asks. "Or to Pyro Darcy, for that matter?"

"The verdict is still out on those two. And unfortunately, Tommy isn't around to testify."

"But happily, Sasha is," Kimmie chirps. "And how's she doing?"

"It's going to take some time," I say, disappointed that I haven't been able to see her yet. "Aside from talking to the police, she hasn't really been up for chatting with anyone outside her immediate circle. I've been keeping in touch with her parents, though. Her mom calls me daily with updates and to thank me. But in some way, I feel like I should be thanking her, too. I mean, I know it sounds all corny, but she helped me understand my own parents better. I've been talking to them more, and I'm going to see my aunt in a couple days. It's, like, I finally feel ready to go home."

"Especially now that Ben will be going home, too?" Wes snickers.

I feel my face grow warm just thinking about him. Ben will be returning to Freetown and graduating on time, with all of us. He's been renting a room in downtown Providence, which is where he is right now, packing his things, getting ready to leave.

"I'm so happy that you and Ben are back together." Kimmie bats her red-coated eyelashes at me.

"And even happier that Adam is now available." Wes raises a suspicious eyebrow at her.

"Who says I give a frick about Adam?"

"Hmm . . ." he says, tapping his chin in thought. "Your latest I-heart-Adam-so-hard-that-my-head-hurts angel-inspired minidress might've been the tip-off."

Kimmie flicks a glob of cream cheese at his face. Conveniently, it lands at the corner of his mouth, so he's able to lick it up. "You're such a fun-sucker."

"You named the dress, not me," he says.

"Do you seriously heart Adam?" I ask, feeling dumb for never knowing, and even dumber for using a shape as a verb.

"Okay, so maybe it's only half a heart." She gives me a sheepish grin.

"And maybe that would only be half the truth," Wes says.

"Would it be okay if I *was* interested?" she asks me. "Or would that be totally weird-incestuous-obnoxious of me? Because the last thing I want is to hurt you, or jeopardize our friendship, or have you feel all freakish at the sight of Adam and me sucking face. . . ."

"Whoa," I say. "How long have you felt this way about him?"

"Pretty much since that first time we met," she says. "After figure drawing class."

"When you saw him naked," Wes clarifies, kindly reminding us of Adam's nude studio modeling days.

"It wasn't just his nakedness." She flicks more cream cheese at Wes's head; this time it lands in his gel-crispy hair. "It was *after* class," she explains, "when we all went out for pizza, and when I really got to talk to him. He just seemed so incredibly sweet and smart and sensitive and attentive."

"Adam is *all* of those things," I assure her.

"But he was also really into you," she says, "which is why I never said anything. I didn't want to be the sour cream that came between you and Adam's spicy hot pepper."

"For the record, things never got above mild salsa."

"Well, Ms. Chameleon," Wes interjects, "I must admit, you never cease to amaze me." He's holding up a gray checked shirt. Whether he's referring to my lack of style or to my alleged lack of spice, I have absolutely no idea.

While the two of them begin to discuss Kimmie's fashion show, I open the desk drawer and pull out Aunt Alexia's journal. I flip through the individual entries, grateful to have had such an amazing support system this past year. Aunt Alexia obviously wasn't as lucky, which explains so much about her, including the reason she decided to give me up at birth.

My parents still think it's best that I don't tell her I know the truth. And after reflecting on it, I agree. If and when Aunt Alexia wants me to know about my birth, she'll tell me on her own.

"So, are we done?" Wes asks.

"I just have a few more things." I stuff the journal into my bag.

"And then you'll be ready to abandon me?" He feigns crying.

"I have a sneaking suspicion that you won't be suffering," I say, tossing him an empty box of tissues. Wes has decided to extend his stay at Sumner by signing up for Summer Session II.

"Don't get *too* comfortable here," Kimmie warns him. "Because in just a few short weeks, there's that thing called senior year. It runs from September to May. . . ."

"Fear not, I'll be back for senior slide, especially now that I know there's light at the end of the tunnel."

"Do you think you'll be okay with going home?" I ask him.

"Better than okay," he says. "And I have you, Ms. Chameleon, to thank. Honestly, if it hadn't been for your borderline-psychotic obsession with Sasha Beckerman's case, not to mention the fact that you're the love child of a mental-hospital romance gone wrong, from which you needed a serious vacation, I'd have never experienced such bliss."

"Well, you're welcome." I smirk. "I think."

# 55

*B*ACK AT HOME TWO DAYS LATER, one of the first stops on my agenda is to see Aunt Alexia. "Do you want to come with me?" I ask Mom.

Both she and Dad are in the kitchen, whipping up a tofu-ginger dish, which on its own is a huge step for Mom. For one, the dish requires cooking. For another, it's actually edible, complete with pasta and soy sauce. A far cry from her *rawt* roast (made with pureed nuts and dehydrated kale paste).

But I digress.

"No, thanks," Mom says. "You go. It'll be good for you and Aunt Alexia to spend some time together. And your father and I will finish up here."

Dad slides his arms around Mom's waist and kisses the nape of her neck. It's the happiest and closest I've seen them in a long time.

As soon as I got home yesterday, Mom called Dr. Tylyn

to schedule a family session. "It'll be healthy to discuss everything," she said.

I couldn't agree more.

I say good-bye and then grab Mom's car keys. The ride over to the hospital goes by far too quickly. I feel like I could use another hour to mentally prepare myself to see Alexia.

Sitting in the parking lot, I flash back to my short but memorable stint in the emergency room, when the doctors wanted to lock me up, too. And what if they actually had? What if I hadn't gotten away? Would I be sitting on the inside looking out, rather than procrastinating in the parking lot about to go in?

Up on Aunt Alexia's floor, I silence my cell phone and then ring the doorbell outside the entrance to the mental-health wing. One of the staff members, a new guy whom I don't recognize, answers. He's wearing a beret (even though it's July).

"Well, I don't need to ask who *you're* here to see," he says.

"And why is that?" I ask. Did Aunt Alexia tell him that I was coming? Or maybe she showed him a picture.

"The resemblance is striking," he says.

"I'm here to see Alexia," I tell him, feeling nervous just saying her name.

"Let me see if she's up for a visit." He closes the door again.

About five minutes later, he invites me inside, has me fill out a form, and then inspects my bag, making sure I haven't brought along any sharp objects.

I step into a large lounge area. A group of middle-aged men watch a tennis match on the big-screen TV that hangs suspended from the ceiling. There are a couple of women playing a game of chess, and a smattering of patients reading books or doing crossword puzzles. It takes me a few moments to spot Aunt Alexia. Sitting at a table in the corner, she's staring straight at me. The paleness of her skin accentuates her ruby-colored lips and the olive tone of her eyes.

I join her and take a seat.

"It's good to see you," she says, reaching across the table to take my hands. Her palms are stained with light blue paint.

I nod, thinking about the last time I visited her—almost a month ago now—when I promised I'd come the very next weekend. Has she been waiting for me since then? "I was away for a little bit."

"Yes, your mother said."

"My mother," I repeat, testing the word in the air, checking her face for a reaction.

But Alexia's expression remains neutral. "A lot has changed since the last time we saw each other, hasn't it?" she says.

"It has," I say.

"Every time I see you"—she squeezes my hands, as if sensing something significant—"you're so much stronger than the last."

I squeeze her hands back, noticing a mole above her

wrist bone—in the exact same spot where mine is.

"You're doing such great things," she continues. "I'm so proud of you—of all you've been able to accomplish, of the person you've become . . ."

"Thanks," I say, unable to help wonder if she can sense what happened with Sasha, or if maybe Mom told her. When I called my parents from the police station, I ended up telling them about my involvement in the case. Most surprising was that Mom didn't explode. She'd known that something was up, especially after our previous phone conversation, when I'd told her that my power of psychometry was screwing things up for me in class. But, this time, instead of talking about her own personal growth, she actually listened when I explained that I felt it was my duty to search for Sasha.

Little did I know then that I would also find myself in the process.

My father, on the other hand, was absolutely crushed that he didn't know, telling me over and over again how much he wished he'd been there for me, and how he never should've let me go.

"I helped save a girl's life," I told him. "This isn't a time for blame or regret. It's a time to be truly grateful."

Helping to rescue Sasha—and my whole philosophy about what truly matters with respect to my future as a potter—is one of the first things I plan to discuss with them in our session with Dr. Tylyn tomorrow.

Aunt Alexia's eyes are unblinking. It's as if she's studying my every move.

"Are you able to do your art here?" I ask her, eager to switch gears.

"I am," she says, letting go of my hands. "Would you like to see my most recent piece?"

"Of course." I let out a breath, relieved to have a moment to myself while she goes off to her room to get her latest work.

She returns a few moments later, holding a large piece of canvas behind her back. "Any guesses as to what this could be?" she asks. Her eyes are wild with excitement.

"Something blue?" I guess, because of the color of the stains on her palms.

She brings the canvas around in front of her, so that I can see it.

My whole body tenses. It's a picture of a faceless woman wearing a light blue hospital gown, lying in bed and holding a baby. The sharp angles of the woman's face, her porcelain skin, and the loopy, pale blond hair that hangs down over her shoulders make it clear the painting's a self-portrait. It's definitely Alexia.

"Do you like it?" she asks.

I swallow hard, flashing back to the photo that Mom showed me of Aunt Alexia in the hospital holding me. It looked exactly like this painting.

"Well?" my aunt asks.

"Why is she faceless?

She shrugs. "Because I'm not really sure who she is."

I nod, though I wonder what she means. Does she not know that it's her? Is there some subconscious part of her—a part she's yet to uncover in therapy—that's leading her to paint bits of her past, stuff that she's not yet ready to remember? Or maybe she's simply trying to find out what I know—curious to see my reaction.

"So, what do you think?" she asks. "Because as a fellow artist, I respect your opinion."

"It's amazing," I say, feeling my eyes fill with tears. Maybe Aunt Alexia was able to sense that I'd found out the truth about my birth.

She looks at it, holding the canvas out. "Maybe someday I'll know the identity of the woman. Until then, I'm calling it a work-in-progress."

"Isn't that what we all are?" I ask her. "Works-in-progress, I mean."

Aunt Alexia sets the painting down on the table. "Do you think I could have a hug?" Her voice is almost too low to be heard.

I stand up from the table and wrap my arms around her. She smells like baby powder.

"I'm glad you like the painting," she whispers in my ear, "but don't let anyone ever take *your* baby."

"Excuse me?" I ask, taking a step back.

"Don't let anyone ever paint your baby," she says, louder now. "Wait until your child is at least three years old before you have any sort of portrait done. It's bad luck, just like opening an umbrella in the house or dancing in wet clothes."

"*What?*" I ask, still confused.

"The day is done when the day is done." She's giggling

now, but the light has gone from her eyes.

I shake my head, completely bewildered. In one moment she seems so together and articulate and insightful, and in the next, she comes apart.

She's sitting in her chair, in a pink dress with matching ballet slippers, laughing uncontrollably while tears stream down her face. And a part of me can't help asking myself: is she truly crazy? Or just choosing crazy? I wonder if I'll ever know.

# 56

*A*FTER MY VISIT TO THE HOSPITAL, I drive to Knead, feeling more inspired than I have in a long time.

"Hey," Spencer says as soon as I come through the door. "You're just in time."

"For cleaning something offensive?" I ask.

"For coffee." He pours us both a cup. "I just brewed it."

"Thanks," I say, taking a sip. I glance over at my work-in-progress, still sitting beneath a tarp at the end of my worktable.

"I've been keeping it moist for you," Spencer says, following my gaze.

"Thanks," I say again.

"No sweat." He smiles. His face is no longer scruffy. He's shaved and gotten a haircut. What used to be long and scraggly dark hair is now chin length and artfully tousled.

"You've been really good to me," I tell him, taking a

seat at the table. "I really appreciate all you did to help me out at Sumner."

"Do you want to talk about what happened?" he asks, joining me at the table.

I nod, feeling like I owe him an explanation, and suspecting that he's already heard the other side of the story. "Sumner was amazing," I assure him. "It was beautiful and inspiring, and there were so many talented students. . . . In some way I feel like I screwed up an amazing opportunity."

"And in another way?"

"In another way, I feel like I got closer to where I need to be."

"And where *do* you need to be?" His dark eyes narrow.

I take a sip of coffee, trying to put into words what I'm feeling without sounding like a total ditz. "Remember how you once told me that a bowl doesn't always want to be a bowl—that I shouldn't force my work into something that it doesn't want to be?"

"I do," he says, frowning at the taste of his own coffee.

"Well, while I was at Sumner, I was inspired by something else—something outside of Professor Barnes's lectures. And I know this may sound selfish and bratty, and perhaps even a little bit like a cop-out, but I felt like that 'something else' was way more important—for me, at least. At that time, I mean. I'm probably not making any sense, am I?"

"You're actually making perfect sense," he says, adding five packets of sugar to his coffee. "The class wasn't a good fit for you at the time."

"But hopefully, someday, I'll have another opportunity like it and I'll be in the right frame of mind to actually appreciate it."

"Sounds like you learned a lot," Spencer says, clinking his mug against mine.

I nod, knowing that he's right. I did learn a lot. And I feel like I accomplished more than ever. I'm not sorry that I enrolled at Sumner, because if I hadn't, I might never have helped rescue Sasha. I might never have met Sasha's mother and in turn grown closer to my parents.

"Well, for the record—and this is the main reason I'm still speaking to you, by the way—Professor Barnes said that you have a lot of talent."

"You're kidding, right?" I ask. "I mean, he treated me like dog dung."

"Which is his form of flattery. He wouldn't have bothered if he hadn't thought you had something great to show." Spencer chokes down his coffee and then gets up from the table.

"Leaving so soon?" I ask, watching as he reaches in his pocket for his keys.

"I have an appointment. I'm meeting with someone about doing an art exhibit. Hence the new do."

"Good luck," I say, glad to hear he's trying to show his work again, because he's amazingly talented, too. And sometimes I think he forgets it.

After he leaves, I pour myself another cup of coffee and get to work. My vaselike bowl looks just as I left it: the sides turn inward to resemble entangled limbs, while the rim turns outward, sort of like a mouth.

I grab a sponge and moisten the surface, hoping that now that Ben and I are back together, I'll finally be able to get the sculpture to where it needs to be. And so I spend the next hour getting reacquainted with the piece, running my fingers over the edges, smoothing the interior, and reinforcing the curves. And at last, it occurs to me what this piece of clay wants to be. Not a vase, nor a bowl. I close my eyes, able to picture the shape in my mind.

I fold the mouth downward and gather up the sides, continuing to work for another four hours straight.

It's my first abstract piece: a heart made of hands, of all different shapes and sizes. Some of them are entwined, others are reaching to hold on to something meaningful, while still others are open or balled up in fists.

A moment later, Ben comes in. "Hey, you," he says, giving me a kiss on the cheek. "I've been trying to reach you all day."

"I kind of got wrapped up in my work."

Ben looks at it, turning the tray to the left and right to view it from different angles. "I love it," he says, meeting my eyes.

I wrap my arms around his neck, forgetting that my fingers are muddied by clay. "Thanks."

"And what's it called?"

*"Touch,"* I whisper, aching to feel his hands on me.

Ben kisses me, sliding his hands down my back, beneath the hem of my T-shirt and then over my hips, either reading my mind or simply aching to feel me, too.

I kiss him more deeply, feeling him almost pull away. *Don't stop*, I scream inside my head, pushing him down into a seat. I sit down on top of him and press my forehead against his, feeling perspiration mixed with clay.

"So, I take it you're happy to see me." He smirks.

"I guess you could say that."

"Good. At least I finally know where I stand with you."

"Because I'm so hard to read, especially for a mind reader."

"Can you read *my* mind right now?" He's staring straight into my eyes.

"I hope so," I say. My heart beats fast.

He continues to look into my eyes as he kisses me again, pulling me closer to him. "I love you," he whispers.

"I love you, too." I place my hand over his chameleon tattoo, knowing that we're meant to be together. "For always."

# ACKNOWLEDGMENTS

First and foremost, I'd like to thank my brilliant editor, Christian Trimmer, who reads my manuscript in all its varying degrees of completion, with a careful eye, and who asks me questions that challenge me, provide perspective, and help make me a better writer. I've learned so much from him.

Thanks to my literary agent, Kathy Green, for all she does. I'm so very grateful.

Thanks to Scott Olson, who was generous enough to answer my questions regarding the profiling of predators and the emotional stages that their victims can go through.

A special thanks to Mom and Ed, who offered helping hands whenever I needed them, so that I had the time to write.

And, last but not least, a HUGE thank-you goes to my readers, who read and recommend my books; and send me letters; and come to my events (even in spirit); and who create book-inspired artwork, song lyrics, videos, posters, playlists, etc., etc. I am utterly grateful for your support, kindness, generosity, and enthusiasm for my work.

New from Laurie Faria Stolarz:
**Welcome to the Dark House**

In this classic horror tale, Laurie Faria Stolarz
masterfully warns: be careful what you dream.

**Available July 2014
from Hyperion**

# IVY JENSEN

I wake with a gasp, covered in my own blood. It's everywhere. Soaking into the bed covers, splattered against the wall, running through the cracks in the hardwood floor, and dripping over my fingers and hands.

I touch my stomach, searching for a stab wound. My chest heaves in and out. I'm breathing so hard that it hurts—so hard that I wish for my lungs to collapse and my heart to stop.

I wish that he'd killed me along with them.

The moonlight shines in through the open window, enabling me to see.

I'm in my present-day bedroom.

It's six years later.

I'm seventy miles away from the crime scene.

There is no blood, only sweat. There are no hardwood floors, either. A shag carpet covers unfinished plywood. I reach down and run my fingers over the thick wool threads, just to be sure. Then I check and recheck my comforter, looking at it from different angles. It isn't pink and covered in paisleys, like the one I had when I was twelve. This one's dark, dark blue. And there are pale green walls. And angled ceilings. And there's an armoire in place of a vanity. There are no music posters on the wall, nor is there a single reference to the soccer I used to play.

I'm seventy miles away. It's six years later. This isn't the same room. There is no blood. This was obviously another nightmare.

Still, I make sure of everything by switching on my night table light. I make sure of everything by going through these rituals one more time: by saying the alphabet forward and backward one more time, by touching the pendant around my neck—an aroma-therapy necklace that was supposed to be a gift for my mother—one more time.

I'm eighteen years old, not twelve.

I dreamed about him again, because I fear that he'll come back for me one day and do to me what he did to my parents.

Six years ago now.

In a room unlike this one.

Seventy miles away.

# Summer

I t's Saturday afternoon, and I'm sitting in Dr. Donna's office. I've been sitting here, on this same leather chair, surrounded by these same four walls.

On the same day.

At the same hour.

For the same reason.

For the past six years.

I'm not sure if it helps, but I never skip a session, because coming here gives me hope that one day I'll no longer have this fear.

Dr. Donna sits across from me. Her legs are crossed at the knee, as usual. Her beige leather clog bops up and down to the ticking of the mantel clock as she waits for me to say something. But coming here—doing this—is starting to feel like watching a rerun. It's the same episode on the same channel, with the same actors, saying the same dialogue. Again and again. And again.

DR. DONNA: So, what do you think?

ME: What was the question?

DR. DONNA: It's been six years, Ivy.

ME: Six years and my parents are still dead, and I still feel like I'm rotting away in purgatory, waiting for a killer to determine my fate. Will he come back and kill me today? Or wait until tomorrow? Or will he put it off until next year? Or perhaps he'll surprise me on the ten-year anniversary?

DR. DONNA: And maybe he won't come back at all. You've changed your name. You've changed your address. You've even changed your family.

ME: What choice did I have with that last one?

DR. DONNA: My point is that maybe he's done.

ME: That depends. Do serial killers retire? I think he's waiting for the opportune moment, watching me, studying my habits. Sometimes when I'm shopping in town or walking home from school, I can feel his eyes on me.

DR. DONNA: Do you still think he's the one who sent you the gifts?

ME: I don't *think*; I *know*. He knows what I like. He knows where I live.

DR. DONNA: You're not into theater, Ivy. And you don't wear much makeup. So, how do you explain the theater pendant or that elaborate cosmetic kit?

ME: And how do *you* explain the paisley-covered journal, the pink soccer jersey, and the Katrina Rowe CD? My love for those things was apparent from my bedroom that night.

DR. DONNA: A lot of people like Katrina Rowe's music, Ivy. And the color pink, paisley designs, and soccer . . . all of those things are popular too. Perhaps a secret admirer sent you the gifts.

ME: Except I haven't played soccer in six years, nor have I listened to Katrina Rowe. And no one who knows me now has any reason to believe that I used to like either.

DR. DONNA: You haven't told a single person? Even in casual conversation?

ME: You still think I'm being paranoid, don't you?

DR. DONNA: I think you have a lot of fear, and I want to help you to defuse it. But I'm not sure what else we can do here. We've talked about that night. We've talked about your nightmares. We've gone over every possible scenario—good and bad—of what could happen in the future.

ME: I need to try something else—to learn to live *with* fear, rather than *in* fear. I mean, lots of people live with fear, right? They put down good money for it. They seek it out from the front row of movie theaters and on roller coasters. They wait in long lines for ghost tours and to go inside haunted houses. They don't let it control their lives.

DR. DONNA: Interesting point. So, how do you propose we get there?

ME: I need to learn from those people. I need to see fear the way they do.

# Autumn

I don't know how I became a subscriber of the Nightmare Elf's e-Newsletter. I'm not a fan of the movies, and there's no chance that I'll ever become one, but with a subject line that hints at ridding my nightmares for good, I can't resist rescuing it from my spam box.

TO: IVY JENSEN
FROM: thenightmare.elf@gmail.com
SUBJECT: LAST CHANCE—NIGHTMARES BE
        GONE CONTEST ALERT

Nightmare Elf e-Newsletter—Issue #206

# NIGHTMARES BE GONE CONTEST
ENTER FOR A CHANCE TO MEET LEGENDARY DIRECTOR
JUSTIN BLAKE
AND GET A BEHIND-THE-SCENES LOOK AT HIS
CONFIDENTIAL NEW PROJECT

Dear Dark House Dreamers,

Greetings from the Nightmare Elf. I am sending this note to say:
If you tell me your worst nightmare, I can make it go away.
Submit your bedtime horror in a thousand words or less.
Then I'll add it to my sack, and you'll enter my contest.*

—The Nightmare Elf

**Contest Guidelines:** In a thousand words or less, describe your worst nightmare. E-mail it to: thenightmare.elf@gmail.com

**Prize:** An all-expenses-paid weekend, including an exclusive, behind-the-scenes look at director Justin Blake's confidential new project, a never-before-seen companion film to his Nightmare Elf movie series, as well as the opportunity to meet Blake himself.

**Contest Deadline:** October 31, midnight EDT.
*Must be 18 years or older to enter.

IN MY HEFTY ELF SACK, YOUR NIGHTMARES WILL KEEP.
BETTER THINK TWICE BEFORE FALLING ASLEEP.

*Dear Nightmare Elf,*

*For the record, I'm not one of your Dark House Dreamers, nor
have I seen even one Nightmare Elf movie—or any of Justin
Blake's films for that matter—but I've been receiving your
e-Newsletters for years now, and this last one caught my eye.*

*I guess you could say that you found me in a weak
moment, because the idea of telling an elf my nightmare, and
having him magically take it away, sounds pretty amazing
right now, especially at four in the morning . . . not that I
actually believe a word of your BS. But, at the very least,
maybe writing about my nightmare and sending it off into
the black hole of cyberspace will trick me into believing that
it'll never come back.*

*So, here goes.*

*For the past six years I've dreamed that my parents are
being murdered in their bedroom across the hall. I'm haunted
by this vision because it happened, in real life. I was in my
room, sleeping soundly—until I heard it. A thrashing sound
across the hall.*

*I sat up, able to hear more noises: a gasp, a sputter, an
agonizing moan. Then silence, broken by an unfamiliar male
voice: "And now it's your turn. You won't feel a thing."*

*My mother screamed. "Please, no," she begged. "Don't do
this. I have a—"*

*There isn't a day that goes by that I don't try to guess at her missing words: "I have an idea"? "I have something to tell you"? "I have a daughter"? "I have a wallet full of cash"? I'll never know for sure. Her voice was cut short with a thwack. Then music began to play. String instruments. An eerie blend of violin and viola that reverberated in my heart.*

*I grabbed the phone on my night table and dialed 911. "I think someone just killed my parents," I told the operator, hearing a hitch in my throat, hearing words come out of my mouth that no one should ever have to say.*

*"Where are you?" the operator asked.*

*"In my room, across the hall."*

*"Is the person still in the house?"*

*"I don't know," I replied, keeping my voice low. "I mean, I think so. In my parents' room."*

*"Okay, I have your address. I'm sending help right over. Can you tell me your name?"*

*"Ivy Jensen."*

*"Okay, Ivy. Listen to me carefully now. Is there a lock on your bedroom door?"*

*I looked toward the door, no longer able to hear my parents.*

*"Ivy?" the operator asked. "Are you on the first floor? Is there a window?"*

*I couldn't answer, couldn't think straight. My hands were trembling so furiously, but still I told myself that I wouldn't drop the phone; I'd keep it firmly gripped in my hands.*

*But then I saw it happen.*

*In slow motion.*

*Falling from my fingers.*

*Bouncing off the bed.*

*Landing against the hardwood floor.*

*It made a loud, hard knock. I felt it in my chest. It stopped my breath, stunned my heart, shot an arrow through my brain.*

*My bedroom light was off, but with the door cracked open, the hallway light leaked into my room and he was able to see me.*

*"Good evening, Princess," he whispered.*

*His hair was long and silver. His face was covered with stubble. He cocked his head and smiled at me; his lips peeled open, exposing a pointy tongue and crooked teeth. I've spent the last six years trying to guess what that smile meant.*

*We both froze, just watching each other, awaiting the other's move—like two wild animals in the night. His eyes were unmistakable: tiny, dark gray, and rimmed with amber-brown. They reminded me of a bird's eyes. And now they're what I see each night as I fall asleep.*

*His gaze wandered around my room—my walls, my floor, my bed, my dresser—as if taking everything in, as if taking me in. The paisley-covered bed linens, the soccer banners, my fuzzy beanbag chair, all the Katrina Rowe posters hanging above my bed.*

*A few seconds later, his eyes fixed back on mine, and he smiled wider. "It's very nice to meet you," he said, overemphasizing every word.*

*I wanted to throw up. Chills ran down my spine.*

*Sirens blared in the distance then. He remained in the doorway a few more moments before backing away slowly and fleeing our little yellow house with the white picket fence—the place that I'd always called home.*

*But I knew that wouldn't be the end.*

*It's now six years later. Those eyes are still out there. And I live in constant fear that the killer will come back for me one day.*

*In my dreams, he plunges a knife deep into my gut before I can rouse myself. My eyes flutter open, and I'm able to see him. Those birdlike eyes.*

*His lips peel open and he smiles at me, his pointed tongue edging out over his jagged, yellow teeth. "You knew I'd come back, didn't you?"*

*He twists the knife—two full turns—before pulling it out to examine the blade. Blood drips onto the bed. I touch my stomach, smearing blood on my palms.*

*That's when I finally wake up. I haven't told anyone this, but sometimes I wish that he would come back, once and for all. At least then I'd no longer have to live in fear.*